For the people who read, the people who love,
and the people who dream.

CONTENTS

EXCERPTS FROM A COMPLETE GUIDE TO PARANORMAL TALENT

by Professor Ayo Abara

Section Two: Kinesis

Of the million or so people in the world today with Paranormal Talents, Kinetics are by far the most common. As a broad category, Kinetics represent nearly half of Paranormals, with Telekinetics being the most numerous. Aquakinetics follow, with Aerokinetics being the most rare, with the possible exception of Lumakinetics, which at this time are purely theoretical. (See Chapter 17)

As with many types of Paranormal Talent, the concept of Kinesis is counterintuitive. Instinct tells us that direct contact is required for the manipulation of matter. Science, however, tells us that everything is connected in ways we may not yet understand. Modern man knows how the mind moves the body, sending and receiving signals through nerves and synapses, but still does it without deliberate control. Without examining the exact mechanics of it, we manipulate nearby objects with our hands, see and hear faraway things with our eyes and ears, and move air with our lungs. Prehistoric man could do all of this long before we understood how or why. It is not a big leap to consider that some of us have additional abilities not yet quantifiable by science, that allow us to sense and manipulate matter around us.

- *A Complete Guide to Paranormal Talent*, Chapter 5

—

Newton's theory of light posits that it is made up of tiny particles, and that these particles then have mass and behave according to the laws of physics like any other type of matter. Given this, it is not inconceivable that light could be manipulated Kinetically.

- *A Complete Guide to Paranormal Talent*, Chapter 17

Paranormal Talents (Currently Identified)

Physical

Kinesis: The ability to move matter without direct physical contact

> Subtypes: **Telekinesis** (solid), **Aquakinesis** (liquid), **Aerokinesis** (gas), **Lumakinesis** (light)

Pyrokinesis: the ability to manipulate the temperature (kinetic energy) of matter in any state

Jumping: Instantaneous travel

Healing: Augmentation of the body's natural healing process

Bending: Transformation of solid matter

Mental

Telepathy: The ability to share thoughts with others

Mnemonic Telepathy / Gaslighting: The ability to read and overwrite another person's memories

Empathy: The ability to feel or manipulate the emotions of others

Charismatic Empathy: The ability to unconsciously induce affection or admiration in others; unconscious charm

Feral Empathy / Taming: Charismatic Empathy tuned to non-human animals

Temporal

Clairvoyance: Sporadic visions of future events

Precognition: Clear view of near future events

Psychics: Vague view of future events, extreme intuition

Prodigy: Extreme instance of an explainable human attribute, like intelligence, strength, perception, speed, or memory

PART 1

1995

CHAPTER ONE: CHAMELEON

Shadows danced and pooled in the dark corners of the casino, flickering in the flashing lights. The cacophony of bells and voices and the muffled thunk of dice on felt washed over me as I scanned the room for anything unusual. *So far, so good.*

I couldn't quite shake my vague sense of unease, and I knew better than to ignore my instincts. My eyes scanned the edges of the room again, searching…

There.

In a dark doorway a man leaned against a wall. I could just make out the outline of him, but even across the room, I felt his eyes on me. Watching me. My adrenaline spiked, telling me to run, to forget the con that I was about to start, and get out. But I'd been planning this for months, and if I walked away now-

"Miss!" the roulette dealer snapped, pulling my focus back to the game. "Do you want to place a bet or not?" I glanced back to the doorway. Empty.

Maybe it was nothing. Considering the way I was dressed, it wasn't surprising that a man would look at me. Short dress, high heels, heavy makeup, all designed to draw attention to *me*, and not what I was doing. To deflect suspicion by blending in. This was part of the plan. Still, it paid to be cautious. I placed a careful bet on the table, small enough that it wouldn't draw attention. Patience had kept me alive more than once. I could wait.

Dizzying flashes of red and black swam together on the spinning wheel, but I blocked them out, let my vision blur, and focused on my *other* sight, showing me shapes and motion in shades of gray. The dealer flung the ball, and the game was on.

3

My attention was entirely fixed on its motion, the spin, the twisting curve, the slow decay of its orbit. I followed along as it plunged toward its destined slot, gave it one tiny mental push at the last minute, and smiled as it hit the wheel one space from where it should have landed.

A woman across the table threw her arms up and cheered, and a man to my left groaned. The dealer looked bored. No one had noticed. I scanned the room again, found no sign of the man in the shadows, and relaxed a little.

Encouraged by the success of my test run, I decided it was time to do it for real. "Red seven, straight up," I told the dealer, pushing a large pile of chips toward him.

He glanced at them emotionlessly. "Two hundred dollars, thirty-five to one odds," he confirmed, placing my stack on the table. Again, I blocked out the rest of the room, ignored the shifting movement of the restless crowd, and concentrated as the dealer propelled the marble around its track. I kept my eyes and my mind firmly fixed on the whirling ball and the slot I needed it to land in. The trajectory was starting to shift ever so slightly, and-

"You like to live dangerously," commented a silky voice in my ear.

I started, but managed to keep my eyes on the spinning wheel. "Why do you say that?" I asked, splitting my focus between him and the game with some difficulty. Mimicking the natural motion of the ball was a complicated feat of physics and required concentration. I didn't need to watch the ball to feel it in my mind, but I wasn't sure I could hold a conversation while doing it. *Guess I'll find out.*

The truth was, I hated living dangerously. I just didn't have a choice.

"You're taking a big risk," he observed. Every hair on the back of my neck raised at his words, and I forced myself to relax again. He couldn't possibly know how big a risk I was taking. I was just a woman in a casino, placing a foolish bet, like all of the others. Definitely *not* a Telekinetic con artist cheating a casino out of thousands of dollars.

Except I *was*, and if I didn't pay attention to what I was doing, I'd be a broke Telekinetic con artist. I was committed now. My money was on the table, and I didn't have enough for a second attempt. Six months of living expenses depended on this, and if I failed… I didn't want to think about what happened if I failed. This had to work.

But I also needed to get out of here afterwards, which meant I had to deflect suspicion. Play the part. "Maybe I'll get lucky," I suggested, turning to look at him with a flirty smile.

I almost lost track of the ball.

There was something about him that immediately pulled me in. Not just his looks, although they were definitely helping. Dark hair curled around striking features, softening the sharp, strong angles of his face. He stood with a sort of casual grace, hands in his pockets and head tilted down toward me. A wide smile held the promise of seduction, barely hovering this side of suggestion.

It was his eyes that caught me. They were dark and bottomless, full of secrets and mystery, beckoning me to adventure. He was temptation incarnate, and for one terrifying moment, I had an urge to drop everything and follow him into the unknown.

"Maybe so," he agreed with a heart-stoppingly wicked grin.

Reluctantly, painfully, I wrenched my attention back to the spinning ball. I had seconds before it fell. I grabbed it, mimicking the natural skittering, twisting, twirling motion, and kept it moving around its track. I had it, now if I could just-

Something touched my back. A warm hand, a soft caress, trailing up my spine. *What the hell?*

I let the ball lose some momentum and slide slightly down the slope. It skipped and-

The touch reached the exposed skin of my shoulders, tracing the curve of my neck, to the sensitive hollow at the nape. Goosebumps broke out along my skin, and I fought the urge to lean in.

-jumped once, twice, and landed neatly in the right slot.

Bells rang. "Red seven! The young lady wins!" Despite his cheery tone, the dealer still looked bored. The rest of the table looked disappointed. "Thirty-five to one, $7000 payout, plus your initial bet of $200." No one had noticed anything. I let out the breath I was holding.

"Incredible," whispered the voice in my ear. I spun to face him, angry and intrigued at the same time.

He was gone.

A second ago, he was right there. My body still shivered from the feel of his skin against mine, and his smooth voice still echoed in my ear. There was no trace of him now. I shook the weird encounter from my mind, and turned to collect my winnings.

—

The glaring daylight was painful after the windowless casino floor, but the breeze was a welcome change from the suffocating, smoky air inside. It would take days to get the smell of cigars out of my hair. That was what I hated most about jobs like this - washing away the vague sense of uncleanness left behind.

It didn't matter. My bag was full of cash, and now all I had to do was get back to the city safely. The line of yellow cabs stretched down the hill from the taxi stand, and I headed for the second car. I heard my grandmother's voice in my ear, telling me never to do the expected. On impulse, I skipped the second one, too, and got in the third. She might have been paranoid, but so far, her advice had kept me alive and free. She was right - the world wasn't kind to those who were different, and my differences ran deeper than most. "Upper East Side, please. Seventy-second and Fifth." It was nowhere near my apartment, but that was another thing she taught me - never let anyone know where you live. I heard the click of the meter starting, and the car rolled slowly forward out of the line. I was out. The rest was easy. I breathed a sigh of relief and fished in my oversized bag.

First, an elastic to bind the hair that I had artfully arranged only a few hours ago into a mercilessly tight ponytail. A makeup remover cloth for the thick layer of paint on my face. A plain black tank top to go over the stretchy red tube dress, a pair of bike shorts to go underneath. I slid the dress down and folded it neatly back into the bag, and swapped my high heels for a pair of sneakers. All of it then went into the bag I had tightly rolled in the bottom of the shiny purse. Within a few minutes, I was indistinguishable from any other jogger.

Half an hour in a cab from Yonkers to the city, and I was home free. Not many people even knew there was a casino this close to Manhattan. No one would suspect that the woman jogging across Central Park was carrying thousands of dollars in a beat-up backpack. A quick circuit of the park, and I could slip unnoticed back to my apartment, confident that no one was following me.

I leaned back in the seat, relaxing. I hadn't technically broken any laws, but I still didn't want to get caught. My grandmother had drilled into me over and over the importance of staying hidden. "The world isn't safe for you," she told me, again and again. "Don't ever let them see what you can do." She never told me what happened to my parents or my grandfather, but it was clear that she blamed their unusual abilities for their deaths. Over and over, she lectured me not to use my gift, ever, but especially in the presence of others. According to her, terrible things would happen if I did.

I didn't have much choice.

We should be halfway there by now. I glanced out the window, but instead of the concrete canyon I was expecting, I saw green trees flowing by. This wasn't the highway.

A voice in the back of my mind whispered, '*she was right.*'

No. I was careful, I hadn't made any mistakes. No one could possibly have known. Maybe the driver was just lost.

"Hey," I called, knocking on the plastic divider. "You're

going the wrong way." He didn't respond.

I banged harder, until there was no way he hadn't heard me. The driver was deliberately ignoring me, and that was very, very bad. With rising alarm, I hammered on the window. "Hey! Where are you taking me?"

I played back the events of the evening, wondering where I could possibly have gone wrong, and came up with the dark-eyed stranger.

You're taking a big risk.

If he knew what I was doing, and was watching me in action… I screamed louder at the driver. I cursed at myself inwardly and at him outwardly. I should have trusted my instincts and bailed when I first saw the stranger watching me. I would have had to figure out something else for money, but at least I'd be free and safe. Instead, I was trapped in my worst nightmare - captured by people who knew what I could do. Maybe I would end up in a government lab somewhere, or coerced into doing horrible things by powerful people. Maybe I would end up dead in a ditch. Maybe worse.

Starting to panic, I pulled at the door handle, not caring that we were still moving fast. A few broken bones would be better than whatever they had planned. The door was locked, though, and the mechanism was too heavy for me to budge. Child safety locks. In a taxi cab. This was bad.

Suburban streets were rolling by now, rows of neat flowers lining carefully manicured lawns. I struggled with the door again, knowing it was useless. The cab pulled into the waiting garage of a completely non-descript house, and the door scraped shut behind it. No external exit, no windows. No way out but the door into the house. I was trapped.

The driver got out and opened my door. There was no point staying in the car. I couldn't escape, and they'd get me out eventually anyway. There had to be some other way out of the house. I was good at opening locks, maybe I could escape through the front door. Trying to look confident, I got out of the car, and went inside.

The room looked like an office. A polished-looking man in a dark suit sat behind a desk. Bookcases lined one wall, and on another, a fire crackled in a fireplace, conspicuous on an afternoon in May. "Hello, Miss Grey," he said, gesturing to an empty chair. "Please come in. Have a seat." He knew my name. I thought about running again, but the driver stood between me and the exit, with a stance that screamed 'police'.

Staying where I was, I hugged my arms over my chest, wishing I was wearing more clothing. "I haven't done anything wrong."

"No one said you did." He smiled welcomingly. "Please. Sit."

"How do you know my name?"

"We know a lot about you," he said, opening a folder on his desk. I strained to see what was in it, but I was too far away. "Diana Grey, Telekinetic. Born May 8, 1973. Raised by your maternal grandmother, Beatrice Grey, who emigrated to New York in 1942 with her infant daughter Catherine, a Telekinetic like her late father. Your father's identity is unknown, but both parents disappeared in 1974 and are presumed dead." He shut the folder. "Kinesis runs in your family, but it doesn't seem to do any of you much good, does it?" *How could he possibly know all that? I didn't even know all of that.*

Deflect. Bluff. Admit nothing. "That's ridiculous," I scoffed. "Magic isn't real."

"No," he agreed, "magic is not. Paranormal Talent, on the other hand, is quite real. And yours is remarkable." He opened the folder again, and rifled through some papers. "As is your very colorful career."

Straining to see the page he was reading without getting closer, I said, "I haven't broken any laws. You can't arrest me."

"You haven't broken any laws *today*," he corrected, closing the folder and placing it on the desk between us. "But don't worry. We have no intention of arresting you."

"What do you want then?"

"We want to offer you a job. One I think you will find much more satisfying than petty theft, and a great deal more lucrative."

"Thanks but no thanks," I said, turning toward the door. The driver didn't move.

The man behind the desk sighed. "You're under no obligation to take it, of course. But you see, the city likes to keep track of all of its Paranormals. You lot have a tendency to cause trouble if left to your own devices. Now that we've identified you, we have an obligation to report our findings to the authorities.

"Legally, I'm required to give this folder to Officer Nelson, here. I'm sure his supervisors will be very interested in its contents. He might even get a raise." Officer Nelson smiled at me from his post by the door.

"But we believe in second chances. I can give you the opportunity to wipe the slate clean. Start over. Just a normal person, with a legal job, a regular paycheck and a clean record. You'd be well-compensated, and you'd never have to worry about money again. And this," he said, lifting the folder, "can go in that fire."

While my police record wasn't horrific, it wasn't exactly clean, either. And a steady paycheck was really, really attractive. "Who's 'we'?"

"We are a consulting agency. When people have problems that no one else can solve, they come to us. We find the right person for the job, and provide the tools they need to succeed. Among other things, I recruit Talented individuals such as yourself. We provide opportunities for you to utilize your particular abilities in more effective ways than would otherwise be possible."

"Doing what?"

"Your assignments will vary from project to project, so

there's no risk of getting bored, but everything you're asked to do will be within your ability. I'm afraid I can't tell you much more than that until you sign the non-disclosure agreements."

"Why me? If you have so many other *consultants*, why go out of your way to find me?"

"Telekinetics are fairly common, but your particular abilities are quite special. What you did today demonstrates an astonishing level of precision. Even the dealer noticed nothing, and he watches that ball all day. What you lack in strength, you more than make up for with control."

What I lack in strength. As he spoke, I realized what made me so uncomfortable about this room. Everything here was too heavy - there was nothing in it that I could move. Every object in the room must weigh at least three pounds, which was the outer edge of my limit. Even the books seemed to be glued down. He knew exactly what my abilities were, and had deliberately disarmed me. If I was frightened before, I was terrified now.

"Think about it," he urged. "You don't have to decide right now. Officer Nelson here will take you home." That wasn't happening, but since Nelson was currently my only way to get back to the city, I'd let him take me as far as Harlem. "If you decide to take the job, come to this address and ask for George Montgomery," he said, holding out a card. "If we don't hear from you within a week, we'll assume you're not interested." And then, he'd give that folder to the police.

I took the card. On one side, it had an outline of a bird with a long bill and a spiky-looking head. On the other, it had an address. No name, no phone number, no company, nothing else. I took it uneasily. More than anything else - including the kidnapping - the card set off all of my alarms.

"I hope to see you soon, Miss Grey," he said with a smile. Officer Nelson stepped aside and opened the door. Trying to pretend my world wasn't crashing down around me, I walked toward the exit with a confidence I didn't feel. I could break down when I got home.

I paused in the doorway. "How did you know which cab I'd get in?"

"We didn't. We bought them all."

CHAPTER TWO: PHYSICS

I climbed the metal staircase carefully, trying to keep it from creaking. Most of my neighbors didn't even know I lived up here, and I preferred it that way. I eased the rusty door open, and stepped into my odd attic living space.

It wasn't exactly an apartment. When my grandmother died five years ago, I was seventeen. What little money she had went fast. I had no prospects for employment, no place to live, and no one to turn to. By the time I went through her jewelry box to find something to sell, I was desperate. I found a gold necklace, her wedding ring, and a little slip of paper with an address.

The building I found at that address was not at all what I expected. It was a weird little house across from Central Park, sandwiched between two huge apartment buildings. Later I found out that it was one of the last few old Victorian townhouses that once lined the park, but at the time, I didn't know what to make of it.

I couldn't bring myself to knock. I had no idea what I could possibly say if someone answered. *'I don't know who you are or why I'm here, but I found this address, so... hi?'* I sat on the bench across the street for hours, with no idea what to do. Eventually, a man came out and saw me sitting there. He told me I looked just like my dad, and invited me in. He said that my father had saved his life more times than he could count, and asked what I needed.

What I needed was a place to live. The attic was a makeshift solution, but it worked. There was plumbing and electricity, a massive wooden bar left over from some questionable past, and a tiny bathroom.

I couldn't get him to tell me anything else. He refused to

talk about my father at all. The fond smile on his face when I asked if he knew my mother suggested that he did, but he wouldn't talk about her, either. A year later, all his secrets died with him. After the funeral, his son told me it was a condition of his inheritance that this place was always available to me, and that he intended to honor it. I'd lived here ever since.

It was drafty and bare. The wood floor had splinters. The single huge window overlooking the park was cracked and dirty. My only furniture was a futon, some shelves made of old milk crates, the massive wooden table that was here when I moved in, and one rickety chair. The kitchen consisted of a hot plate on top of the ancient bar, and a mini-fridge tucked underneath. It was cold in the winter and hot in the summer, and occasionally damp in big storms. I loved it.

I was safe here. No one but my landlord knew I was here. I had more space than most Manhattanites dreamed of. When Nelson made a quip on the way home about being able to get a bigger apartment, I began to relax. More than anything else could have, that reassured me that they didn't know where I lived.

It was small comfort. I couldn't hide up here forever. After stowing the day's earnings in a hidden spot in the rafters, I dropped down in front of the window and stared out at the park.

I had a week to decide. Either way, my life was about to change completely. I rested my chin on my knees and drew my arms up over my head.

One week.

———

Break.

The cue ball struck the tightly racked balls with a loud *crack*, and the eleven sank neatly into a corner pocket.

One.

I felt my mind begin to still as I settled in to watch how the rest of the balls split apart. Eyes closed, I picked out my next shot.

Jimmy's was the definition of a dive bar. The floor was sticky, the stink of cigarette smoke lingered in the dark corners, and the bitter aftertaste of despair hung in the air. But there were familiar faces and a pool table in the back, which was what I needed right now.

At four in the afternoon, the bar was nearly empty. The pool table was in a back area, hidden from direct sight from the main room. I didn't need to see it with my eyes - Telekinesis connected me to the objects around me, showing me the shapes and outlines. From where I stood, I could feel the familiar forms of barstools and tables and Jim himself behind the bar. He was watching tv again, and the pair in the corner seemed to be focused on their conversation. Alone and out of sight, I allowed myself to close my eyes. The hard shape of each ball was sharp against the felt surface of the table, and I could pick out the cue ball from a tiny chip in the porcelain. I bent over the table and lined up the next shot. Another ball sank into a corner pocket. Didn't matter which.

Two.

Pool was physics, and physics was something I understood. I didn't need to use Telekinesis to move the balls. It was actually better practice not to, because it abstracted everything to understanding how things moved, and that was something I got - something I *needed* to get - on a subliminal level. I sank another ball.

Three.

The noise in my head began to fade. Once the fuzzy blur of fear fell away, the stark reality of my dilemma came into sharp, crystal clear focus.

I was screwed.

Four.

My first instinct was to run. I had enough money from the casino job to buy a bus ticket and go far away, out of their reach. But I'd spent my entire life in this city. I liked it here. And I wouldn't even know where to go.

Five.

I could stay and hide better. Go back to super-low-profile jobs. Apartments. Bars. Picking pockets. I hated those, though. Too much work, too much risk, too little reward. I could stretch the money from the casino until I figured out something else, or…

Six.

Or I could take them up on their offer. Despite their pretty words about second chances, I recognized it for what it was - blackmail. Play by their rules, or face the consequences. I circled the table to line up a combo to a side pocket.

Seven.

The front door creaked and someone came in - male, medium height - but went directly to the bar and started chatting with Jimmy. I kept my eyes shut.

Eight.

Maybe it wasn't so bad. I could start over with a clean slate. My record wasn't that bad, but it wasn't great either. I could have a regular job, a regular salary, no more hiding or looking over my shoulder. No more wondering where the next paycheck would come from. It was everything I could dream of.

Nine.

It was also my worst nightmare. A whole company full of people who knew my name, knew my face, knew my *Paranormal Talent*, as he'd called it - just the idea made my blood run cold. Once I walked in, there would be no going back.

Ten.

I wondered what the others could do.

Eleven.

I wondered what *he* could do. The man from the casino had to be one of them. After seeing how he disappeared into the crowd so suddenly, I was sure of it. One minute he was there, and then gone the next. That had to be supernatural. No. Paranormal, I reminded myself. Which meant that if I took the job, I might see him again.

A smile stole onto my face as I remembered the feel of his hand against my skin. I knew he was just trying to distract me, probably, but I couldn't help but daydream. He couldn't possibly be as perfect as I remembered. Real men didn't look like that.

Twelve.

A few more people filtered into the bar. One of them - medium height, average build - wandered toward the back of the bar where I played. I opened my eyes, and took a sip of my drink, but otherwise ignored him.

Thirteen.

The newcomer was watching me. My back was to him, so he thought I couldn't see him, but when I bent to take the next shot, the angle of his head made it clear where his attention was. It wasn't on the table.

Fourteen.

As I stepped around the table to line up my last shot, I glanced at him. He was attractive enough, in a frat-boy kind of way. Blonde, athletic, expensive-looking clothes. It was obvious what he was after. I could leave here with him, and maybe this guy would take my mind off of a soft touch and a silky voice I couldn't get out of my head. And deep, dark eyes…

I missed my shot. *Dammit.*

"Not bad," Frat Boy said. "Want to play?" I knew this game. We'd play a few rounds, I'd let him win a couple of times, we'd make small talk for a while, and by the end of the night, I'd either leave with him or his money, depending on my mood.

It might be a useful distraction from my problems. Forget everything for a night. But in the morning, I'd still be stuck with an impossible dilemma and the memory of a stranger who'd somehow gotten under my skin.

"Table's taken," I growled, re-racking the balls.

———

"Want to talk about it?"

The unexpected voice made me jump. I'd been so wrapped up in thought that I hadn't noticed Jim come in. "Talk about what?"

"Whatever it is that's got you so wound up that you're in here every night. This is the fourth time this week." He leaned against the wall next to the door and crossed his arms. Jim wasn't a friend, exactly, but he'd known me longer than anyone else. I'd been coming here for years. Instead of turning me over to the police when he caught me stealing from him, he sat me down, handed me a coke, and asked why a seventeen year old kid was stealing from a bar. In exchange for a promise not to take his money again, I left that day with a twenty and a safe space to go when I needed it.

He quietly left out the alcohol in my drinks until I turned 21, made sure no one followed me when I left alone, and turned a blind eye when I sharked his customers out of their money. Occasionally, he listened to my problems. Not this time.

"It's nothing," I told him, turning back to the table and lining up a shot.

"Is it about a guy?"

"No," I said, a little too defensively. "Sort of." I couldn't deny that I was curious about my mystery man, but that really wasn't the main problem. "I got offered a job." *Seven, corner pocket.*

"What kind of job?" he asked, narrowing his eyes.

"A real one, this time. Legal."

"So what's the problem?"

The situation was complicated, but the problem boiled down to something simple. "I don't trust them."

He snorted. "You don't trust anybody."

I didn't answer. *Three, side pocket.*

"Look, kid," he began more seriously. "I know you've had it rough, and I try not to tell you what to do. But this path you're on, it doesn't go anyplace good. I've seen where it ends. If you have a chance to go a different way, take it.

"You're young. Your future is wide open. People don't get second chances every day. Don't blow this one because you're scared. Take it from an old man - life is too short to live with regrets." There was something in his voice that was wistful, almost bitter. Caught up in my own problems, I'd never wondered about Jim's life. What he'd been through, how he got here, what he'd lost along the way. He'd never tell me even if I asked.

"You know what, Jim? You give pretty good advice."

"It's in the job description. Now get out of here, and stop scaring away my customers."

CHAPTER THREE: ORIENTATION

Another address on another piece of paper. At least I had a name this time. The card my blackmailer gave me brought me to an office building in the middle of Midtown. The person at the front desk looked me up and down, taking in my ratty jeans and ancient tank top with thinly disguised contempt. "Can I help you?" she asked dubiously.

"I'm here to see George Montgomery."

She gave me a condescending smile. "I'm sorry, you must have the wrong address."

I pulled the card from my back pocket and looked at it again to make sure. "No," I started to protest, "this is the right place…" I trailed off when I saw her expression.

She was staring at the back of the card, with surprise and a touch of fear. I flipped it around and saw nothing but the blue outline of the bird. "Can I see that card, please?" she asked, suddenly painfully polite. Reluctantly, I handed it to her. She turned it over, examining it carefully, then tucked it out of sight. Keeping her eyes on me as if I might turn into a cobra at any second, she picked up the phone and dialed a number. After a hushed conversation, she hung up and smiled at me. "Come with me, please."

After opening the gate for me, she led me to an elevator at the back of the building. It had no call button, just a slot for the key card she entered. The door opened with a chime. Without setting foot inside, she leaned in, pressed a button, and gestured for me to go in.

I hesitated on the threshold. "Can I have that card back?" I asked. It seemed like a useful thing to have.

Her smile hardened. "No, ma'am." She removed her key card from the slot, and the elevator doors closed, trapping me inside.

A few nervous seconds later, they opened again onto a blindingly white lobby. I stepped out into the open space and looked around. On the other side of a reception desk, a large sign with discrete up-lighting displayed the same blue bird from the card, and the words 'Kingfisher Consulting Agency'. So it did have a name.

Sitting behind the desk was a pretty woman with perfect curls, hot pink lipstick and matching nails. She was touching up her makeup and trying very hard to ignore the woman standing to her left.

Looking completely out of place in a flowing skirt and peasant blouse, the second woman smiled at me. Her dark hair trailed down her back in a long braid with ribbons and beads woven into it. She was of indeterminate age, and had an air about her that annoyed me for some reason I couldn't quite place.

"So it begins," she intoned solemnly, arms held out and palms toward the ceiling. Then she smiled brightly at me and practically squealed, "So lovely to meet you at last!" in a much different tone. Tilting her head, she commented, "I thought you'd be taller," and then shrugged, putting it out of her mind.

Arms still out, she came toward me and before I could react, she enveloped me in a big, intrusive hug. I tried to politely disentangle myself from her, but she gripped me tight. After a long awkward moment, she released me, but grabbed my shoulders and looked deeply into my eyes for a moment.

Her expression got sad and slightly pitying. "Oh, sweetie," she said gently. "Such a long road. But worth the pain, in the end." My eyes went wide. *What the hell?*

"Athena, we've talked about this," said a tired-sounding voice from the side. A man stood in a doorway I hadn't noticed before. He was middle-aged, nondescript, and looked like he lived in a constant state of annoyance.

The woman - Athena - gave me one last searching glance, a reassuring squeeze of my shoulders, and then released me. "Her footsteps are so loud, I couldn't resist."

The man was unamused. "Try harder." He turned to me. "Diana Grey?" he asked. "George Montgomery," he continued when I nodded. "Let's talk in private," he added with a pointed glare at Athena. As he ushered me through the door, he told me, "Don't mind her. She does that to everyone."

I tried to put the strange encounter out of my head, but I couldn't quite shake my uneasiness. "What exactly does she do here?"

"Mostly annoy people. Don't worry, you won't be working with her. Come to my office, we have a lot to discuss."

—

The morning passed in a blur of incomprehensible paperwork. I tried to follow Montgomery's explanations, but I was completely lost. I thought I got the important parts: I would get paid a lot of money, I would get assignments, and I couldn't tell anyone about it. The rest - W2s, 401Ks, other random combinations of letters and numbers - I could figure out later.

The afternoon passed in a blur of introductions. Montgomery handed me off to a small woman with a childlike face named Lynn, who I liked instantly. Lynn would be guiding me through my training starting tomorrow, but today was mainly introductions and assessments.

The pretty woman at the front desk was Candace, but she preferred to be called Candi. She was Security, which I didn't entirely understand, given her diminutive stature, but it seemed impolite to ask. Athena, the woman who'd greeted me first, was a Psychic. According to Lynn, she was always right, but almost never in a way that was useful. Luis was a Pre-cog, which meant he could see a few seconds into the future, which was handy in a fight. Haru was an Aquakinetic, which was like my Talent only with liquids, and the serious-looking man with the metal-framed glasses was Oliver, who remembered everything.

Names and faces swirled around me and I tried to memorize them, but by the time Lynn led me off to my first assessment, my head was spinning and I wanted to leave. I wasn't looking for a man with dark eyes and a mysterious smile, so I definitely wasn't disappointed when he didn't appear. And I'd keep telling myself that until I believed it.

My first assessment was in a large open space that looked like a high school gym. It was about half full of people, casually doing incredible things. On one side, a man stood in front of a set of weights that appeared to be lifting themselves. Nearby, another man was pulling a string of water. As I passed, the water froze and crashed to the ground, and the Aquakinetic spun angrily to his neighbor, who was laughing. A bucketful of water leapt out of its container and splashed against the laughing man's face. They were still fighting when we left them behind.

As Lynn led me to the far side of the gym, curious eyes followed us. I tried to ignore them, but they made me acutely uncomfortable. This was exactly what I'd been avoiding my whole life.

The far corner had a little area sectioned off with a line of tables, shaped in a U. Each table had a lock of some kind, from padlocks hanging from hooks on one side, to safes on the other. In the center of the U stood a man with a clipboard.

"This is Brandon. Brandon, this is-" Lynn began, but he cut her off.

"I know who she is." Brandon looked me over dubiously. "Precision Telekinetic," he said. "OK, Miss Grey, my job is to find out exactly how precise you are. Let's start over here with the lock on the far left."

"You're kidding," I said as I realized what they wanted me to do. At least they were lined up in order of complexity rather than size, and the safe at the end was a halfway decent one.

Brandon looked like I'd just confirmed his opinion of me. "Just do the best you ca-"

I didn't wait for him to finish. With a series of clicks, all of the locks fell open at once. The heavy door to the largest safe made a loud creak as it swung wide, and then clanged loudly as it stopped. There was a long moment of shocked, awkward silence. To be fair, it was a good lock. When it first hit the market, it took me a few days to figure out the mechanism, but once I knew how it worked, it was easy to crack.

"Are we done here?" I asked Lynn. The rest of the room had stopped pretending not to stare. Brandon was still staring open-mouthed at the safe, and the look on his face nearly made the rest of this day worth it.

Lynn recovered first. "OK, then," she said with a bright smile, "why don't you go get some coffee while I see if Bob is ready?"

—

"This is absurd." A different section of the gym was taped off like a boxing ring. Inside it stood a wiry man in his thirties who looked like he never stood still.

Lynn grimaced apologetically. "The bosses insist that everyone has basic self-defense training. You need to be able to protect yourself. Just in case."

"I don't need self-defense training."

"Prove it," challenged Bob. "Pass the test, prove that you don't need training, and you can go."

"What's the test?" I asked with a resigned sigh.

"Knock me down. I won't even try to fight back. Knock me down or push me out of the ring. If you cross the line yourself, we start over."

I stepped into the ring.

"That's it? That's all I have to do? As soon as you hit the ground, I pass the test?"

"That's right," Bob grinned, motioning me forward with his

hands. "Show me what you've got.

I stayed exactly where I was.

His brow furrowed. Taking a step toward me, he said, "You can't just-"

He didn't manage to finish the sentence. His eyes went wide, and his arms windmilled for a long moment before he sprawled to the floor at my feet. I suppressed a smirk as he lay there in a heap, staring incredulously at the shoelaces I'd tied together while he was talking.

I turned to Lynn, who was obviously trying not to laugh.

"Can I go now?"

Chapter Four: Hidden

I talked Lynn into leaving me in the library for the rest of the day. It wasn't hard. She was obviously at a loss for what to do with me next, and welcomed the suggestion when I made it. My Talent let me hold my own in this unfamiliar environment, but there was a lot I didn't know, and it put me at a disadvantage.

It was probably a conference room at one point, but now the library was lined with books on everything from physics to Psychics. I picked up a book from the shelf - _Introduction to Paranormal Talent_, by Professor Ayo Abara - and settled in to read.

> _Of the million or so people in the world today with Paranormal Talents, Kinetics are by far the most common. As a broad category, Kinetics represent nearly half of Paranormals, with Telekinetics being the most numerous. Aquakinetics follow, with Aerokinetics being the most rare, with the possible exception of Lumakinetics, which at this time are purely theoretical (See Chapter 17)._

"Miss Grey?" called a tentative voice. I looked up to find Oliver hovering nervously near the door, clutching something tightly to his chest, and looking at me hopefully.

"Diana, please," I corrected him, smiling.

"I wonder if you could help me with something?"

"Of course," I said, amused by his diffidence.

He set his treasure very carefully on a table. It was a cylinder, around three feet long by one foot around, and appeared to be a solid block of wood. It had carved designs on both ends, and the remnants of peeling paint on the sides. It looked old. Curious, I looked deeper, and made out a hollow center, and something solid inside. It was a container, then, but there was no clear way to open it.

"This was found in the estate of Adelaide d'Orleans, and it's believed to date back to at least the 1720s. It's lined with some kind of metal that blocks all of our scans, so we have no idea what's in it, but it has the royal seal of Louis XVI, so we think it may be an artifact that was lost during the Revolution. When he was deposed, many historical artifacts were secreted away by lesser nobility, so-"

"What about this one?" I asked, flipping the cylinder onto its other end.

He seemed startled. "That one? That's the labyrinth from the Chartres Cathedral. It dates back to…"

I tuned him out. History was not my thing. Locks, now, that *was* my thing. While Oliver went on about the cultural and historical significance, I closed my eyes and looked beneath the surface of the wood.

Kinetic sight, the book called it. An awareness of the physical world around us, without which no Kinetics - whether Telekinetic, Aquakinetic, or Aerokinetic - would be able to manipulate our surroundings. For me, it was instinctive, something I'd always had, but it was nice to have a name to put to it.

As I expected, the cylinder was two pieces, not one, very carefully fitted together. Inside, it was lined with something smooth and hard, but it wasn't uniform. On one end, beneath the circular labyrinth pattern, grooves were hollowed out inside the wood. In the hollow groove, there was a ball - smooth, hard, dense, like metal - about the size of a marble. A maze. Like a labyrinth.

It was probably meant to be traced with something magnetic, to move the ball through the maze, but it was stuck. If I traced the paths back to the center… *there.* I pressed on the locking mechanism, and it opened with a faint click.

"Try now," I told Oliver. "Lift the top."

His eyes got very wide. Hands shaking a little, he grasped the top of the box. I moved his hands up a bit, just above the invisible seam. He lifted, and the top came away.

He looked like he might faint. Curious, I looked inside to see a weird-looking hand at the end of a gold stick. The paint was peeling off the wood, and the band of stones around the wrist was set in some metal so tarnished it was black. Whispering something about justice, he snatched up the box and ran off.

Ooookay. I went back to my reading.

—

The last person to leave took the elevator down at a quarter to nine. At ten after, the main lights switched off. Finally. I was forgotten here in the library, which was exactly what I wanted. I'd used the time well while pretending to read, peering with my Kinetic sight into the walls, finding the cameras, tracing the wires, figuring out which one I'd need to break to disable all the cameras. Once I snapped it, I figured I had about half an hour before the security guards downstairs noticed and came up to look.

Half an hour should be enough for what I had in mind.

According to the ancient-looking newspaper article framed near the lounge door, the company was founded by two men named Robert King and John Fisher. While not Talented themselves, they became early benefactors of the Paranormal community, providing jobs and safe havens for people, while allowing them to maintain anonymity in the broader world. Initially, it was a construction company primarily employing Telekinetics, but over the years, it expanded into other fields: security, finance, intelligence. Now they recruited Paranormals of all Talents, solving the problems no one else could solve.

It was a little too rosy a picture for a company whose recruiting methods included abduction and blackmail. There was a darker side here, and I wanted to know what it was.

I'd also been watching people. Montgomery's office was tucked into a back corner, on the far side of the building. Three times over the course of the afternoon, he'd left his office, carefully looked to make sure no one was watching, and then went through a door across the hall, which was just at the edge of my range. Ten or fifteen minutes later, he reappeared and crossed quickly back to his own office.

I wanted to know what was behind that door.

After giving it another five minutes or so after the lights went out, I snapped the right wire, careful to fray the edges so it looked like a short. After a cautious look through the door showed that the little indicator lights on the cameras were off, I stepped out into the hall.

The door I was looking for was conspicuously labeled 'Cleaning Supplies', and most definitely did *not* have cleaning supplies behind it. It was locked, which only slowed me down by a few seconds. Behind it hid a nondescript staircase, leading up to another floor. At the top I found another locked door. Through that door…

City lights stretched out below me. I stopped short, taking in a darkened hallway with a broad glass wall facing out over streets and skyscrapers and cars moving like ants below. I carefully closed the door to the lit staircase behind me, and for a moment, just reveled in the view.

My city, as I'd never seen it. Stunningly beautiful. Home.

Twenty five minutes. I took stock of the rest of the hallway. To my right was a door, closed and locked. On the other side of it was a huge corner office, with a desk and a couch and shelves. The desk was bare, the drawers were empty. Whoever's office this was, they weren't here very much. There'd be nothing interesting in there.

To my left, the corridor stretched toward another office, and the desk in this one was piled with papers. Much better.

The long hall was dotted on the window side with spectacular-looking plants. Taking up the central third or so of the interior wall, large glass doors looked out onto a darkened lobby. Looking in, I could make out an inlaid design of the kingfisher bird in a gleaming marble floor. On one side there were elevator doors, which were on the opposite side as the elevator I'd used that morning. That meant this floor had its own private elevator. Better and better.

I walked silently past the big glass lobby doors, past the plants lining either side of the hall, toward the second locked office door. As I approached it, something to my left caught my attention. Something that wasn't a plant. No, not something. Someone.

Ah. That explains that.

Without turning, I said aloud, "you might be able to fool everyone else, but you can't hide from me."

"What makes you think I'm hiding from *you*?" asked a familiar, smooth voice.

I turned my head in time to see the darkness shimmer, and reveal the seductive smile that inhabited all of my daydreams for the past week.

Lumakinetic. So rare, even the expert wasn't sure they existed.

The last time we met, I was distracted by the con and didn't have a chance to really look at him. I took my time now, taking in every detail. At least a few inches taller than my five foot eight. It was hard to tell in the dim light, but I thought he was probably close to my own age, perhaps a few years older, maybe mid-twenties. Dark hair that fell past his shoulders, pulled sharply back from his face. He leaned against the wall with a casual grace that disguised the strength of the densely muscled body.

I thought I'd romanticized him in my mind, but the reality was every inch as perfect as I remembered. He was still devastatingly handsome in a roguish kind of way that cut through all my defenses. This man was trouble, and I couldn't seem to resist.

He pushed off the wall in one fluid move and took a step toward me. "You shouldn't be here."

"Neither should you," I countered. The hall was dark, but my eyes had clearly seen empty wall where he was now standing. If he was using his Talent to hide, he didn't want to be found here, either.

"You need to leave. Now." He glared down at me, arms crossed over his chest.

I bristled at his harsh tone. "Why? What's up here that's so secret?"

"Go. While you still can."

"Is that a threat?"

"No, it's-" A loud ding from my left cut him off. His eyes widened in alarm, as his head snapped toward the unexpected noise. The lights flickered on, first in the lobby, then in the hall where we stood. The distinctive sound of elevator doors opening and closing rang ominously through the hall.

This is bad. Very bad. If I ran for the stairs, I'd have to go right past the big, glass doors to the lobby. With all the lights on, I'd be seen immediately by the person who just came in. I could duck into the office, but whoever it was would probably go straight there. Before I could even register what was happening, I was pressed with my back against the wall and a hand over my mouth. My mystery man had me pinned. The back of my mind registered that if I wasn't terrified, I'd be enjoying this.

"Shh," he whispered sharply, eyes fixed on mine in warning. There was genuine fear in them, and in the split second I had to decide - run or stay - that was what made me go along with him. I nodded.

"Has it passed validation?" a new voice asked as I heard the glass doors open. I wanted to look, but my captor/rescuer held my eyes and I couldn't look away. The urgency in his expression was too extreme for the risk of being caught in the wrong hallway. I was right, there was something dark under the surface here, and I'd accidentally stumbled into a dangerous situation.

Footsteps, muffled by carpet. "Excellent. Three down, four to go." Closer. The doors to the lobby twanged faintly as they swung shut. There was no shout of alarm, though, so it seemed like we were successfully hidden. "I don't care what Fisher said. This is your priority." Closer and closer. He was coming toward the office door right beside us, toward the doorknob that was a foot from where we stood.

The hand over my mouth released me, and then my arms were held above my head, flat against the hard surface. I was pressed into the wall by a body, warm and hard against me. His eyes were still on mine, but closer, so much closer, and his mouth a hair away from mine.

Oh, god. Not the time to get distracted.

I didn't know what to do with my hands. My heart pounded and my mind spun with images that were wildly inappropriate to the situation. He seemed to realize it at the same moment. Drawing a breath, he looked away, at the ceiling, at the wall beside my head, as if trying to pretend our bodies weren't pressed together.

It just made it worse.

"Get it done," said the voice, only a few feet away now. I couldn't bring myself to look with my eyes, but I felt him coming closer to where we hid, still oblivious to our presence. His path would take him inches from us - no, less.

I lined up the shot in my head, mapping the trajectory like a ball on a pool table, and my heart sank. Too close. A collision course with disaster.

I couldn't bring myself to look. My captor's body pressed harder into me, his head beside mine now, his breath in my ear. I felt him exhale and hold it, compressing his lungs to make himself as small as possible, and I did the same.

Those last few inches got us clear. I felt the breeze of the door opening and closing again, and then we were alone in the hallway. A faint snick came from the doorknob as it locked. Nothing moved for a second. I began to breathe again.

He finally inhaled, too, and his forehead quietly hit the wall beside my head. Another breath. Two. He didn't move.

For a long moment, maybe a second, maybe an hour, we stayed perfectly still. I was aware of every inch of his body against mine, every pounding heartbeat, every breath.

He pulled back slowly, his cheek brushing mine, until we were face to face again. The same raw, liquid heat that was running through me was reflected in his eyes, locking me in place. Wanting. Waiting.

Without warning, he pushed back from the wall and stalked down the hall without looking back.

Hurrying after him, I caught up as he passed through the stairwell door. I followed him down, struggling to match his pace, past the floor I'd started on. Straight down, five flights, ten, twenty, ignoring all the doors until we got to one labeled 'street'.

Through the door was a broad alley, stretching in both directions to the streets on either side. A left, a right, a long block toward 8th and then across, until the bustle of the Theatre District morphed into the restaurants and bars and residential brownstones of Hell's Kitchen.

Through the entire walk, he remained invisible.

"Who was that?" I asked when we got to an empty section of street. "What was he talking about?" He ignored me, and kept walking. "Who are you?"

He stopped dead, and turned to me, appearing suddenly beside me. "You know," he commented without answering any of my questions. "Most Kinetics can't see me." His tone was casual, conversational, but I felt the sharp undercurrent.

"So?"

"Because it's impossible," he finished flatly. "Bodies are too solid for Aquakinetics and too liquid for Telekinetics. Living things are invisible to Kinetic sight. Except yours, apparently."

Fear settled back in the pit of my stomach. I was one of a kind after all. And now I was right back in the same kind of situation I'd been in all my life, but now a stranger knew my secret, and I had no idea what he was going to do with it.

"Don't tell them," he said, echoing my train of thought. "It's better if no one knows."

Not what I expected. "You know," I pointed out.

"Yes," he said, smiling for the first time, "but I'm on your side."

"Are you?"

A pause. "At the moment." There it was, the smile, the spark that made me want to throw caution to the wind. Tension stretched between us again, and the memory of our first meeting hung in the air, waiting to be acknowledged.

"Who was that?" I asked him again, breaking the heavy silence.

His expression shut down again. "Someone you don't want catching you where you're not supposed to be," he said seriously. "Don't go up there again. It's not safe."

"Then why were you there?"

"Same reason as you. Looking for answers."

"Answers to what?"

He sighed. "Questions it's better not to ask. I'm serious. Don't go back." It sounded like genuine concern in his voice, which threw me off.

"Only if you tell me who you are."

"I'm Jack," he admitted, relaxing. "Nice to meet you. Again."

"Diana."

"Yes," he said. "I know."

"You're not what you seem, are you, Jack?"

"Almost never." Smiling a Cheshire cat smile, he faded into the night, invisible to my eyes, his shape still clear in my mind. It would take a while to get used to the disconnect. I felt him step back and turn, walking back the way we came. This time I didn't follow.

"I can still see you," I called after him.

"Still not hiding from *you*," he replied without turning.

I stared after him a moment, and then walked off in the opposite direction, trying to suppress the smile that just wouldn't quite go away.

CHAPTER FIVE: SETUP

"You want me to do *what?*" I demanded when Montgomery handed me my new assignment.

I'd been working at Kingfisher for long enough that I thought I knew what to expect. The first few missions they gave me had been laughably easy. In two weeks, I'd unlocked abandoned safes, retrieved lost valuables from inaccessible places, and disarmed a few bombs from outside shielded rooms. While the last one was nerve-wracking, it wasn't actually hard, and I was beginning to think I was going to like it here.

I hadn't seen Jack again, but I'd stopped worrying about groceries, I'd started paying for my drinks at Jimmy's, and I'd even had dinner out a few times. At a *restaurant.* It was starting to look like this job was the best thing that had ever happened to me.

Until today. "You can't be serious."

Montgomery watched me from the other side of his desk, looking unimpressed. "Is there a problem with your assignment, Miss Grey?"

"Yes, there's a problem," I informed him. "It's impossible."

"The impossible is what we do here."

I shook my head impatiently. "No. That's a slogan. This is actually impossible. It can't be done."

He leaned back in his chair. "I see a great deal of potential in you, but if you can't carry out your assignments, I'll have to reconsider. I'd hate to see you give up on your career here so easily."

The implication was clear. My job was dependent on this assignment. If I refused, or failed, I'd be out of a job, and without that job, I'd be right back where I started, stealing from bars and casinos and hoping not to get caught.

"Your partner didn't think it was impossible. Why don't you talk it over with him? I'm sure he'll have some ideas, if you don't."

"Partner? What partner?"

"Did you really not read the whole briefing before you decided it couldn't be done? Surely you didn't think you'd have to do it alone."

I blinked. That was exactly what I'd thought. I'd gotten as far as seeing what they wanted me to take and from where, and I panicked. Taking a moment to breathe, I scanned through the document again. When I saw who they had assigned me to work with, I grinned. "Yes," I agreed. "I think I'll go talk to him."

—

"Nice place," I commented when I heard footsteps in the hall. My words elicited a string of curses, and I smiled.

"What the hell are you doing in my apartment?" Jack demanded. I flipped through the pages of the mission brief, satisfied with his reaction. It was fun to have the upper hand on him for a change. "How did you get in? Never mind, dumb question," he corrected. "Don't you knock?"

I looked up, and blinked.

He leaned against the doorframe, wearing a pair of well-worn jeans, and nothing else. My eyes scanned involuntarily from the waist of his low-slung jeans, up over the flat planes of his stomach, the arms that were were crossed over his chest, giving the muscles of his shoulders even more definition. His hair fell across them, messy, as if tousled from sleep.

"Did you just wake up?" I asked. It was three in the afternoon.

"I worked late. What the hell are you doing on my couch?" he demanded again. "How do you even know where I live?"

I pulled a page from the folder I was holding and read it aloud.

"Jack Raven," I recited. "Shadow. Start date August 24, 1993. Age 23. Male, Caucasian and Native American. Date of birth November 14, 1973. US Citizen. Address 34 Commerce Str-"

"Is that my personnel file? How did you even… never mind, that's a dumb question, too," he corrected, shaking his head. "I'll go back to the first one - why are you here?"

I tossed the mission brief onto the coffee table. He glanced at it, and then back at me, and nodded. "OK," he agreed, relaxing. He uncrossed his arms from his chest, momentarily distracting me. "We can talk about that, after we talk about the way you were just blatantly checking me out."

My eyes flicked back up to his face. The scowl was gone, replaced with a smirk and a spark in his eyes.

"I did no such thing," I protested.

The smirk turned into that sexy grin I couldn't resist. "You know, for a con artist, you're a terrible liar."

"Ex," I corrected. "Ex con artist."

"Of course," he snorted, slipping back into his bedroom to grab a shirt.

—

I struggled to concentrate as Jack dropped into the chair opposite me with his own copy of the mission brief in his hand. He'd put on a t-shirt, but it wasn't doing anything to erase the memory of what was underneath. "I knew we'd need to talk about this at some point, I just thought it could wait until Monday. You don't seem happy about it."

"They want us to steal the most famous diamond in the world, off the neck of the very famous person wearing it, on live tv." The Hope Diamond was being featured in an upcoming big-budget movie, and as a promo stunt, the actress was wearing the real thing to the premier. "No, I'm not happy about it."

"I wouldn't think stealing would be a problem for you." A hint of teasing humor crept into his voice.

"OK, first, I was under duress, second, I haven't done it in years, and third, I *don't* have a problem with stealing. I have a problem with getting caught."

"We're not going to get caught," he assured me. His blythe confidence annoyed me.

"How are we not going to get caught?" I demanded. "There are going to be cameras everywhere. Millions of people will be watching." It made no sense. "It would be easier to take it from the museum."

He shook his head. "It wouldn't. The museum security is too tight. We'd never get through unnoticed. Just taking it isn't enough - no one can know it's gone. The fact that the museum is allowing it to be taken out for this event is too good a chance to pass up. It has to be there. There's no other way. I'll take care of the cameras. No one will see a thing."

Aha. Nice to have that confirmed. "You *are* a Kinetic, then," I commented.

"What?"

"Your Talent is a Kinetic Talent, not Mental. You're moving light, not manipulating minds."

"Why do you say that?" he hedged.

"You can obviously hide yourself from sight," I reasoned. "I've seen that several times now. And you hid me from that guy in the hallway, so it's not Personal." Wait, that wasn't the right word. "Prodigal," I corrected myself. "It could have been Mental, you could be tricking people's brains into not noticing you. But if you can trick the cameras, too, then you're bending the light itself. Kinetic."

He watched me for a minute. "You're right," he admitted. "It's a type of Kinetic. They call us Shadows, but it's not really about shadow. It's about light." He held out a hand. A brilliant turquoise butterfly sat perched on it for a moment. It spread its wings once, and then fluttered up toward the ceiling, where it burst into a shower of blues and greens. The pieces rained down toward my upturned face like snow, and disappeared before they reached me. The whole thing was breathtakingly beautiful, and I'd never seen anything like it. It felt like magic.

When the last of it vanished, I looked back at him to find him watching for my reaction. He was trying to impress me. It was working, but I wasn't about to admit it to him.

"Showoff," I accused with a smile. He tilted his head in an admission of guilt. "You said *they* call you Shadows. What do you call yourself?"

"Raven." Before I could ask more, he changed the subject back to the original topic. "So what don't you like about the plan?"

"Does it matter? You said we have to do it anyway."

"It would be foolish to ignore the expertise of a professional thief. So yes, it matters."

"I'm not a professional thief," I insisted. He raised his eyebrows. "Anymore." It struck me that he knew so much about me, and I knew so little about him. I hated it. "So you hide the diamond, I lift it off her neck without her noticing, and replace it with a replica. We take the real one, we leave without being seen. Piece of cake."

"I'm sensing some sarcasm."

"How am I supposed to do that without her noticing? I mean, weight sensors are one thing, but weight sensors don't move around."

He leaned back in his chair, eyes narrowed. "That's not the problem, is it? You could do that in your sleep. And it's not the pressure. I've seen you work just fine in high-stress situations," he said with the hint of a smile. Thoughtfully, he mused, "No. The problem isn't you. It's me. I'm your only escape route. You'd be completely dependent on me to get you out, and you *hate* that, don't you?"

He shrugged. "I don't blame you. You barely know me. You have no reason to trust me, and less reason to trust the company. If we set you up to take the fall, you'd have no way out. For something this big, the fallout would be catastrophic for you."

I hadn't quite thought of it that way, but he was right. My unease about this job came down to trust. The theft itself - it would be tricky, but it was familiar. I knew how to do that. But trust wasn't something that came easily to me.

"So let's change that," he suggested. "Let's modify the plan so you're not relying on me to get out. If everything goes south - which it won't - you can just walk out with no one the wiser."

"And how do we do that?"

"The same way you did in the casino. We look like we belong. No one looks twice at the staff. We get on the roster, wear whatever everyone else is wearing, and you'll be just as invisible with or without me. There would be nothing to tie things back to you, and you can just walk out."

That would probably solve the problem. "Why would you do that?"

He smiled. "Because I'm not planning to set you up."

There had to be a catch. I just wasn't seeing it yet. "I'll think about it," I told him, and left.

—

"I don't like it," I told the world at large. A few people glanced up at the sound of my voice, and then quickly away. Even in good neighborhoods like this one, people got nervous when you talked to yourself.

I still didn't like the plan, but I no longer had a real reason. I could usually rely on instinct, but it was failing me this time. I had no idea what to do. Without any clear direction, I started walking, blocks and avenues going by in a blur as I thought. When I realized where my feet had taken me, I laughed.

"Hey, Jim," I called, as I walked into his bar.

He scowled when he looked up. "No. There are customers back there, and they're bad news. Stay away from them." It was sweet that he tried to protect me. Pointless, but sweet.

"Not here for that," I told him. "I'm just here because I missed your pretty face." I beamed at him as I flopped down onto a barstool.

He looked at me for a second, then started mixing a drink. "How's the new job treating you?" he asked, handing me the glass.

I stared into the dark liquid. "I'm thinking of quitting, actually."

"Already? Why?"

"I think I'm getting set up."

He rolled his eyes. "Has anyone ever told you you're paranoid?"

I laughed. "Yeah, but I don't trust them." I took a swig from my glass. Maybe I was overreacting. "Something about it just feels wrong."

"Based on what?"

"Past experience."

"You *have* no past experience with this." He leaned forward and rested his elbows on the bar. "From what you said, this is a real, legitimate company, not a scam. Right?" I nodded. "Not everyone is out to get you."

The bell over the door rang, and Jim looked over my shoulder to see who was coming in. "Hey, Eddie. The usual?" he asked.

Conversation over, I thought. Once Ed started drinking, he'd be here all night. I didn't mind confiding in Jim, but I didn't need Ed knowing my business, too.

While Jim poured him a beer, I thought about what he said. *Not everyone is out to get you.* I hadn't actually seen anything suspicious about Kingfisher since my weird encounter with Jack in the hallway on my first day.

It wasn't that I didn't trust Jack. It was that I didn't trust anyone. All of my life, I'd worked alone, but this was something I couldn't do by myself. I could stick with what I'd always known, or I could take a risk, and try something new. Do more.

Be more.

"Thanks, Jim," I called, leaving money for the drink on the bar. He'd yell at me later - he hated when I over-tipped - but I was in a hurry.

I had to go tell Montgomery I'd do the job.

CHAPTER SIX: PRICELESS

I'd never been inside a space this grand before. A masterpiece of Art Deco architecture, the grand foyer was immense and imposing, dripping with glamor and oozing sophistication. It was the sort of place that made a point of keeping out riff raff like me. It gave me a spiteful sort of satisfaction to be on the inside for once.

Even more remarkably, I looked like I belonged. I didn't need Jack's illusions. Dressed in the same uniform as the rest of the ushers and other staff, I was effectively invisible. Glittering people milled around the main area, posing for the cameras and each other. The amount of wealth casually displayed on any one of them would be enough to support me for years. While I was here, maybe I could-

"Easy there," said Jack's voice in my ear. "Just the one we're after. If someone notices something missing, we lose our window."

I closed my eyes, trying not to focus on how close he was behind me. He was dressed in the same red bowtie-and-vest atrocity I was, but it actually looked good on him. I was pretty sure anything would look good on him. It was annoying. And distracting.

Everything about him was distracting. Every second that passed made me more and more aware of him. I was pretty sure he was doing it on purpose - standing a little too close, looking a little too long. It became a game, each of us flirting a little more outrageously, pushing to see which of us would break first. Staying focused on the job was... challenging.

Diamonds helped. They were the hardest things in the room, and they popped out to my Kinetic sight like stars reflected in a murky sea. From where we stood in a quiet corner, I could pick them out with my eyes closed. I didn't need Jack to tell me when the one we were after entered the room. It lit up like a beacon, pulling my awareness like a magnet.

"There," he whispered, still too close to my ear. "She's coming in the far door now. Silver dress, blonde hair."

I was expecting it to be a bright sapphire blue. Instead, it was a muted, smoky color, like a restless ocean. The dark gem stood out starkly against the actress's pale skin, showcased by her upswept blonde hair and the keyhole neckline of light-colored dress that framed it. It couldn't have been more visible if they'd put a spotlight on it.

"Can you reach it from here?" Jack asked in my ear. My skin prickled from the feel of his breath against my neck, sending goosebumps along my spine. I shivered. "Everything OK?" he asked, with a touch of humor.

"Fine," I said shortly, shaking it off. "She's easily inside my range, but I'm going to want to concentrate. I don't want to drop it if someone bumps into me."

He looked around, and then gestured to a spot above us. "How's that?" he asked, indicating a narrow balcony. It was opposite the grand staircase where the handlers were now guiding the actress. From there, I'd still be easily within range, but…

"Will we both fit?"

"It will be cozy," he agreed, "but we've had worse."

I did *not* need a reminder right now of Jack pinning me against that wall. And I *definitely* did not need to picture him doing it again, up there on that balcony, with everybody down here. "It'll work," I said, sharply shutting down that train of thought.

By the time we made our way up to the balcony, the profession-al photographer was positioning and posing the actress like a doll. At her feet, his assistant scurried, rearranging her train every time she switched positions. Flashes went off in every direction, earning glares from the official photographer as he measured the light levels. Every eye, every camera was fixed on her, and on the diamond I was about to steal.

Not my problem, I reminded myself.

I stepped up to the edge of the balcony, and made the mistake of looking down.

"What's wrong?" Jack asked as I swayed away from the edge.

"I need to close my eyes," I told him. "It's easier if I don't have regular vision to distract me. But that rail is low. I don't want to bump into it and fall over." Looking up apologetically, I said, "I need you to hold me up."

"What?"

"Stand behind me and hold on to me. So I don't fall."

He looked panicked. "I don't think that's a good idea."

"Why not?"

"If I do that, we'll both be distracted."

"Why?"

In explanation, he turned me to face out over the crowd, and stepped in close behind me. He wrapped both arms around my waist, and pulled me back against him. "Are you sure you want me to do this?" he asked in my ear, and I immediately understood why. My body reacted instantly - and so did his. It seemed that his mind had been in the exact same place as mind all night, and the way we fit together like this was giving him the same ideas it was giving me. It was impossible to ignore the hardness pressing behind me, and nearly as difficult to stop myself from pushing back into it.

Distracted didn't begin to cover it. I didn't care.

"I'm sure."

"Just to be extremely clear," he said, still close to my ear, "you want to stay exactly like this, while we do this job?"

It was beyond irresponsible. Downright foolish would be

closer to the mark. Insane might cover it. But for all I was worth, I couldn't bring myself to tell him to move. "Yes," I breathed. "Exactly like this." It would be torture. Exquisite, beautiful torture.

"You are going to be the death of me."

"Hopefully not today." I slipped the diamond from my pocket and held it up. "Ready?"

I could feel his chest shake with silent laughter. "As ready as I can possibly be."

I let the diamond slip from my fingers, and caught it just above the crowd below. Shutting out the feel of Jack's fingers digging into my waist, I let it sail across the room and hover above the actress's head. I paused, half expecting a shout of alarm from the crowd. There was none.

So far, so good.

Step one: remove the real one. The key to this was mimicking the weight of the rock against her skin. I had to hold the necklace still relative to the actress, and move it with her as she moved. Fortunately, she was posing, but she switched positions frequently. Slowly, I lifted the prongs holding the real gem in place.

No reaction.

Carefully, carefully, I lifted the diamond away from its setting. Still no reaction. Breathing a little more deeply, I started to swap the gems.

Real one out…

She moved.

I must have been a fraction of a second off in following her motion, because she reached a hand up to adjust the necklace. If she touched it now, she'd feel sharp prongs sticking up from an empty setting.

Thinking quickly, I tugged at the fabric of her gown, just below the neckline. Her hand rapidly shifted direction, and grabbed at the front of her dress. While she snapped angrily at the photographer's assistant who was arranging her skirt, I dropped the fake gem into the setting and quickly bent the prongs back into place.

Fake one in. Done.

I just had to get it back to this side of the room. Easy. Starting to relax, I became aware of my surroundings again. Balcony. Jack standing behind me, arms around my waist, hard as a rock against my back.

"Hey Jack?" I asked a little breathlessly, as I carefully pulled the gem back across the room toward my waiting hand. Slowly, steadily, carefully not dropping it.

"Yeah?"

"Nobody saw that, right?"

"No."

"So nobody but us knows the job is done yet, right?

"Right."

"So we have some time before anyone looks for us?"

His intake of breath told me he knew exactly how I wanted to fill that time. "We do."

The diamond finally landed in my palm. I closed my fingers around it. "What do you say we get out of here?"

—

I had the door unlocked before his hand hit the knob. It looked like a storage closet, maybe for props, I didn't care. What I cared about was Jack pulling me inside, falling back against a set of metal shelves that rattled slightly but stayed upright. I shoved the diamond into my pocket and wrapped my hands around his neck.

I have a diamond in my pocket.

His arms pulled my body against his as I pulled his mouth down to mine. Heat pulsed through me as we crashed together recklessly, lips and teeth and tongues tangling, hands pulling frantically at clothes.

I have a diamond in my pocket.

His tie fell forgotten as I pulled at the buttons of his shirt. The crush of his mouth against mine drove every other thought from my head, but one kept creeping back.

I have a priceless diamond in my pocket.

He pulled the hem of my shirt free from my pants, and slid his hands up my back. The feeling of his fingers on my bare skin was everything I imagined it would be.

I wonder how much I could get for it.

We'd been heading for this since the moment we met, and the more time we spent together, the higher the tension rose. Now that I had him in my arms, under my fingertips, I wanted him more than I'd ever wanted anything else in my life.

Almost anything else.

I was already regretting what I was about to do, but I would never get a chance like this again. It took every ounce of concentration I had left to pull back so I could see his face.

"Jack," I whispered, staring into his eyes.

"Yes," he murmured back.

Hoping he could see the sincerity of my words, I said, "I'm sorry," and meant it.

His brow furrowed, and I took advantage of his momentary confusion to step back, out of his grasp. He tried to step forward after me, but was held against the metal rack behind him by the fabric of the bow tie I had slipped through his belt loop and tied to the shelf. It wouldn't hold him long, but it would hold him long enough.

I stepped back again, gave him an apologetic smile, and slipped back out through the door, locking it behind me. His muffled shouts followed as I walked calmly toward the nearest door, straightening my clothes.

I have a diamond in my pocket.

With one last glance back toward the prop closet, I hurried toward the door, gripping the gem tightly in my hand.

I will never get a chance like that again.

CHAPTER SEVEN: HOPE

He found me sitting on the edge of the long, narrow fountain across Fifth Avenue. I knew he would - I was waiting for him. I just didn't know what he would say when he got here.

I looked up at him nervously when he stopped in front of me. For a long time, he didn't say anything at all, he just stood there looking down at me silently with a flat expression. The chatter of the city floated around us. A handful of people came and went on the sidewalk, but none paid us any mind. I held up the smoky blue gem, offering it to him. He didn't take it.

"You locked me in a closet," he said eventually.

"I did."

"But you're still here."

"I am."

His face was still stony, hands tucked into his pockets. "Why?"

"Why did I lock you in a closet?"

"Why are you still here?"

That was the question. I'd been struggling with it since I first sat down here, and I thought I had an answer now.

"Your plan worked perfectly," he continued, before I could explain. "You got me to help you take the diamond, and then locked me in a closet so you could get away. No one but me knew you had it yet, no one would even look for it for hours. It worked, I fell for it. There are cabs everywhere. You could have been well on your way to the airport by now. No one could stop you. It all makes perfect sense. The only thing that doesn't make sense," he concluded bitterly, "is why you're still here."

I took a deep breath. *Now or never.* "Come with me."

He blinked, shocked into silence. I wasn't sure which one of us was more surprised. "What?"

"Come with me," I repeated earnestly. "Like you said, we can catch a cab, and be on a plane before anyone even looks for us. No one could stop us. Come with me."

"So you can set me up again? I'm not that dumb." Now anger was settling into his voice, and I couldn't blame him for it.

"It wasn't a setup," I insisted. "I didn't plan any of that. I just saw the opportunity and acted on instinct. I wasn't thinking clearly. It was a mistake."

"Which part of it, exactly, was the mistake?"

"The part where I left you there. Come with me," I repeated again.

He shook his head slowly. "Why should I trust you? You just locked me in a closet." The indignant tone was beginning to waver, and I started to hope that I had a chance of convincing him.

"Because I'm still here."

The only way I could make him believe I wasn't still conning him was with the absolute truth. I stood and met his eyes earnestly. "We just did the impossible together, Jack. It was easy. No one else in the world could carry off what we just did and we were barely paying attention. You and I together, the things we could accomplish, it's limitless. We could be unstoppable together. Untouchable. If we can do this without even trying, what *else* can we do?"

He inhaled sharply. He saw it now - I could almost see the possibilities spinning through his mind the way they did in mine. His eyes searched my face, trying to decide if I was genuine. I didn't know how else to convince him that for once in my life, I wasn't holding anything back. "Don't you want to find out?"

My heart skipped when an incredulous laugh escaped him. With a disbelieving smile, he said, "You want me to run away with you. For real."

I nodded. "We can disappear. Find a beach somewhere. With this kind of money, we could buy our own island if we wanted to." His smile broadened, and I knew I'd won him over. He believed me now, he saw it, he wanted to go. My heart surged with joy, knowing that the biggest gamble I'd ever made was going to pay off.

And then his expression changed. His eyes closed and he took one long, tortured breath before turning away and looking up at the sky. "They would find us."

"They wouldn't-" I began.

"They would," he interrupted. "It wouldn't matter how far we went, or how well we hid. It wouldn't even be about the diamond. They can't let people walk away with the prize, or everyone would start doing it. You don't know these people. They're ruthless and powerful. They would never stop until they caught us, and once they did, they'd make an example of us, so no one would ever try again."

He was slipping away from me. I had him a minute ago, I could convince him again. "But don't you want-"

"It doesn't matter what I want," he said roughly. He turned and left me standing there on the sidewalk, watching my short-lived hope go up in smoke. When he reached the corner and turned out of sight, I shoved the priceless gem back into my pants.

I walked away, feeling the diamond weigh heavily in my pocket.

—

"Who are they?" I asked Jack as he stepped into his kitchen.

To his credit, he only jumped slightly this time, and didn't seem all that concerned to find me in his apartment unannounced again. "I'm not surprised to see that you still don't knock," he said after a brief glance at me. "I *am* surprised to see that you're still here."

He was fully dressed this time, which was probably for the best, all things considered. Ignoring me, he walked toward his kitchen and opened a cabinet. "I wasn't keen on getting hunted down by ruthless and powerful people," I admitted. "If you couldn't hide from them, I wouldn't stand a chance. I handed it in to Montgomery last night."

This time he did turn and look at me, arms crossed and leaning back on the counter.

"You thought I would leave," I realized. "But you didn't tell Montgomery."

He turned back to the cabinet, pulled out two glasses, and filled them from the wine bottle on the counter. "Consider it an apology for getting you into this mess," he said, handing me one of the glasses.

"So it *is* your fault they abducted and blackmailed me."

"They did what?" He shook his head. "You know what, I'm not even surprised. They really wanted that rock, and like you said, we're the only ones who could have carried it off, so they were desperate."

"Why did they want it so badly?" I asked. "I mean, they obviously have money, so it can't just be that. Why this, why now?"

"Officially, this mission was a test. There's a new board member, and he's not convinced the team is living up to its full potential. We're supposed to be able to do the impossible, so he set us an impossible task - stealing that diamond. It was a performance evaluation."

I shook my head. "A performance evaluation that just happens to give him the world's most famous diamond? I don't buy it."

"No, me neither," Jack agreed. "But I've learned it's better not to ask too many questions."

I stared into the glass for a long moment without drinking from it. "Who are these people, Jack?" Twice now, he'd warned me about them, and both times it seemed genuine. More and more, I was wondering what I'd gotten myself into. I didn't like being in the dark.

He shook his head. "The less you know, the safer you are."

"You seem to know a lot. How do you find out all this stuff?"

"I listen."

"Listen where?"

A trace of a smile returned to his face. "Places I'm not supposed to be."

"Like the upstairs hallway?"

"Exactly."

"Why were you there that night?"

He gave a huff of resigned exasperation. "If I tell you this, will you stop asking about them?"

"Promise."

He sighed. "Fine. I was curious about the new board member. His predecessor died rather suddenly. I wanted to see what kind of person he was."

"Did you?"

"I hope not," he replied grimly. "So what's next for you?" he asked, transparently changing the subject. "Another theft?"

I made a face. "Training. Now that I stole his diamond, Montgomery doesn't know what to do with me."

"Training? With who?"

"I'm supposed to meet someone named Vivienne tomorrow morning."

He looked at me sharply. "Vivienne? For training? In what?"

"He didn't say. What about you? What are you doing next?"

"If I tell you, I'd have to kill you," he grinned.

I laughed and shook my head. "No, no. It's too late. That whole 'man of mystery' thing isn't going to work on me anymore."

"Man of mystery?" he laughed. "I think I like that," he said, topping off my glass.

As I sipped from it, I felt a warmth in my chest that wasn't from the wine. I didn't have a priceless diamond, but maybe I hadn't walked away empty-handed, either.

Chapter Eight: Training

Jack was chatting with Candi when I stepped off the elevator. I had a brief surge of jealousy, but when he noticed me, he seemed to forget she existed. Candi looked between the two of us for a moment, and stifled a smile. "Never thought I'd see that," she said under her breath.

"Jack," I said, stating the obvious.

"I heard you were training with Vivienne today," he explained with a forced smile. "I thought you might want company." There was something tight under his tone that sounded almost like worry.

"Why would I need company for training?" I asked, starting to get nervous.

"Oh good, you're here," interrupted a new voice from my right. A woman was standing in the doorway. She was tall and graceful in a stylish white dress that contrasted beautifully with her dark skin. A multitude of neat braids fell down her back, tied loosely at the base of her neck. She gave off an overwhelming sense of gentleness that instantly set me at ease. "I am Vivienne. It's nice to meet you. Please come with me."

I followed her down the hall to a small room next to the library with a handful of chairs. Jack followed, but she insisted he wait outside. He looked unhappy about it, but obeyed.

An older man stood and offered me his chair. "This is Oleg," Vivienne introduced him, as I sat. "He'll be assisting me with your training."

"What are you teaching me?" I asked curiously.

"Biology, mostly. Medical training. With your level of precision, they think you might make a good surgeon."

"Surgeon?" I scoffed. "I don't know the first thing about surgery."

She nodded to Oleg. "You're about to."

Before I could ask more, a wide band wrapped around my torso and tightened, pinning me to the chair.

"What the hell?" I demanded, starting to struggle. The band held, and Oleg checked something on the back of my chair.

"Thank you, Oleg," said Vivienne calmly, as though he hadn't just restrained me. "You can go."

"Let me go," I shouted as the door opened and closed behind me.

"Relax. I'm not going to hurt you," Vivienne assured me gently.

"Then why am I tied up?" I demanded.

"You are restrained for your own safety," she said soothingly. "So you don't fall."

This day just kept getting weirder. "Why would I fall?"

"Some people," she began, laying a cool hand to my forehead, "find this disorienting."

"Disorienting? What the hell are you teaching me?"

"It's not so much the *what*, as the *how*." She sat in front of me. "I'm what's called a Mnemonic Telepath. We specialize in memory - reading, modifying, erasing. I'm not going to teach you so much as give you someone else's memories of learning it. Close your eyes. It will be easier that way."

"I never agreed to this! Let me go!"

She smiled at me sadly. "You did. It was in your employment packet - the contract you signed on the first day." She laid her hand on my forehead again. "Now close your eyes."

—

This was the hardest exam I'd ever taken. The anatomy section alone would take an hour. And then organic chemistry, human physiology… good thing I brought plenty of coffee. Everything rode on passing this test. Without a good grade here, I would never get into medical school.

I'd just finished up labeling all the bones on a diagram of the hand when a voice came over the loudspeaker.

"Her mind is open now, Jack. I stop now, she will never recover. She won't remember who she is. Let me work."

Another voice answered. A familiar voice. "What are you doing to her?"

"I'm giving her knowledge. Medicine, specifically."

"Like an EMT course?"

"Like a medical degree."

"Vivienne!"

"I have children, Jack. You know I have no choice. She'll be fine. Probably. Now let me concentrate."

"If she's not…"

"The longer you distract me, the worse it will be when she wakes up."

A cadaver lay on the table, staring sightlessly at the ceiling, torso gaping open. I began reciting the organs of the body, pointing them out to my instructor as I went. Liver, gallbladder, spleen. Left lung, right lung. Bronchial tubes. Aorta. Heart.

"Diana." *Who was Diana?*

I focused on the cadaver. Heart. The heart was beating. Was it supposed to be beating? I shook off my distraction. Heart.

"Wake up."

The heart was still beating, but the cadaver was standing, leaning over me, holding a hand to my forehead.

"Diana."

I must be dreaming. Maybe I fell asleep in class.

Someone was holding my hand.

I opened my eyes. A man, someone I thought I knew, was sitting next to me. I struggled to remember who he was. Foggy memories came. A shape in the shadows, a laugh, an incandescent moment in the dark. I blinked, searching for his name. "Jack," I said, remembering.

He closed his eyes and let out his breath.

"Good," said the woman's voice. I turned to look at her. A

tall woman stood on my other side. Not a cadaver, after all. I could still feel her heart beating inside her chest, her lungs moving in and out. Now that I knew what I was looking at, my Kinetic sight showed me details. Bones, dense and hard. Her left ulna had been broken at some point. Organs, softer, spongier. The empty spaces that were her veins, moving blood that I couldn't sense.

"Do you know who you are?" the woman asked.

"Diana. Diana Grey."

"Good. Who am I?"

"You're Vivienne. You just trained me. Sort of."

"And who is he?" she asked with a nod toward Jack.

"Jack. My, uhm," I faltered, trying to remember what he was to me.

"Friend," he supplied with a smile. A strange warmth filled me at the word. Vivienne looked between us with a frown, and then visibly decided not to ask. She picked up a clipboard and checked something off.

"What year is it?"

"1995."

"Father's name?"

"I don't know," I answered honestly. She looked up sharply. "But my mother's name was Katie," I added quickly. "And my grandmother's name was Betty. Beatrice Grey. She raised me. My parents died when I was young."

She made another check on the clipboard, apparently satisfied with my answer. "How many bones in the human body?"

"Two hundred six." Check.

"Name three neurotransmitters."

"Dopamine, norepinephrine, serotonin." Check.

"Newton's third law?" She continued to grill me for a few minutes on scientific knowledge I had no reason to know but did anyway, and then concluded, "Good. You seem sane, for now. Do you have someone to stay with you? Family, roommate, significant other? You shouldn't be alone today."

That would have been a good thing for her to ask before she started messing with my head.

"I'll stay with her," Jack volunteered.

She looked back and forth between us again, and then nodded. "Talk to her about her memories today," she instructed Jack. "Reinforce the real ones. She's going to be disoriented for a while, but it should improve over time. If she's still having trouble in the morning, call me."

CHAPTER NINE: MEMORIES

I looked at Jack as we walked the handful of blocks to Central Park. "We're friends?" I asked him with a sideways smile.

"I think we are," he confirmed. "I'm not sure, though. I don't really have any, so I'm not entirely sure how it works." I wondered how many people missed his dry sense of humor.

"Me neither," I confessed.

"First time for everything."

I felt the stress and worry of the morning fade into the background as we crossed into the park. I'd always loved it here. I loved my city, too, with its chaos and its constant motion, but the park was a welcome respite. The fact that I lived so close to it was an extraordinary anomaly in my life - a bright patch of luxury in an otherwise austere existence. It was a natural choice for a hot summer afternoon.

Jack bumped me with his shoulder as we walked down the tree-lined paths. "You're supposed to be talking," he reminded me. "Tell me a memory."

This should feel weird. I didn't normally talk about myself, but for some reason today it was fine. Maybe it was a side effect of the training. "What should I talk about?"

"Start at the beginning," he suggested. "How old were you, when you realized you weren't Normal?" he asked.

"As soon as I was old enough to understand words, I think. My grandmother always told me, 'you're not like other people, you have to be careful to hide it.' She told me that so often, it still feels weird talking about it sometimes."

"You said she raised you, right? What was she like?" I knew he was probably just trying to reinforce my memories, like Vivienne told him, but I thought he might be genuinely curious, too.

"Sad, mostly," I told him. "She wasn't a Paranormal, but my grandfather was, I think. I don't know what happened to him. She and my mom fled from… somewhere during World War II. I don't even know where. My mom was an infant at the time. She wanted to blend in and not attract notice, so she tried to be invisible. Nondescript. Grey.

"I don't know what happened to my parents. I don't even know my father's name. I was too young to remember, and my grandmother blamed him for my mother's death, so she never talked about him.

"I was all she had left. She lost everyone else she cared about, and she thought it was because of their Talent. She didn't want that to happen to me, so she taught me to hide it. Never use it."

He laughed. "Sounds familiar."

If I had to talk about myself, it was only fair that he should too. "What about you? When did you figure out you weren't Normal?"

"I think I was six. My kindergarten teacher freaked out when my crayon drawing came to life."

Ha! "What was it a drawing of?"

"A dinosaur. I was obsessed with pterodactyls at the time. I wasn't very good with crayons, so I cheated and moved around the light instead. Once I got the hang of it, I made it jump up off the page and fly around the room. The other kids were freaked out, but I thought it was hysterical. The teacher didn't, though."

I could picture the scene, children running, the teacher gaping in horror, the crayon dinosaur circling the room.

"What did your parents think? Were they surprised?" I wasn't above using this as an excuse to fish for more information about him.

"Mom was thrilled to have a new Raven in the family. We

pop up every couple generations on her side, but there hadn't been one since her great great grandfather. The principal was less thrilled. They sent me to a private boarding school after that."

"Boarding school? What was *that* like?" That told me a lot about his background, and it was very, very different from mine.

"I got into trouble a lot. Mostly for being places I wasn't supposed to be. Hearing things I wasn't supposed to hear."

"Sounds familiar."

He grinned. "Never grew out of that, I guess. It's useful. The principal hated me, but he couldn't kick me out, because I caught him having an affair with the music teacher."

"Did you like it there?" I couldn't imagine being on my own as a child. My grandmother was strict, but always, always there for me. Until she wasn't.

"I hated it, but it was better than being home. It never occurred to me that I could escape all of it until college."

Of course he went to college. "What did you study?"

"I started with physics. I wanted to understand more about how light worked. It didn't help me as much as I thought it would, since I already knew more than they did. So I switched to Art, and that was much more useful. My father wasn't thrilled with that."

"Why not?" I asked, thinking of the butterfly he made for me. "I can see how it would help you develop your Talent."

He snorted. "My father thought my Talent was only good for pranks and games. He wanted me to be a lawyer, like him. Can you imagine?"

"I thought your family was proud of your Talent?"

"My mom was. It came from her side. My father was not pleased to learn that his wife and child had Native American ancestry, either. That was one of the things I wasn't supposed to hear. We don't speak anymore."

"What happened?"

"After he found out I changed majors, we had it out. He tried to make me switch to pre-law, I refused, he cut me off and disinherited me. Best thing that ever happened to me."

"What did you do?"

"I changed my name to Raven, left and went to find others."

"Changed your name? Why?"

"Paranormals take the last name of the side their Talent comes from. Plus, I didn't want any connection to my father anymore. I was making this grand gesture of rebellion." He shrugged. "Seemed like a good idea at the time."

"What happened when you found the others?"

"I didn't. There aren't any, as far as I could tell. Mom died when I was ten, so I couldn't exactly ask her." He paused, looking sheepish, and a little puzzled. "I've never actually told anyone that story before. Please don't spread it around. Cuts into the whole 'man of mystery' image," he added with a grin.

Dogs and children frolicked in the grass beside the path as we walked. "How did you end up at Kingfisher?" I asked him, stepping aside to let a jogger pass.

He shrugged. "Didn't have much choice. My money ran out, and I wasn't about to go be a lawyer, so when the opportunity presented itself, I took it."

"And now? Seems like you're doing OK. Why do you stay?"

I knew him well enough now to catch the slight tightness around his smile when he answered. "Why would I want to leave?" There was something else there, something he wasn't saying, but I decided not to pry.

We lapsed into comfortable silence, winding our way through the park. Our meandering took us to the Great Lawn, full of people playing softball and having picnics. On our left, the ground sloped down toward the Turtle Pond, making a secluded little area, still out in the open, but buffered from the nearby crowds and noise. Across the water, Belvedere Castle perched on its pile of rocks like a miniature fortress. I meandered down toward the water and he followed me.

"I used to love it here when I was little," I told him, sitting on the grass and leaning back on my arms. "I used to imagine it was a real castle with fairies and princes and all. Used to come here all the time." As I spoke, the castle grew and changed. It doubled in size, and tall spires grew from its corners. Banners floated above it in an imaginary breeze.

"Why'd you stop coming?" he asked, sitting beside me.

I tried to cover my expression and failed. That wasn't a story I really wanted to tell. The reality of the first few years of living on my own wasn't something I liked thinking about. But hearing about his family made me think he knew something about being alone, too. "Didn't really have time," I told him honestly. "It took a while to figure out how to survive, after my grandmother died. I didn't think of the casino thing immediately. In the beginning, it was harder."

I stole a glance at him to see his reaction. My background was very different from someone who went to a boarding school. I expected judgment or pity, but all I saw was thoughtful curiosity. "So what did you do?"

"Tried pickpocketing, but I was terrible at it. I was a pretty good thief, but after I got caught a couple times, I decided it wasn't worth the risk. At least there are no actual laws about cheating at roulette. All they can do is kick me out, not arrest me." I lay back in the grass and looked up at the sky. "I think that cloud kind of looks like a cat, don't you?" I asked, pointing.

He lay beside me and squinted up at the cloud. "Sort of?"

"The tail's over there, on the right. And the ears are up there."

The cloud rearranged itself slightly, ears emerging, and a tail gaining definition. "Like that?" He pointed to another cloud. "What about that one? Looks kind of like a dolphin."

When he lowered his hand, he laid it next to mine, just barely touching. With a hidden smile, I placed my hand in his and laced our fingers together. It should have felt strange to hold hands with someone I'd been undressing in a closet two nights ago, but it didn't. It felt oddly, completely right.

—

We lay in the grass for hours, watching the clouds and trading stories until the sun set. When the stars came out, we picked out the constellations, Jack using his Talent to make them bright enough to cut through the ambient city light. It felt peaceful, and natural, and I didn't want to leave. The cold night air eventually forced me to admit that it was time to get inside.

"I should probably go," I told him, sitting up. "It's late."

"How are you feeling?" he asked, standing and offering me his hands.

I took them and let him pull me up. "Pretty sure I'm still sane. Thanks for staying with me."

"It wasn't exactly a hardship," he said without letting go of my hands. Neither of us stepped back. A charged silence fell as we stood there for a long moment, hands intertwined. His eyes searched my face, like he was looking for something, and I realized he wanted to kiss me. Butterflies fluttered in my rib cage at the thought. I'd kissed him before, but that was different, somehow. After today, it seemed… real.

He leaned forward slightly, and I met him halfway. I moved without hesitation, not thinking about the future or the world around us. His mouth brushed mine lightly, softly, and everything changed.

The ground went out from under me. I was in freefall, light-headed and dazed from this slightest touch. Our hands were still clasped, and distance still between us, but this gentle kiss felt so much more intimate than anything I'd ever experienced before. In that moment, I felt closer to him than I'd ever felt to anyone else. I wanted to share all of my secrets with him, and it terrified me.

I stepped back slightly, breaking contact. "I should go," I said, pulling away.

He let me go with a smile that made my heart skip. "Can I walk you home? The park's not safe at night."

"No," I snapped automatically, feeling sudden panic at the

thought of anyone knowing where I lived. As long as no one could find me there, I would always be safe. I trusted him, but this was different. He looked taken aback, surprised by the sharpness of my tone. "I'm sorry, it's just-"

"No," he said, stepping back. "You don't have to explain." All of the intimacy of a moment ago was gone.

As I walked away - in the opposite direction as my home - I was afraid I'd just offended him, and ruined whatever this was. I looked back, over my shoulder, to see him still standing where I left him, hands in his pockets, watching me walk away.

I kept walking, glad that darkness covered the smile I couldn't hide.

CHAPTER TEN: HEARTS

"Hey, Jimmy," I called as I slammed open the door and stalked to the back of the bar. I didn't wait for him to acknowledge me. I was already racking the balls by the time he came into the back room with two brimming shot glasses.

"On the house," he told me, handing me one. I downed it without waiting for him, and turned back to the pool table. Gin. I hated gin.

"Now I know you're upset, if you're willing to drink gin. You want to talk about it?"

"No," I said, bending over the table to break. The sharp sound of porcelain hitting porcelain rang through the small room with a satisfying crack. Nothing sank. I lined up the first shot.

"This is the third night this week."

Nine ball, corner pocket. "I don't want to talk about it."

A week had passed since my day in the park with Jack. I couldn't stop thinking about it, and it was freaking me out. Every time the memory of that kiss played itself back, I felt that crazy rush of... *feelings*, and then an immediate answering rush of panic. I didn't *do* feelings. Feelings were dangerous. Feelings clouded your judgment, and that got you caught.

Two, side pocket. I missed.

"You sure about that?" Jimmy asked, eyeing the ricocheting ball.

I ignored him, and lined up another shot. This one went in.

"Is it about that guy?" he asked, with that uncanny perception of his.

It hit too close to home. "I said I didn't want to talk about it!" I snapped, rounding on him.

He stared at me for a moment, pressing his lips into a flat line, then nodded. "Let me know when you do," he said, turning to go.

Eight ball, side pocket.

—

I started stowing the balls and cue sticks when I felt the last customer leave the bar. I'd run the table three times, and was now calm enough to feel horrible at the way I'd lashed out at Jimmy. I owed him an apology for the way I'd spoken earlier. In the other room, he was moving around behind the bar, emptying the register for the night and mopping up spilled beer with his ancient rag. His heartbeat felt slow and steady, and I focused on it for a moment, letting it calm me.

Ever since Vivienne's training, I was fascinated with bodies. With my new knowledge of anatomy, I could pick out details that were blurry before, and see the shapes under the surface. I did it all the time, now, picking out the dense muscles, and hard bones, identifying individual organs by their movement - lungs breathing in and out, heart pulsing steady and strong.

I groaned when I felt the front door of the bar open and another body come through. While I wanted to apologize to Jim, I also didn't feel like having anyone else asking questions I didn't want to answer.

Almost immediately, I realized something was wrong. The newcomer's heart was beating too fast, like he was nervous. After a moment, a muffled exchange drifted through the door, and then I felt Jim's heartbeat speed up, too. That was weird. Jim never got excited. I closed up the pool cabinet and went out into the main room.

Jim was in his usual spot behind the bar, facing the newcomer. I recognized Ed, but I'd never seen that look on his face before - desperate and ugly. He looked like he hadn't slept in a week. And he was holding a gun.

Ed swiveled toward me when I entered. "What are *you* doing here? You're not supposed to be here, kid."

The second Ed's attention was off him, Jim started slowly reaching for something under the bar. *No, Jim, don't do anything stupid.* "What are you doing, Ed?" I asked, trying to keep his attention on me instead of Jimmy.

"I don't want to hurt you, kid."

"Then don't," I told him. "Put the gun down, and we can all have a drink and pretend this didn't happen."

He started turning back toward Jim. "Give me the money, and everybody goes home."

It happened so fast.

Jim lunged for something under the bar. Ed swiveled and the gun fired, and Jim fell back against the bottles behind him. Ed and I both stared in shocked horror as Jim's body slid slowly to the ground. I couldn't see him behind the bar, but I felt the horrible moment his heart stopped beating.

Dead.

Jimmy was dead, the back of my brain told me. My friend was dead and I never got to tell him I was sorry.

Ed and I turned to look at each other. The understanding passed between us that he had just murdered someone, and I was a witness, so he had to kill me, too. His heart was beating so fast. For a second, he wavered, and I could see on his face that he didn't want to do it. I felt his heart rate begin to slow. Maybe I would get out of this alive after all.

I raised my hands placatingly. "I was never here. You were never here. It's a dangerous neighborhood. Anybody could walk in off the street. Anything can happen." It was a lie. The second I got out of here I would run to the cops and Ed would rot in jail forever because he killed my friend. His heart beat began to slow, and the tip of the gun started to drift toward the floor. "That's it, put the gun down, Ed, and we can-"

I realized immediately that saying his name was a mistake. It reminded him that I knew who he was, and could identify him.

The second I said his name, his heart rate kicked up again. He was going to shoot me. I was going to die here. I would never get to tell Jimmy I was sorry, and I would never see Jack again.

Time slowed. The muscles of his heart contracted and relaxed. I could name each one of them, but none of that would help me right now. His arm swung up, the gun pointed at me, and I panicked.

I pulled.

A bloody mass of muscle, still twitching, ripped from his chest. It flew across the room and smacked wetly into my chest. I caught it by reflex. For one sickening moment, Ed stared at his own disembodied heart before he crumpled to the ground.

I stood frozen for a moment, and then the horrible, bloody, squishy mess in my hands twitched. Blood spurted from various holes, splashing my face and soaking my shirt. I dropped it on the floor, where it landed with a wet smack, splashing the tables and chairs around it. It twitched again, spraying my legs and feet.

I backed away from it in horror until I hit the wall behind me. My knees gave out, I hit the ground, and everything faded.

———

Time passed. People came. Voices spoke.

"What the hell?"

"It's like a horror movie in here."

"This one's alive. I don't think she's injured, but she's definitely in shock."

"Stay away from her. I need to make a call."

"Is that his heart?"

"You don't think she did this, do you?"

"Secure the scene. Don't go near her."

"How would a little thing like her do this?"

"Wait outside. Yeah, this is NYPD. I'm at a crime scene. I think this is one of yours."

More time. Other people. Different voices.

"What are you doing?"
"Sedating her."
"Are you serious? She's in shock already."
"George, get him outside and wipe this memory. Make them both think they got called to a fire, and were too late to stop it."
"What?"
"Ernie, once we're out, torch the place. Leave the two bodies."
"WHAT?"

A needle in my arm, then nothing.

CHAPTER ELEVEN: HELP

My head hurt. I opened my eyes and my stomach heaved.

The ceiling spun and the walls twisted dizzyingly. I tried to get my bearings, but I didn't know this room. It was bare and sparse, with a bed and not much else. No windows, just a dim light coming through the crack under the door.

I tried to sit up and failed.

My hands were cuffed to the bed. *That's not good.* I unlocked them and stood.

My knees buckled, and I fell back onto the mattress. I braced myself against the wall and made my way unsteadily to the door. I tried the handle. Locked. *Whatever.*

It took longer than it should have to pull my focus together enough to find the locking mechanism and disengage it, but I managed eventually. The light from the hallway was bright when I opened the door, and it made my head hurt again.

Memories were drifting back as I tried to figure out where I was and why. A gunshot. A heart. Blood on my hands. *Oh, god.*

People came and took me and locked me up.

They saw. They know.

Fear gave me a dose of clarity. Wherever I was, I needed to get out. I staggered down the hall, found stairs, and stumbled down them, somehow managing not to fall. I came out into a larger area where a young man in a plain gray uniform sat behind a desk. There were doors on the other side of him.

He scrambled to his feet when he saw me, and raised a gun. His hand was shaking. "Stay where you are," he said nervously. "Put your hands up and don't move."

My hands? What would be the point of that?

"Do you know who I am?" I asked, forming each word carefully.

He looked absolutely terrified of me. "Yes," he said, his voice a little unsteady.

"Do you know why I'm here?"

"Yes." His hand was shaking more obviously now.

"Do you really want to be in my way?"

He dropped the gun like it burned him and put his hands in the air.

Better. I didn't like having guns pointed at me. That was something for later. Right now, it was time to go. Through the doors, the sight of a busy night time street made my head spin again. Bright lights swam around me dizzyingly as I stumbled toward the nearest cab. I only had one clear thought left in my head when I landed in the back seat.

Jack.

—

I could dimly see a shape moving in the dark. I grabbed the wall for support. *Where? Right. Jack's place.* Things were getting fuzzier.

Arms steadied me. *Jack?*

He was saying my name, asking me things. "What are you doing here?" I tried to focus on him. I couldn't answer, but it didn't matter. I was safe now. "What's wrong?" And then, "Why are you covered in blood?"

Blood? I looked down. I *was* covered in blood. I had a sudden lucid vision of a heart in my hands, spraying blood all over me. I yelled and tried to push it away, but I could still feel the sticky heat seeping into my shirt. *Off, get it off!* I reached for the hem of my shirt and pulled it over my head.

"What are you… oh, god. No! Don't…"

The pants were soaked, too. I couldn't bear the thought of them against my skin for another second. *All of it. All of it off.* Jack seemed distressed about something. I wanted to reassure him, but I was so tired and the room was spinning again.

There was a bed behind him. I had to lay down.

"Wait! Put this on first," he insisted, pulling off his own shirt and pushing it toward me. "Please." It seemed important to him, so I let him pull a shirt over my head, and struggled to get my arms in its holes. I pushed away from him, and staggered to the bed.

Soft. Warm. Safe.

Jack carefully pulled the sheet up and leaned over me. He brushed hair out of my eyes and peered into them one at a time, then pressed his hand on my neck. "You seem OK," he said after a minute. "Vitals are fine, no concussion, no visible injuries. Can you tell me what happened?"

I looked at him. His face swam in and out of focus. "Drugged," I told him.

"Yeah, I figured that much out. I think you just need to sleep it off. I'll be on the couch. Call if you need me." He started to stand. Jack was leaving.

"No!" With rising panic, I swung my hand wildly and grabbed at him. I caught his hand and pulled. "Stay," I pleaded. "Don't leave."

There was a long moment of silence.

"Diana…"

"*Don't leave me.*"

Silence.

Then a sigh and a brush of cool air as the sheet lifted and he slid in beside me. I curled into him, needing to feel his heat. Warm skin against my cheek, a gentle arm wrapped around me. I clung to him, listening to the steady thump of his heartbeat reminding me I was alive.

———

The sun was too bright. *Why… where… why am I in Jack's bed?* I sat up sharply, and a stab of pain pierced my head. *Ow.* Right. They drugged me. I dimly remembered waking up in the locked room and escaping to find Jack. It was all kind of blurry.

Slowly I got up from the bed. I was sore, but everything seemed to be in one piece. Steadier than I expected, I walked to the door. Jack was in the kitchen, facing away from me. It looked like he was making coffee. He didn't look up at me. "Bathroom's down the hall. There are towels and clean clothes in there. You'll feel better after you shower." There was tension in his shoulders, and he still wouldn't look at me. *Of course.* I was a fugitive now. I endangered him by coming here.

"I'm sorry I got you involved in this. I'll go if you want me to."

"Go? You're not going anywhere. Shower, put on clothes, and then we'll talk."

"You're not mad that I came here?"

"Mad?" He glanced at me and then immediately looked away again. "No, I'm not mad."

"Why won't you look at me?"

"You're half naked."

I looked down. I was still wearing Jack's shirt… and nothing else. At all. It covered the important parts, but only barely. "Oh. I-"

"Nope," he cut me off. "We're not going to talk about the fact that you showed up in my apartment in the middle of the night, stripped naked, and got into my bed. We're going to talk about why you were covered in blood and incoherent when you did it. You're going to go shower, put on some clothes, and coffee will be waiting when you're done. And then after that, you're going to tell me what happened. Got it?"

As he spoke, I remembered doing each of those things. I remembered feeling his bare skin under my cheek, and falling asleep wrapped around him, and I suddenly wished I could remember everything much better.

Clearly, Jack could remember just fine. He was standing by

the coffee machine, his hands flat on the counter, staring carefully down, and every muscle in his body was tense. Suddenly, not talking about last night seemed like a great idea.

I nodded. "Got it. Shower. Clothes. Coffee. Talk."

"Go," he said, pointing toward the bathroom without looking up.

———

"Much better," he said when I re-emerged wearing a t-shirt that swam on me and shorts that reached my knees. He handed me a mug of coffee and gestured toward a chair. "Have a seat. I have a feeling this is going to be a hell of a story."

I stared at the mug of coffee in my hands. I wasn't sure where to begin, so I started in the middle. "They locked me up."

"Like in a cell?" his eyebrows went up in surprise.

"Kind of? Or maybe just a room. It was blurry. The door was definitely locked from the outside, though."

He laughed. "And they thought that would work?" Disbelief and amusement played on his face.

Piecing together the events of the night before, I remembered something important. "I need to learn how to disable a gun," I told him.

"OK. We'll get to that," he said in the kind of tone you use to gentle a nervous horse. "Why did you need to disable a gun? Did someone point one at you?" I nodded, trying to speak, but the words wouldn't come. I killed someone. I killed Ed.

"Is that whose blood was on you?" I nodded again. "Why did he point a gun at you?"

"Because I saw him…" I saw him kill Jimmy. Jimmy was dead.

"You saw something he didn't want you to see?" I nodded. "What did you do then?"

I looked down at my mug, knowing that I had to tell him eventually. "I may have, uhm… ripped his heart out."

There was silence. I snuck a glance at him. His eyebrows were raised in surprise. He didn't seem horrified, just astonished.

"Literally?"

I nodded. "It was an accident."

"An accident," he repeated slowly. "You ripped someone's heart out of their chest by accident." I nodded again. He absorbed the information for a moment. "Well, that explains the blood," he concluded, nodding. "What happened then?"

"He died."

"I figured. After that."

"I caught it. It kept beating." I tried to remember past that. This part was all very vague. "The police came, and then there were… other police? And they drugged me and burned down the building and locked me up. They're going to look for me," I realized with a sick fear. "I shouldn't have come here. I'll get you in trouble, too." I stood to go.

He grabbed my arm. "Sit down. You're not going anywhere. We'll figure this out. It will be fine."

That stopped me short. "We?" I asked.

"Yes," he said gently. "We."

I sat back down.

We.

Hunh.

"You're going to need clothes of your own at some point. You can wear that for now, but if you're staying here for a while, we should get you some things that actually fit."

"I'm staying here?" I asked, still adjusting to being part of a 'we'.

"People will be looking for you. You can't be seen walking around. You're good at being inconspicuous, but not invisible. So either you stay with me, or I walk you back to your apartment. Would you rather go home?" I looked down. If he walked me home, he'd know where I lived. "Didn't think so. I'll sleep on the couch. No," he insisted, overriding my protest. "That part's not negotiable. I have limits."

I stared at him speechlessly as he went to refill his coffee. I opened my mouth, and then closed it again. "Why are you helping me?" I finally blurted.

He set his cup down, and leaned back against the counter, looking at me with arms crossed. "Why did you come here?" he asked, holding my eyes.

A dozen answers swirled in my mind, but I couldn't bring myself to say any of them out loud.

Because I'm scared.

Because I need help.

Because I have no one else to turn to.

and then…

Because I trust you.

The last one shook me. I could count on one hand the number of people I'd ever trusted in my life, and they were all dead. The idea that a man I'd known for only a few weeks had joined that list was astonishing to me, but I couldn't deny that it was true. I trusted him. Some of that must have shown on my face, because he just smiled and turned back to refill his mug.

There was a curious look on his face when he turned back around. "How long did it keep beating?" he asked with a morbid fascination.

I laughed. "I wasn't counting."

Chapter Twelve: Special

"Do you want to talk about it?" Jack asked as we walked the narrow park running alongside the Hudson River. I was starting to get the hang of walking around the city while invisible. Dodging people who couldn't see us became a silent game in my head. It wasn't hard to avoid pedestrians, but the rollerbladers were more of a challenge.

"Talk about what?"

"You killed someone. That takes a toll, the first time. It wasn't your fault. Don't blame yourself." I sat heavily on a bench we were passing, disturbing some pigeons, and stared at the ground. I *didn't* blame myself, and that was what bothered me. "Why don't you tell me what happened?" he prompted gently.

Deep breath. Just say it. It all came out in a rush. "I was at Jimmy's, and Ed came in with a gun. I think he just wanted money, but Jimmy went for his own gun, and everything happened so fast. I don't think he planned to kill him, but he did, and then he realized I was a witness, and he was going to kill me. I don't regret it, Jack. I'm glad I killed him. Does that make me a monster?"

I looked up at him and my heart sank. He was standing a few feet away, with his arms crossed over his chest and a scowl on his face. The gentle expression he'd worn a minute ago was gone, replaced with shock, and a little horror. He almost looked sick.

I closed my eyes again. "You think I'm a monster."

"I don't think you're a monster," he said, not moving from where he stood. He was lying - I could see it in the stiffness of his muscles, the tension that now radiated out from him. His entire demeanor was changed, now that he knew I was truly a remorseless murderer. It was too late to take it back now.

"Tell me about the people that came," he said after a minute. "You said there were police?"

I struggled to remember through the haze of that night. "Yes. Someone must have heard the gunshot and called them. I don't remember much, just voices. One of them said I was in shock, and the other one called someone else. He said they were NYPD, but I don't think the second group was. He said, '*I think this is one of yours.*'"

Jack let out a huff of air. "They called a cleanup crew. That's not good."

Feeling queasy, I asked him, "What's a cleanup crew?"

He sat on the bench beside me and looked at the ground. "There aren't a lot of people who know about Paranormals. The city isn't very comfortable with it, so they have an arrangement with the agency to clean up their own messes. Anytime one of us steps out of line or does something dangerous, they send a crew trained to deal with Paranormals."

"Deal with us? What does that mean?"

"Exactly what it sounds like."

It was more or less what I was expecting, but hearing it out loud made it real. "Why didn't they just kill me then? Why lock me up?"

"Fortunately, eliminating an asset requires direct approval from one of the Twelve. That takes time, so they would have had to lock you up until they could get in touch with one. Useless, in your case, but they probably didn't expect you to wake up so soon."

I was an *asset*. To be *eliminated*. Pushing aside the casual coldness of the phrase, I shifted to the other piece of new information. "One of the Twelve? Twelve what?"

"We shouldn't be talking about this out here," he said,

standing suddenly and looking around warily. "I'll explain when we get back home."

The idea of Jack being nervous drove home the severity of my situation. "I'm in a lot of trouble, aren't I?"

He finally looked at me again, almost apologetically. "Yeah. Yeah, you are."

—

The walk back to Jack's apartment was tense and silent. I spent the time trying to imagine what he was going to tell me that was worse than a cleanup crew. By the time we got there, my mind was racing out of control.

"Who are the Twelve?" I demanded the second the door closed behind us.

"The people who run things. The board. Rich and powerful people with the kind of resources to do whatever they want, and what they want is to become richer and more powerful." His voice held an uncharacteristic amount of bitter cynicism.

"These are the people you said would find us, no matter where we ran?" He nodded. "Are they government?"

"Some of them. Others are industry leaders, private contractors, CEOs, ex-military. And there's always one Fisher and one King. I think it's in the charter."

"How do you know all of this?"

"Listening in places I'm not supposed to be." He sighed. "I shouldn't be telling you any of this. The less you know, the safer you are, but honestly it doesn't really matter at this point. You can't get in more trouble than you're already in. They know what you can do now, and you're too powerful to be allowed to run around on your own. So they have to do something with you."

"Powerful? I'm not powerful! I can't lift anything bigger than a houseplant!"

He looked back at me skeptically. "You can kill someone from - what's your range?"

"Sixty feet or so."

"You can kill someone from sixty feet away. There's no way to defend against it, and there's no way to prove it was you. I'd say that's pretty powerful." I gaped at him in horror. "Like it or not, you're now a highly efficient killing machine."

It was worse than that. As long as they were all under three pounds, I could lift many things at once. I'd done seventy or eighty one time just to see. Which meant I could walk into a room full of people and kill them all in seconds. I had a sudden mental image of dozens of floating, bleeding, disembodied hearts and felt sick.

He read my expression correctly. "You don't have to do it the same way. You can do something else next time. Leave the heart inside the body. Stop the lungs. There are many ways to kill people. It doesn't have to be messy."

"Next time?" He was talking like this was going to be a frequent occurrence.

Almost apologetic, he said, "I have an idea, but you probably won't like it."

"Do I have a choice?" I asked. "The most powerful people in the world are sending a 'cleanup crew' to kill me. I can't run, and I can't hide forever. I'm out of options. If you have an idea to get me out of this, I'm all ears."

He sat heavily in a chair. Whether or not I was going to like it, he certainly didn't. "The only way I can see them agreeing to let you live is if you're too useful to throw away." He paused. "You're sure? Once I tell you this, there's no going back."

"It can't possibly get worse than it already is. Just tell me."

"The only option I see is working with me. In Special Projects."

That didn't sound so bad. There was something I was missing. "What's Special Projects?"

With a grimace, he told me, "Special Projects is a separate team that doesn't answer to Montgomery. We do assignments that require extra secrecy. They tend to be jobs that the government needs done, but can't have traced back to them."

"If the government is involved, does that mean it's legal?"

A trace of a smile crossed his face. "As long as you don't get caught."

"And if you do?"

"If you do get caught, legality is the least of your problems."

I remembered what he'd said earlier. *There are many ways to kill people. That takes a toll, the first time.* "They kill people."

"Assassination is one type of mission, yes."

"And you work for this team? You kill people for a living?"

"Among other things. Spying, asset retrieval - trust me, it wasn't my first choice."

"Then why?"

He breathed out heavily, and admitted, "I got caught someplace I wasn't supposed to be." I remembered our meeting in the upstairs hallway, and how desperate he was to make sure we weren't found. This is what he was protecting me from. He put me closest to the wall because he was already suffering the consequences. At some point he was in the exact position I was in right now, and he didn't have any other options, either.

At least I had someone in my corner. "You think they would agree to it?"

"I think I can convince them. If I ask to take you as a partner, to work with me directly, they might go for it. But you need to understand that if we do this, there's no turning back. Ever. You don't retire from this team."

"What does that mean? You don't retire?"

"It means we work for them until they decide to let us go. Or we die," he amended. "Whichever happens first. Life expectancy isn't high on this team."

"That's… like slavery."

"It's more like indentured servitude, with better perks."

"That can't be legal!"

"At this level, legality doesn't really apply."

I could hear my grandmother's voice in my head, warning me, over and over. This was exactly what she said would happen if I used my Talent. I could go back over the decisions I'd made that got me here, but it didn't matter. I was here now, and I couldn't go back.

I stepped close to him and looked up into his eyes. "Thank you, Jack," I said, putting a hand on his arm.

He pulled away like I'd burned him. "Don't."

"Don't what?"

"Look at me like that. You don't have to do that. That's not why I'm doing this."

Oh. For a moment I'd forgotten - I was still a monster. A killing machine. He did what he did because he had to, and I'd told him I was glad I'd murdered someone. And now he saw me as a useful partner, but not a person. I wasn't a woman anymore. Any hopes I had of something more between us just went up in smoke.

It hurt. It would continue to hurt, every day, working side by side with him, together, but so far apart.

But at least I'd be alive.

CHAPTER THIRTEEN: NEGOTIATION

The Twelve filed into the boardroom, one and two at a time. Jack and I stood in an empty hallway, silent and invisible, watching as the men who held my fate in their hands took their places inside.

I thought they would look different. It was silly, but somehow I imagined there would be some visible evidence of the kind of money and power they wielded. Instead, they were just… men in suits.

A week had passed since we hatched this plan. Jack had called in a favor to get on the agenda for their monthly meeting today. They didn't know I was going to be there. I had a feeling they didn't like surprises.

"Ready?" Jack asked, once they were all inside.

"As ready as I can be."

He pulled me into an empty office and quietly shut the door. "I have something for you," he told me, reaching into his pocket.

"You're giving me a present? Now?"

"It's more of a prop than a present." He opened his hand and showed me what it held.

It was a necklace - a long chain suspending a deep red garnet. It was unusually large, and eye-catching, but I wasn't sure how jewelry was going to help us in this situation. I took it and held it up to the light.

It was shaped like a heart. A blood-red heart, hanging from a chain. I made the connection immediately. This wasn't jewelry. It was the worst moment of my life, the worst thing I'd ever done, and he wanted me to wear it around my neck like a battle trophy. He wanted me to take pride in the fact that I was now a murderer.

"We get one shot at this. Once you walk in that room, you know who they are. That makes you a liability, maybe even more so than what happened. This has to work. You could kill everyone in that room in seconds, and I want them to think about that every time they look at you. I want them to be terrified of you."

He looked intently into my eyes. "You are stronger than them, Diana. You have nothing to be afraid of. You are powerful. Remember that. Own it."

I looked at the gem in my palm.

We were selling me as a killer. If I was squeamish about it, if I showed weakness, we would fail. But he was right. I *was* powerful.

I fastened the chain around my neck. It felt heavy. But it also felt good. Right. From now on, I didn't have to be afraid. I was strong.

"I'm ready."

———

I followed Jack silently through the door, and carefully stood out of the way against the wall. Oblivious to my presence, the men around the table focused on Jack as he took a seat. Other than being men in suits, they were nothing alike. Tall, short, old, young, striking, unremarkable. I picked out the man I'd seen in the hallway - he had to be either Fisher or King, if he'd inherited his position. He wore a pleasant smile, like all the rest, but I had the sense that underneath the veneer of politeness, predators lay in wait. My overall impression was that I had just walked into a pit of sharks, and in order to survive, I had to be a predator, too.

"Raven," an older man in a blue suit greeted him. "A pleasure as always."

Jack inclined his head politely. "A pleasure to be here, Mr. Fisher." So that one was Fisher. Mid-fifties, maybe, graying hair and sharp eyes. The other one must be King.

"To what do we owe this visit?" asked a man to Fisher's left.

I was pretty sure I'd seen him on TV somewhere, but I couldn't quite place him.

"Mr. Secretary, as always, it's an honor," Jack continued smoothly. A spike in the man's heart rate told me that there was something about Jack's words that I didn't understand. I remembered how Ed reacted when I said his name, and then it was obvious. Jack had just reminded the Secretary that he could identify him. Just like the necklace, it was a very subtle threat. Despite his internal reaction, Mr. Secretary's smile was easy, giving nothing away. Pit of sharks, indeed.

"Everyone's time is valuable, so I'll get straight to the point. I have a proposal," Jack continued as if nothing had happened.

"A proposal?" asked a man to his left. "This is highly irregular, Raven." His back was to me, so I couldn't see his face.

"True. But an opportunity has arisen that is too good to pass up, and I knew you'd want me to bring this to your attention." Abstractly, I knew Jack was good at this. He knew these people, and I never doubted that unlike me, he had no problem swimming with the sharks. Knowing it and seeing it in action were two very different things.

"Go on," said a reedy voice to his right.

"I think my efficiency could be improved," Jack said. "Dramatically. With my proposal, I could do more jobs, faster, and with lower risk." By the way their backs stiffened and they leaned in slightly, I could tell he had their attention.

"How?" asked a thin man wearing a black suit and round glasses.

"By taking on a partner." There was a rustle of movement around the room, but Jack went on. "Two of us together would be able to complete missions in half the time, and do things we could never accomplish individually."

"Out of the question," snapped the Secretary. "Your missions are classified. We can't have anyone else involved."

Unaffected, Jack smiled. "I can personally vouch for her discretion. I will take full responsibility for her actions." He'd just put his own life on the line for me - no one had ever had that much faith in me before.

"Her?" someone else asked. "You have a particular partner in mind?"

"I do," he said, and unbent the light around me.

One by one, they all noticed me. I saw the reactions on each of their faces as they became aware of my presence. They clearly did not like an intruder in this room, especially one they hadn't known about. Some of them recognized me immediately, and those who didn't were quickly filled in by their neighbors.

Jack stood and held out his chair for me. I sat, feeling small under their scrutiny. As they noticed my new jewelry, some of them frowned, some of them flinched, and some of them wore openly fearful expressions. *Fear. That's right. I'm powerful.* Sitting up straighter, I smiled. Twelve hearts beat faster.

Pulling up a new chair, Jack began to introduce me. "This is D-"

"We know who she is," Fisher cut in. "Why is she here?"

"She's here because her Talent is extraordinary and a perfect complement to mine. We've worked together successfully in the past, with excellent results, as I'm sure you'll recall," he said with a glance toward King.

"I think your judgment is compromised, Shadow," said the reedy voice at the end of the table. His hair was white-blonde and styled carefully, as though he was a fashion model, but his face had a weasel-ish look to it that no one would put on a magazine cover. He looked vaguely familiar, too. "I didn't think you'd be one to be swayed by a pretty face."

"Power is power," Jack shrugged. "Doesn't matter what she looks like."

"Power? She's a low-grade Telekinetic."

Jack laughed. "She ripped a man's heart out of his chest. I'd say that's pretty powerful."

Weasel-face sneered. "You expect us to actually believe that? We're not gullible, Raven."

I picked my head up. Until now, I'd kept my gaze mostly on the table, and glanced up briefly now and then to follow the conversation. This guy annoyed me. I turned my head to look at him and held his eyes.

He swallowed hard, and his heartbeat began to race. I could almost taste his fear. I smiled.

"That's enough, Miss Grey." I turned my head away from the terrified man. The second my eyes were off him, he scrambled away from the table, knocking his chair over in his desperation to get away from me. Mumbling some excuse about a spider, he righted his chair and sat. "You will not threaten a member of this group again, Miss Grey," the Secretary continued. "Is that understood?"

"All I did was look at him," I pointed out.

The resulting silence was broken by the last thing I expected to hear - laughter. Every head turned to look at the source. Fisher was nearly doubled over with amusement. When he finally stopped, he grinned widely at me. "Well done," he told me with a slow clap. "That was brilliant. You just demonstrated your value. No one here can say one way or another what just happened." To the room, he added, "they'd be the perfect strike team. Quiet, efficient, deadly, zero evidence left behind. I say we allow it."

"Zero evidence? I wouldn't call a trail of disembodied hearts quiet!"

A man with a military-style crew cut pointed out, "She doesn't have to rip them out. Stopping them would work just fine."

"That would just look like a heart attack," someone else mused. "Nothing to suggest it wasn't a natural death."

"Absolutely not," snapped the Secretary. "She's an unknown quantity. We can't have someone that dangerous running around."

"It would be a shame to throw away our sharpest weapon, for fear of getting cut," said the man with the crew cut. "You can't deny that they'd be effective together."

"After a while, we wouldn't even have to use them," the man in glasses observed. "Once word gets out that our enemies tend to die mysteriously, people would just fall into line. They would be like monsters in the dark, and soon everyone would be afraid of their own shadows. It's brilliant."

"Out of the question." The debate raged on as though we weren't even there. My life was hanging in the balance, and judging by the look on his face, Jack thought we were losing.

"The status quo is working. Don't fix what isn't broken. He's effective enough without her."

"The status quo is not working," Jack cut in over the raised voices. "I cannot continue to do this job alone. Either she joins me, or I will resign. You can consider this my notice." It was a desperate gambit. I hoped he knew what he was doing.

A bark of laughter. "You can't re-"

The sound of a throat being cleared cut him off. I looked around to see Fisher glaring at the man beside him. Some of the heartbeats around the table were elevated, some were not. There was something happening under the surface here.

The man in the glasses looked confused, and it dawned on me that the board was not as unified as it looked. Apparently, not all of them knew about Special Projects. As far as some of them knew, there was no reason Jack couldn't resign. If they explained that, they would have to explain about Special Projects, and those that knew desperately didn't want the rest of them to find out. Jack was playing a very dangerous game.

"What my colleague means to say," King smoothly interrupted, "is that we would hate to lose such a valuable asset as yourself. You have our trust," he said pointedly to Jack. "I am quite sure you would never violate it. If you take responsibility for her, I see no reason not to try it out. Don't you agree, gentlemen?" he asked the room with a charming smile.

Immediately, several of the others chimed in their agreement. The Secretary hesitated for a moment, and then nodded.

"We will have to discuss compensation," said Fisher. "We're not paying both of you for the same job. If we can come to agreement on that, I see no reason not to allow it on a trial basis."

I caught Jack's sharp exhale, the tiny upward tick of his mouth. We'd won. "Same commissions, split 50/50 between us."

"Are you sure? That's a huge pay cut for you."

"I don't think it will be," Jack countered. "We'll be far more efficient together. I think we'll do twice the number of jobs in the same amount of time. It will balance out."

"Your loss if it doesn't work out that way," Fisher shrugged. "I propose we give them six months to prove out the model, and then reevaluate. Any objections?" The room was silent. "You may go. Next order of business."

Chapter Fourteen: Facets

As we walked up 7th Avenue toward Central Park, I couldn't help stealing glances at Jack. There were so many sides to him that didn't seem to fit together. The man who held my hand as we watched the clouds go by, and the man who killed for a living. The man who kept secrets, and the man I trusted with my life. The man who made butterflies come to life in his living room, and the man who hid in the shadows. Today, I saw a new side - the calm, collected negotiator, who could hold his own in a boardroom full of powerful men. I wondered how many other sides there were that I hadn't seen yet. They were like facets of a gem, all part of the same stone, depending on how the light touched it. He was all of them, and he was none of them.

He saved my life today. He put his own on the line for mine, and yet, it still felt empty. I was happy to be alive and free, but being constantly beside him, and not with him, that would be absolute torture. I finally knew what I wanted, and it was just barely out of reach.

He caught me looking at him as we crossed 59th Street. "What is it?" he asked, as we passed the line of defeated-looking carriage horses at the bottom edge of the park.

The future was a problem for tomorrow. Tonight, we were celebrating. "Where are we going?" I asked, deflecting his question.

Grinning mysteriously, he only said, "You'll see." His enthusiasm was infectious, and my mood lifted immediately. He led me through the trees and lawns, past playgrounds and softball fields, past families having picnics and couples on park benches. On the far edge of the Lake, we crossed a little wooden bridge into the

Ramble, a part of the park I'd always loved. Walking the meandering wooded paths, it was easy to believe that we'd left the city behind, and slipped into some other world far away from its noise and chaos. He led me down the darkening path until we reached a large, flat stone that sloped down to the water's edge. Across from us lay the Hernshead Rocks, a little spit of land covered in boulders and tourists, but here, in our little secluded spot, it was quiet.

"It's beautiful here," I told him, lowering myself onto the smooth stone. The sun was just starting to set behind the skyline, painting a pink glow across the water. Toward the east, where the sky was getting dark, a smattering of stars were coming out. The moon was just starting to crest above the trees. It was easily the most romantic thing I'd ever seen, and my heart hurt to be here with Jack, and yet not with him.

He sat beside me on the stone. "It's OK," he allowed, "but it could be better." Tiny points of light lifted from the surface of the lake and drifted above the water, floating like will-o-wisps over the smooth surface. Water lilies rose and bloomed, glowing white in the fading light. Flickering sparks drifted through the darkness around us, flitting like fairies just out of sight. Glittering white fireworks spread across the sky, and fell in a dazzling shower of light. *Magic*, I thought, breathing it all in. *This man is magic.*

"Jack, this is…" I turned to find him watching me. "Incredible," I finished.

"You like it?" he asked, almost shyly. This was yet another facet of Jack - the artist who brought beauty into the world. I thought that very few people got to see this side of him. Maybe no one but me. There was something fragile in his expression that made me think we weren't just talking about the pretty scene. I fell a little harder.

"The world is so much more beautiful when you're around."

"I could say the same," he said, without looking away.

My mind spun with confusion and hope. A few minutes ago,

I was sure he didn't want me, but the way he was looking at me now made me question everything. "Come with me," I blurted. The words were out of my mouth before I had a chance to second guess them. "I want to show you something."

He looked at me curiously. "Come where?"

"Just come on," I said, standing and holding out a hand. "You'll see. Just come."

He stood, taking my hand. I laced my fingers through his and held tight. Practically dragging him, I led him through the park, out of the Ramble, along the Bridle Path, up toward the Reservoir. Every time he tried to ask where we were going, I just shook my head and repeated, "You'll see." He was clearly dying of curiosity by the time we left the park and crossed the avenue.

I paused when we got to my little alley, and hesitated. This was it, this was the point of no return. Once I did this, someone would know where I lived. My secret sanctuary would no longer be secret. But this was Jack, and I trusted him.

"This way," I told him, squashing down my nerves.

His brow furrowed in confusion. "Down the alley?"

"You'll see," I said again. He still hesitated. "What's wrong?"

"I'm following a beautiful woman who could literally rip my heart out down a dark alley that would be perfect for hiding bodies. This is how horror movies start."

I laughed, relaxing a bit. "I promise not to rip your heart out."

"That's exactly what a serial killer would say," he commented, but he followed me, smiling.

CHAPTER FIFTEEN: HOME

He stopped at the base of the rickety stairs, half-hidden in the darkened alley. "Where are you taking me?"

Pausing halfway up, I bit my lip. "Home."

"Home?" he asked. "Your home? Like where you live?" I couldn't see his face, but I could hear in his voice that understood what this meant to me. The level of trust I was showing him. I nodded, not even sure he could see me in the dark. As he slowly climbed the stairs behind me, I randomly wondered if they'd hold two people at the same time. Too late now.

They held. I paused again at the top, nervous now about what he would think. Something I'd never had to think about before. "It's a little... unusual."

His mouth quirked up in an amused smile. "I kind of got that from the alley and the stairs."

Taking a breath, I opened the lock and pushed on the door. It swung open silently. "Come in," I told him with only the slightest tremor in my voice.

I waited anxiously as he stepped inside and peered around. The only light was coming from the window at the far side of the room, but Jack brightened it until it illuminated the whole room. I watched his face carefully as he took in the space - my strange little bar-kitchen, the incongruous heavy wooden table, the futon at the far end.

"You live here?" he asked in astonishment.

"It's weird, like I said-"

"It's amazing."

I trailed cautiously behind him, as he walked the length of

the room, immediately drawn to the window at the far end like a moth to the light. It was my favorite part of the apartment, too, which was why I'd put my bed in front of it. From the futon, I could watch the stars at night, the sunrise in the morning, and the people going by in between.

He stopped in front of it, staring out across the park. The sky outside was dark, but the moon was up now, and nearly full, bathing the room in its light. Jack stood still and silent, gazing out, ignoring me completely, and I realized in a flash what he was doing. He was giving me space, letting me adjust to his presence here.

At the idea of another person knowing me well enough to understand what I needed, and giving it to me, I suddenly didn't need space.

I crossed the room to where he stood looking out over the city. Lights were starting to come on below, lining the paths through the park like glowing rivers through the growing dark. The vast expanse of the Reservoir lay silent and deep, a pool of impenetrable shadow at its heart. "This window is what kept me sane through the worst of it. Any time things got to be too much, I knew I could come up here and hide, and watch the world go by. I could be safe, but not completely alone. It helped."

I glanced at him shyly. "This is the first time I've brought someone up here."

"I know," he said with an infuriating smile.

"How do you know?"

"Your hands are shaking," he said, taking one of them and holding it in his.

My heart was beating so fast I thought it might explode. Looking down, I asked, "Did you mean what you said before? Downstairs?"

"That you were a serial killer?"

"No. That I was beautiful." I glanced up to see his expression.

He had a look of exasperation on his face. "Diana, you are amazing in all of the ways it is possible to be amazing. You are smart, and strong, and brave, and yes, you are beautiful, too."

"Then why-?" I stopped before I embarrassed myself any more.

"Why what?" he asked gently.

"Why don't you want me?" It hurt to say. It would hurt more to hear the answer, but I needed him to say it.

"What gave you that idea?" he asked, now looking dumbfounded.

"You did! You told me not to look at you. You wouldn't let me touch you. You've been so weird, since…" I didn't finish the thought. "You said that wasn't why you were helping me."

"It wasn't," he told me. "I would have helped you no matter what." He ran a hand through his hair, leaving it tousled. "What I was trying to say was that you didn't have to pretend you wanted me. That I wasn't doing it so you would sleep with me. The last thing I wanted was for you to fake it out of obligation, or because you thought your life depended on it."

"Why would you think I was faking it?"

He dropped my hand and turned back to the window. "You're kind of made of mixed signals."

"What are you talking about?"

"Well," he began, like he was reciting a list. "You pulled me into a closet, but then locked me in and ran off with the diamond."

"But I stayed-"

"You kissed me in the park, and then looked terrified when I offered to walk you home."

"OK, but-"

"And then avoided me for a week."

"I wasn't avoiding you. I was just… trying not to see you."

"That's the same thing," he pointed out with a faint smile, still staring straight ahead. "And then you showed up in the middle of the night and dragged me into bed with you - which was the most frustrating experience of my life, by the way - and then the next morning, you were talking about the guy you were with the night before." His voice and his face both got a little hard with his last words.

"Wait, what?" I interrupted. "What are you talking about? I wasn't with anyone, I was at… " I trailed off in realization. "I was at Jimmy's. You thought… Jimmy… and I… " The idea was so absurd, I couldn't even finish the sentence.

He still wasn't looking at me. "You were jealous," I accused. "That's why you've been so weird, isn't it? You were jealous. Of Jimmy." I laughed out loud at the ridiculousness of it. Jack did not look amused. He just kept staring out the window.

I ducked into his field of vision. "Jack," I said, grabbing his face to turn it toward me. "Jimmy's is a bar," I told him. "I go there to play pool sometimes." He finally looked at me. "Jim was the owner. He had emphysema, a receding hairline, and three grandchildren."

"Oh," Jack said stupidly.

"I was there because playing pool clears my head and helps me think. I was falling for this guy I worked with, and I didn't know what to do, because it terrified me."

"Oh," Jack said again.

"How can a man this smart be this dense?" I asked, shaking my head. My entire space was within my range, so it was easy to locate the pack of condoms I kept in the bathroom and pull it to me.

I shoved the box into his hand. "Is this clear enough?"

He looked down at it and then back up at me.

I pushed him, hard enough that he stumbled back. His foot caught the edge of my futon and he tipped backwards, landing on his back, staring up at me.

"How about now? Still getting mixed signals?"

I followed him down onto the mattress, and climbed over him. "How about now?" I asked, leaning over him with an arm on either side of his head. "Clear enough yet?"

He was grinning up at me now. "Nope." I looked at him

incredulously. "Say it. Out loud."

I grinned back, my mouth a hair's breadth from his. "I want you," I whispered against his lips. "I haven't stopped thinking about it since the second I saw you."

"Say it again," he said in a low voice that set me on fire. "Be specific."

I sat back and took his wrists in mine. Placing his palms against the sides of my legs, I told him, "After you touched me," I told him, trailing his hands up my thighs, "in the casino. I couldn't stop thinking about you. For a week, I kept picturing you pulling up my skirt and bending me over the roulette table, right there in front of everyone." I slid our joined hands under the hem of my dress, and pushed it up to my waist. Leaving his hands there, I lifted the rest of the dress up and over my head.

"Still have that dress?" he asked as the room was replaced by the flashing lights of the casino.

"I do," I told him, slipping off my bra.

"Tomorrow," he promised, eyes roaming down my body. "What else?"

I reached down to find the buttons on his shirt, and started opening them, one by one. "In the closet, in that theater. I wanted to strip you naked," I told him, working my way down. While my hands were busy on his shirt, I found the waist of his pants in my mind, unbuttoned and unzipped him, so that when I trailed my hands down his chest, all I had to do was pull on the rest of his clothing and it slid below his hips, freeing him. God, he was beautiful. "I wanted to touch you," I told him, wrapping my hand around the cock that was as perfect as the rest of him. He rocked up into my hand involuntarily. "I wanted to watch your face while I made you as crazy as you made me."

"What else?" he asked, his voice a little ragged now.

"In the hallway," I continued, moving back up his body until we were face to face again. "In the hallway, when you had me pinned against the wall-"

He flipped me onto my back. "Like this?" he asked, holding

my wrists above my head.

"Yes," I breathed, reveling in the feel of his hard body on top of me. "Exactly like this."

"What were you thinking, when I was pinning you against the wall?"

Oh, god, this was finally happening for real.

"I was thinking," I continued, "about wrapping my legs around your waist, like this," locking my ankles behind his back, opening fully to him. He rocked against me lightly, and I could feel every hard inch of him, with just a thin slip of fabric between us. "While you fucked me senseless against the wall."

He tilted his hips in again, pressing against me, and kissed me fiercely, until I was gasping and desperate.

"And in the hallway," he said, reaching for the condom wrapper and pulling my panties off one leg, "when I was fucking you senseless against the wall," he said, leaning back over me and wrapping me around him again. "What was it like?" he asked, pressing inside me.

I couldn't speak to continue, adjusting to the sudden feeling of fullness, so perfect, so-

"Was it hard? Fast? Slow? Quiet? Loud?" His voice was breathy as he pulled back and pressed slowly back in.

My head tipped back and my mouth fell open. "Hard," I gasped. "Hard and fast. Hard enough to rattle the windows and the doors. Loud enough that everyone in the building heard."

"Like this?" he asked, snapping his hips with the next thrust. "Is that hard enough?" He did it again, harder. "Or like that?"

"Yes," I gasped. "Like that. Again." He did. "Again." He was torturing me, one wicked, controlled thrust at a time. "Don't stop," I pleaded. Again. And again. Slow and deep, while he read the pleasure on my face, taking it in hungrily like he couldn't get enough.

And then I was telling him to go harder, faster, deeper, more, swept away by the pull of my nails in his back and his teeth

on my skin and the glorious friction of our bodies. Lost in one another, outside of time. We forgot the world, forgot everything but this, now, us, on and on until we carried each other over the edge. My hands gripped the sheets through the waves of my release and he slammed into me one last time and held us there, locked, joined, perfectly, perfectly synced.

We fell together, back to earth, into sleep, and desperately, hopelessly, deliriously in love.

PART 2

2003

Eight Years Later

CHAPTER SIXTEEN: SUN

I woke when the first rays of sunlight hit my face. Moving carefully, not to wake Jack, I slipped out of bed and went to the window. The sun felt warm on my bare skin. I luxuriated in it for a moment, stretching, naked except for the garnet necklace I never took off. A reminder of my own strength, and the man who had so much faith in me that he put his life on the line for mine.

I turned back to the bed to watch him sleeping, only to find him awake and looking at me. "What are you thinking?" I asked with an innocent smile, stretching again for his benefit.

The thin sheet covering him couldn't hide the evidence of his appreciation. I loved the way he loved my body, and it made me want to show off for him. "Just wondering how I got so lucky," he said, smiling back, "that I get to wake up next to you every day."

"Well," I replied, stalking toward the foot of the bed. "It doesn't hurt that you're easy on the eyes," I said, grabbing two fistfuls of sheets and pulling them toward me. He lay back, letting me expose his body, inch by glorious inch, letting me soak in the view of skin and muscle and manhood, ready and waiting for my attention.

Climbing onto the mattress, I crawled over him slowly, working my way up. "I'm rather attached to this," I said when I reached his hard length, painting a long stripe up it with my tongue. He bit his lower lip, but said nothing, still watching me.

I continued my way up his body. "You're a decent kisser," I told him, running my mouth along the underside of his jaw. "But mostly it's your conversational skills," I finished with a teasing grin, rubbing my nose against his.

"My conversational skills?" he asked, running his fingertips along my body. "Or the way I make you forget how to speak?" he murmured, hands finding exactly the right spots. I tried to answer, but all that came out was an incoherent sound.

Slipping one hand downward, he suggested, "Maybe we should have a long, loud, heated *conversation* right now."

—

He left me lying in the sun, sprawled like a starfish on the sheets and still unable to form words. I stared up at the rafters, trying to remember how to move, feeling the light soaking into my skin.

"Coffee?" he offered, returning with two mugs.

"You look pleased with yourself," I teased.

"You look pretty pleased with me, too."

I stretched and sat up, taking the mug he handed me. "Definitely not complaining."

Maybe it was the afterglow, but right at that moment, my life felt perfect.

"We got offered another assignment."

And there went perfect.

"Is that why you gave me three orgasms this morning? To put me in a good mood? Jack, we're supposed to have a couple days off. What's the point of fixing this place up if we're never here?"

"I gave you three orgasms because I like watching you come. You didn't seem to mind at the time."

"Jack."

"If we do this job tomorrow-"

"Tomorrow!"

"If we do this job tomorrow, we can take time off down there," he finished.

I paused. "Down where?"

"Aruba."

"How much time?"

He grinned. "A week."

I shot upright, nearly spilling my coffee. "A week?" I demanded. "An entire week? Seven whole days? In a row?"

"Minus the travel time and the actual job, but that won't take much time."

I looked at him suspiciously. "How did you swing this?"

"I bribed Rogers," he said, looking even more smug. "I brought him back his favorite chocolate from Peru."

"What's the job?" I asked.

His smile dimmed a bit. "Arms dealer. Single-handedly propping up three civil wars and five terrorist organizations. That they know of. He's going to be in Aruba to finalize a deal that could destabilize half of South America."

"Another assassination, then."

"Do you want to take it? We don't have to."

Aruba. "I guess I'll need a bathing suit."

His eyes swept down my still-naked body. "Not necessarily."

—

A sheet of glorious blue swept out into the distance. It faded from deep indigo to a brilliant turquoise closer to shore, where a long, thin strip of pale sand separated it from the land. Out of all the places we'd been, this place called to me the most - a fragment of a long-forgotten dream. Maybe someday.

With an effort, I reminded myself we weren't just here on vacation. "I want to do it a little differently this time," I told Jack as he stepped up behind me on the hotel room balcony.

"Oh?" he asked absently, wrapping his arms around me. "Why?"

"This place is big enough that they might have a defibrillator. I don't want to have to kill him twice." The first time that happened was extremely unpleasant for everyone involved. I really didn't want to repeat the experience.

"What are you thinking?"

"The carotid artery. A little bit of pressure would completely block off blood to the brain. He would barely feel it. To a bystander, it would just look like he's passing out. No evidence of physical trauma for a coroner to find. It's faster, and... more humane." I didn't mind killing people that the world was clearly better off without, but that didn't mean I had to make them suffer.

"How much faster?"

"If I do it right, he'll be unconscious in ten or twenty seconds. Dead in under 30. No chance of recovery."

"What's the catch?"

"I've never done it before. It's not like I can practice at home."

"Please don't," he agreed, dropping a kiss behind my ear. "If it works, it's a huge improvement. Faster, cleaner, less risk. If not, I'll catch him later, and he'll have a tragic accident."

"Is that his boat?" I asked, catching sight of a vessel entering the bay.

"No, he's not due for another hour. We have some time to kill." His mouth dropped down my neck, to the hollow where it met my shoulder. "How would you like to pass the time?" he murmured, slipping a hand beneath the edge of my top.

I bit my lower lip, enjoying the feel of skin on skin. "Can anyone see us right now?"

"Nope," he said, tipping my head to one side for better access to my neck.

I struggled to maintain focus. "And it's easier for you to hold the light, once it's bent? You can maintain the illusion easily at this point, right?" All I got was an affirmative hum against my skin. "Can you do it while you're distracted?"

He stopped entirely and looked at me curiously. "I can."

"How distracted?" I asked, finding the button of his pants in my mind and opening it.

His eyes lit up as he realized what I was suggesting. With a speculative tone, he said, "I don't know. I've never tried before."

"Want to find out?" I asked with a wicked grin, pulling on his zipper.

In answer, he leaned in close to my ear and growled, "put your hands on the rail." He pushed me forward, bent at the waist, as his free hand reached down and grabbed a fistful of skirt.

Below us, crowds milled about, heading back from a long day of sun. Shadows were starting to stretch, as they chattered happily, not twenty feet below. Eyes glided past us as he hiked my skirt above my waist. The ocean breeze was cool against my naked skin, and I felt both exposed and not exposed at the same time.

It was the hottest thing I'd ever experienced. This was not going to take long.

I was ready before he even touched me. He let out a faint groan as he slid inside me, stretching me open. I couldn't stay silent once he started to move. The crash of the waves against the shore and the bustling crowd below mostly covered the first slap of skin against skin. When a pack of bikini-clad twenty-somethings passed below, one of them glanced in our direction curiously, but kept walking.

Jack was reacting the same way I was, judging by the pounding pace he set, one hand gripping my hip and the other wound in my hair. An older couple talked about their upcoming snorkeling trip. Hard, fast, relentless, until one of the valets looked up and said, "Do you see that?"

I came with a scream that cut through the noise of the crowd, causing a surfer to look around and comment, "Somebody's having a good time." Jack came a second later, falling forward over me, sweating and gasping.

"See what?" the other valet asked.

The first one looked up, eyes sweeping right past our balcony. "Nothing, I guess."

"That was the best idea you've ever had," Jack said, kissing my back.

"We are definitely doing that again," I agreed as my breathing returned to normal and my heartbeat slowed.

"Give me ten minutes," Jack promised.

I hadn't meant right now, but since he was up for it… "Five."

"Five," he agreed, laughing.

Chapter Seventeen: Shiny

"Do you think it's being outside or being in public?" Jack mused as we took two seats by the bar in the hotel's lobby. From here we could see the entrances to each of the four on-premise restaurants.

"Maybe both?" I shrugged. "We'll just have to experiment until we figure it out. Extensively."

"Fortunately, we have an entire week for experimentation." His eyes caught on something over my shoulder, and he was immediately serious. "He's here."

Casually, I turned in my chair, pretending to admire the lobby. Three people walked across the marble floor. A man who could have been an accountant, and two women in evening gowns. One was slim and graceful, with long brown hair that swept past her waist in a smooth sheet, wearing a deep blue sheath. The other was shorter, wearing a dark green dress that set off her auburn hair. They looked like arm candy. Appearances were deceiving. "Who's that with him?"

"Bodyguards. The brunette on his right is Gwyn Blythe. Extremely acute sense of smell, can identify nearly 500 poisons by scent alone. You'll see her check anything he eats, drinks, or touches, and he won't go near anything until she has. The redhead on the other side is Mia Garr. She's the muscle. Don't let her size fool you. She could throw that table across the room with one hand. You should see what she did to the last person who tried to get near him."

"I'd rather not." I scanned the room. "No Psychics, then. Or Pre-cogs."

"Doesn't look that way."

"Dressed like that, they're headed toward the formal restaurant. Which conveniently, is on a patio overlooking the beach," I mused. "Clear line of sight, easy exit route."

"You just want to go down to the beach."

I grinned. "Maybe."

—

The sound of the hubbub from the restaurant faded as we meandered along the water. They hadn't quite realized he was dead yet, but when he fell face-first into the carpaccio, it drew attention. By the time everyone figured out he was not just passed out from too much alcohol, we would be far away, nothing to connect a random couple on the beach to a sudden medical emergency.

This wasn't my favorite kind of job.

"Have you noticed they're all assassinations, lately? The revolutionary in Malaysia, the cult leader in Sweden, that guy in Bangladesh - they're all like this. Ever since Fisher died."

"At least we managed to stay clear of that."

"Stay clear? What does that mean?"

"Board politics are a dangerous game. I saw it when Ferdinand King died. Has a tendency to backfire on the wrong people."

"Politics? You think Sam Fisher was killed? I thought he had an asthma attack."

Jack shook his head. "He had no prior history of it, and his successor pushed through a promotion for Casey a week later."

I shuddered at the mention of his name. Casey was an Aerokinetic who had been on Special Projects for a lot longer than we had, and he gave me the creeps. He was strong enough to pull air from his victims' lungs, which always seemed to me a horrific way to die. Worse, unlike Jack and I, Casey seemed to truly enjoy his work.

"And King? Did he also die of 'asthma'?"

"No idea. The family never released his cause of death. He was only forty-seven, though, no prior health issues."

"Does this happen often?"

"Those are the only two hereditary positions." While I'd known the company charter required a descendant of each of the original founders on the board, it had never occurred to me before that this created a conflict of interest for ambitious offspring.

Samuel Fisher was the only board member that I'd actually liked. He was often the voice of reason, talking the more volatile members down from violent solutions. Matthew Fisher appeared to be a very different sort of man than his father.

We walked a little farther along the beach. Jack stopped abruptly. "So, maybe this isn't exactly the right time. But with our lives, there's never a right time. Life is short, and unpredictable, so we have to steal moments whenever we can."

As if to prove his point, his phone buzzed in his pocket. Impatiently, he silenced it. "I don't know what the future will bring. All I know is that I want to spend all of it - every last minute - with you." I covered my mouth with one hand when I realized where this was going.

He dropped to one knee in the sand. "Diana, will you-"

The phone buzzed again. He silenced it again, and started over. "Will you-"

Another buzz.

He stood, took the phone in his hand, and threw it into the ocean as hard as he could. Turning back to me, he dropped down into the sand again.

"Will you marry me?" he asked, slipping a ring onto my left hand.

Inside my bag, my phone buzzed.

Jack flopped backwards onto the sand, defeated.

I fished out my phone and answered it. "What?"

"You're needed," said Rogers, on the other end.

"We're busy," I told him, watching Jack lying on his back in the sand.

"This takes priority."

"We're on vacation."

"Not anymore. There's a 6AM flight to Edinburgh. I'll text the name and address of the hotel. Details will be waiting for you there. Take out the target at all costs." The line went dead before I could say anything else.

Jack was sitting dejectedly in the sand, staring out at the sea. I sat beside him.

"Yes," I told him. He looked over at me, as if he'd forgotten what the question was. "You're right. Our lives are unpredictable. We never know what's going to happen minute to minute. But there's no way I'd rather spend it than with you. So yes, I'll marry you."

"I've been carrying that thing around for weeks," he confessed, "waiting for the right time."

I held out my hand, looking at the ring for the first time. Long graceful arms of gold wrapped around an oval stone, hugging it in place. No hard angles, no sharp prongs, nothing sticking out that could catch on something at the wrong time. He'd put a lot of thought into this, finding exactly the right ring for our dangerous lives. Something told me that was the wrong thing to point out at this moment.

I tilted it this way and that, so the bright moonlight caught in the facets, making the gem shine. "It's so sparkly."

That coaxed a smile out of him. "You know what they say about ravens and shiny rocks."

Chapter Eighteen: Choices

We stared at the imposing structure in front of us. "Are you sure this is the right place?" I asked.

Jack looked at the paper in his hand, and then back at the building. "Yeah, this is the right place." Despite his words, he was looking at it as doubtfully as I was.

"It's a hospital," I said unnecessarily.

"I can see that."

We looked at each other. "It would be nice if we had an actual briefing." When we checked into the hotel in Edinburgh, an envelope had been waiting for us. It held a single sheet of paper with a name and address.

We'd had weirder jobs. "May as well check it out," I concluded. Jack reluctantly agreed, and we went inside.

"Hi," I said to the woman at the front desk, trying to look like an anxious relative. "Could you tell us where to find Quin Greenacre?"

"Is that supposed to be a joke?"

"Please just look."

She looked skeptical, but nodded after pecking at her keyboard for a few minutes. "ID please," she said, holding out a hand. I gave her the two false IDs that went with the particular identities Jack was projecting onto our faces today. She glanced at them and then handed us two visitor passes. "Third floor, turn right when you get out of the elevators, end of the hall on the left."

The first thing we saw when the elevator doors opened was a large sign that read 'Maternity Ward'. Jack's brow furrowed. "Is this right?"

"She said third floor," I reminded him, checking that the number on the wall was correct. "And this is the third floor. Right turn from the elevators. This way."

Jack faded into invisibility as he stepped out of the elevator, a sure sign that he was uneasy, too. I felt him beside me as we walked past room after room hearing the cries of angry infants. There was a swinging door at the end of the hall on the left. The sign said, 'Neonatal Intensive Care Unit'.

"I think we need to call Rogers," I told Jack under my breath.

"We're here now," he whispered back. "May as well scope it out first?"

Beyond the swinging doors, the hallway was separated from a row of incubators by a glass wall. About half of them were occupied. No nurse's station in sight, but there were a few people working. "Excuse me," I called to a passing nurse. She paused and smiled at me. "Could you help me, please? I'm looking for Quin Greenacre." I was careful with the phrasing. The name could apply to a man or a woman, a nurse or a patient.

She beamed. "Oh, I'm so glad to see she has visitors." *Patient, then. Female. A new mother?* "Let me bring you in, she's the second one from the left," she told us, pointing at one of the incubators, which held an infant with red hair. "Isn't she precious?"

This had to be a mistake.

The nurse misread the look of horror on my face and rushed to reassure me. "Oh, don't worry. She's fine now," she explained. "It was touch and go for a bit, not surprising, given the circumstances." I nodded somberly, hoping she was about to tell me what those circumstances were. "She's a fighter, this one, to make it through what she did. But she's out of the woods now, ready to leave. We can release her any time someone comes to identify her." She looked at me hopefully. "Are you family? I'd hate to see her wind up in the orphanage."

"Identify? This isn't Quin Greenacre?" Maybe this was a

mistake, after all.

My hope was short-lived. "Ah, you're American. Quin Greenacre is kind of a placeholder name. Our little joke. Quin's another word for girl, here. And Greenacre is… I guess you would call her Jane Doe, or some such over there? It just means mystery girl."

Rogers better have a lot more information. "Where's her mother?" I asked, being careful with the phrasing again.

"She's still in the morgue. We can't release the body until she's identified. She had no ID when we brought her in. Such a tragedy. It's just lucky we got to her in time to save the baby."

"Yes," I agreed weakly. "Will you excuse me? I need to go make a phone call."

—

"This has to be a mistake, Jack." I paced the length of the hotel suite in agitation.

His face was grim as he hung up the phone. "It's not a mistake," he said, placing the phone carefully on the counter. "According to Rogers, it's a second attempt. The first one failed, and it's a high priority target."

"Who did they send the first time?"

"Neela."

"Neela missed? Neela never misses."

"No, she hit the target she was sent after, but they failed to tell her that the woman was pregnant. The mother died, but the ER staff managed to save the baby."

"If she got the target, then why are we here?"

"Neela wasn't given all of the information, either. The real target wasn't the mother. The real target was the baby." He looked sick as he said the words.

I stared into space as the words sank in. "It's not a mistake. They actually did send us to kill an infant. Why would they do that?"

"Apparently, one of the Psychics had a fit, and gave an

actual prophecy. She declared that this child was going to grow up to do horrible things, and was too dangerous to live. Called her a 'Dragon'."

"Jack, she's a baby."

"I know."

"We can't."

The words hung in the air for a long moment, implications echoing around them. Refusing orders had consequences. Running a hand through his hair, Jack said, "If she's that dangerous-"

"You can't be considering this. She's a baby! She hasn't done wrong!"

"It's not the first time we've done a job based on a prediction. The job in Berlin-"

"That was completely different and you know it. All we did in Berlin was prevent the parents from meeting. This is a living, breathing infant."

"The damage is immense, according to the Psychic. Whoever this kid is going to be, it's bad news. Here, the whole prophecy is there," he said, handing me his phone, open to a text message.

"*The Dragon comes*," it read, "*bringing death and destruction. Empire crumbles, voices wail in mourning*." I snapped it shut in disgust.

"Are you seriously considering this?" I demanded.

He looked at me with anguish on his face. "We don't have a choice, Di. You know what will happen if we refuse a job."

I did know. Special Projects was a lifetime assignment. We knew too many things that were too dangerous to too many powerful people. We couldn't choose to walk away. If we tried, our lives would be forfeit, and the full weight of Kingfisher would come down on us, making a cleanup crew look like a pack of playground bullies. Trying to walk away was suicide.

"I can't," I whispered. "I can't do it. How can you even think about this?"

"If it's a choice between you and a nameless stranger, I will choose you every time." He stared at me searchingly for a moment. "But apparently, you won't."

My mouth hung open, silently, as I tried to find words. Nothing came.

He stood silently for a long moment, and then grabbed his jacket and went out the door. It slammed shut behind him.

I sat frozen in shock. We'd fought before, but never about something as important as this, and we'd always talked it out before. Neither one of us had ever walked away from an argument.

That wasn't even the worst part. The worst part was that he'd taken his kit with him, which meant he was going to do the job without me. Staring after him, I wondered for the first time if I actually knew the man I'd chosen to spend my life with. And if I'd made the right choice.

Chapter Nineteen: Angel

I sat at the edge of the bed, staring at the engagement ring in the palm of my hand. My bag sat in the middle of the bed, open but empty. I couldn't bring myself to pack it, but I couldn't bring myself to put it away, either. Paralyzed by indecision, I just stared at the ring, wishing for answers.

I didn't want to leave. Jack was… everything. He was my partner in every possible way. He was my life. The thought of not having him by my side was impossible to comprehend. I could never leave.

But I couldn't stay, either. I couldn't live with someone who was able to murder an innocent child. Not once could I ever have imagined him capable of this. He'd always seemed less affected by what we did than I was, but I always thought that was a front he wore for my sake. Now I wasn't sure. If he could do this, he was not the man I thought he was.

The sound of the hotel room door pulled me out of my thoughts. Jack. I shoved the ring onto my finger, but stayed where I was, back to the bedroom door. I felt him standing in the doorway, waiting. "I don't want to talk to you right now."

He didn't answer. He didn't move. I wasn't expecting another argument, there was no point now, but I thought he would at least say something, especially with my bag sitting in plain sight on the bed. I turned around to look at him and stopped short.

It took me a moment to register what I was seeing. He was holding something in his arms. It was wrapped in some kind of pink fabric, the whole thing sort of round and oblong.

It moved.

"Jack?" He looked up at me with a slightly spooked expression, and then offered me the bundle in his arms. I shrank away, just as freaked out as he was at being in possession of a living, breathing baby. A faint wail came from inside the blanket.

"We can't leave her there. They'll just send someone else."

Struck speechless, I just stared.

"You were right," he admitted. "It's been getting worse. More assassinations, fewer details. I don't like it either." I stood and walked over to him, and peered into the blankets. A tiny, red face peered out at me, and immediately began to cry.

We looked at each other helplessly. Neither of us had any idea what to do with a baby.

"So now what?" I asked, at a loss.

A phone rang.

That was odd enough that it caught my attention. We always kept our phones on silent. Mine was powered completely off, and his was still somewhere in the Caribbean. I fished the phone out of my pocket. The display was dark, but it was definitely ringing.

"Are you going to answer?" Jack asked. I showed him the blank display.

"Diana, darling, pick up the phone," came Athena's voice through the cell, which was still folded shut. "It's Athena," she added, completely unnecessarily.

"If they were going to send someone, it wouldn't be her," I commented.

"And they wouldn't call first."

Apprehensively, I flipped open the phone. "Athena," I said into the receiver. "I'm sorry, this really isn't a good time," I explained as Jack shifted the screaming child in his arms.

"Oh, don't worry, sweetie," she said, giving additional confirmation that it was, in fact, Athena. No one else called me that. No one else dared. "I happen to be in the neighborhood, and I thought I might drop by for a visit."

"We're on a job, Athena. We're not at home."

"Oh, I know! Edinburgh is such a beautiful city. A bit busy, but lovely at this time of year. Why don't you join me at the cafe on the corner? The one with the green awning. I'm there now. They have the most delicious pudding! You *have* to try some."

I glanced out the window. There was, in fact, a green awning on the corner, with little cafe tables under it. In one of the chairs, I saw Athena's distinctively colorful form. She gave a little wave.

I looked at Jack. "Athena is downstairs," I told him, "at the cafe on the corner. She'd like us to join her for coffee. And pudding," I added. His eyebrows raised to his hairline. "We'll be down in just a second," I said into the phone, and hung up.

"Why is she here?"

"I'm sure she'll tell us. We should at least talk to her."

He looked down at the still-screaming child. "What do we do with her?"

—

We left the baby on the large bed, in the middle of a barricade of pillows. She was too young to crawl or even roll over, so we figured she should be fine. Probably. We really had no idea what to do with a baby.

Athena gave us both giant hugs when we joined her. Another thing I'd come to accept from Athena and no one else. It's not like I could stop her, anyway.

She looked at us expectantly as we sat, and an awkward silence fell. "So," I started, making polite conversation. "I hear your daughter is doing well in school." What was her name? Annie? Alice? The last time I saw her, she was an angry teenager, screaming at her mother for ruining her life. Then again, I couldn't blame her. Living with Athena would probably make me scream, too.

She beamed. "Oh, I'm so proud of Alexandra," she gushed.

Right. Alex. "Another true Clairvoyant in the family! She takes after my grandmother, you know." I nodded, pretending I had any idea who Athena's grandmother was. "It's so quiet in the house without her, though. I get lonely. I'm so used to having a child around. I've been thinking of adopting."

Jack and I exchanged a glance. I thought I could see where this was heading, and I wasn't sure I liked it. "So what brings you to Scotland?" I asked casually, taking a sip of my coffee.

"You tell me," she countered. "I had a feeling you might need my help."

Athena's 'feelings' were always right. This might actually be one of the very rare occasions where they were actually useful, too.

—

"There she is! The little darling, you poor thing." Athena scooped up the tiny infant off the bed. Astonishingly, she quieted down instantly.

"Before you get attached, you should know - there was a prophecy about her, and-"

She made a dismissive noise. "Prophecies," she scoffed. "Prophecies lie. They never mean what they say. The future can't be written down. It's far, far more complicated than that." She cooed down at the tiny Dragon in her arms. "You are something else, though, aren't you?"

"Is she dangerous?"

Athena snorted. "Of course she's dangerous. I'm dangerous, you're dangerous. Danger is meaningless. That doesn't matter. What matters is power, and this one has it in spades.

"Power creates, and power destroys. It's neither good nor evil, it all depends on the one who wields it. Angels and demons, two sides of the same coin.

"This one casts a long shadow, true, but so do the two of

you. Your experiences shaped you, and led to the choices you've made. If she has a loving home and a supportive family, perhaps she will make good choices."

Perhaps. Athena didn't know how this would turn out, either.

"Won't people notice if you suddenly have an infant with no adoption papers?"

"Well, I'm not going to tell them," she said as though it was obvious. "Let's see if we can make you an angel, little one. That's your name, isn't it, sweetie?" she asked the child as if expecting a response. "Angelina. My little angel."

The angel-dragon-baby in her arms hiccupped once, and fell asleep.

—

Jack closed the door behind Athena, looking like he'd just survived a hurricane. I was sure I looked the same. He sat beside me on the bed. "Now what?"

"We could tell them we disposed of the body. Let them think she's dead."

"Then what?" he asked. "We go back, pretend this was all fine, wait to see what they send us to do next? It's just going to get worse."

"Maybe it's time to retire," I suggested gently.

"They'll never let us leave."

"Then we won't ask. We leave everything in New York, we don't go back, we just disappear. Go find an island somewhere. Get married."

"So we run?" I could see ghosts of the past on his face. He never said it, but I had a feeling that before he met me, someone he knew had tried to leave. Whatever happened to them must have been brutal for him to still react this strongly to it. "We can't take this back," he warned. "Once we go, we can't ever go back. We need to be sure."

I put a hand gently on his arm. "I'm sure."

"We'd be on the run forever. Looking over our shoulders constantly. We'd never be safe."

"Is there another choice?"

He looked a little doubtful, but said, "maybe there is. Maybe we can talk them into letting us leave. Maybe we can actually retire. Like normal people."

I sat in his lap and looked up at him. "Like normal people with a private island, right? That part is important."

He laughed, as I'd intended, and kissed my forehead. "I don't think normal people have private islands, but we'll figure something out."

Chapter Twenty: Renegotiation

"Something isn't right," I told Jack as we approached the boardroom. "I can't feel anyone in there." I could see them with my eyes, plain as day, but to my Kinetic sight, the room appeared empty.

He paused, and held me back with a hand on my arm. Our images continued forward for a few paces, and we followed invisibly a moment later, about six feet behind our ghost-selves. The trick had saved us from ambush more than once. Hopefully what was in that boardroom wasn't an ambush.

We paused just outside the doors. It wasn't just the bodies that were strange. It seemed like there were holes in reality, chunks of the tables and the chairs missing in a halo around their bodies. The middle of the table was there, though, which meant the rest of it probably was, too, along with the chairs and the bodies in them.

"What is it?" Jack asked quietly.

"There's something suppressing Kinesis in there. It's not affecting you?"

"No. Light is different. I'm curious how they're doing it, though."

"Yeah, me, too." I squeezed his hand. "Let's go find out."

We stepped forward into our projected images, and they vanished around us. Twelve faces turned toward us when we entered the room, and I caught the movement. With that as a reference, I could latch on to the faintest trace of their physical presence, like haze over pavement on a hot summer day.

They glared at us impassively. Some of the faces were familiar from our last visit, some weren't. Matthew Fisher looked a lot like his father. He was far too young to be here - maybe nineteen or twenty - but he had the same kind of predatory look as they all did. Of the rest of them, I didn't remember which was which. It didn't matter. They were all the same.

"What is this?" I demanded coldly without a greeting.

Someone snickered off to one side. "Told you it would work," I heard in an undertone. I recognized him from last time as the weasel-faced man I'd terrified just by looking at him. He was trying to look distinguished and respectable now, but it just came across as pompous.

"There's no need for alarm, Ms. Grey," a smooth voice informed me. I recognized this one, too, but couldn't place the name. Blonde, about my age, friendly smile. "Kinetic dampeners. Just a precaution," he assured me. "I'm sure you can see why we'd want to even the playing field, under the circumstances."

The playing field was nowhere near even, but I wasn't about to tell them that. "Of course," I said with a gracious smile, and sat. The only way they were willing to be in the same room with me was metaphorically tying my hands behind my back. They were terrified of me, which was useful information.

Jack took the seat beside me. "Thank you for seeing us, gentlemen," he greeted them. "I know you are all very busy. We'll try to take up as little of your time as possible." He was laying it on a bit thick, but they seemed to be eating it up. He was good at this, which was why we'd decided that Jack would do the talking. It left me free to observe. "I'll get straight to the point. We have decided to retire."

"Denied. Next order of business."

"I think you have misunderstood," Jack interrupted with a sharp edge in his tone now. "We aren't asking for permission. We are retiring. Out of respect for your generosity over the years, we are giving our resignation in person, as a courtesy."

"You can't just retire," Weasel-face snapped.

Silently, I turned my head to look at him. I couldn't hear his heartbeat this time, but I didn't need to. His fear was written all over his face.

I smiled.

Someone to my left cleared their throat. I kept my eyes on Weasel-face, who was frozen like a deer in the headlights.

"The fact is," explained Fisher, "there are legal implications. You both signed contracts."

I turned back to face Fisher as Jack slid a piece of paper across the table to him. "Here is our proposed addendum to the contracts. In summary, we will sign non-disclosures and non-competes, and forfeit this year's bonuses. In return, you will leave us in peace. We disappear, you forget we exist."

"The last mission is completed?" asked the smiling blonde man, while his colleague glanced at Jack's proposal. He was asking about Angelina, casually confirming that we'd murdered an infant for him. I made a point of remembering his face.

"It's taken care of," Jack assured the man, handing Fisher a metal pen.

As it changed hands, it faded from Kinetic sight. Curious, I focused on the pen while Fisher fidgeted with it, ignoring the rest of the conversation. *There.* I could make out the shape, faintly. Less distinctly, I could almost see a shadow of the hand that held it. A suggestion of fingers. Now that I had it, it was easier to see. I traced the length of his palm up to his wrist, felt the cuff of his shirt. Concentrating hard on the button, I found the thin threads holding it to the fabric. I pulled on one experimentally, and it broke. *Ha!* One by one, I snapped all but one of the threads, leaving one single strand holding the button in place.

Fisher read the paper quickly and then pointed the pen angrily at Jack. I broke the last thread. The button fell free from the cuff, and hit the table with a quiet sound. It landed on its side, and rolled a few feet until it tipped over with an audible click.

There was a long silence as every eye in the room stared at the button. "You should speak to your tailor about that, Mr. Fisher," I commented into the painful pause.

He looked at me, looked at the button, and then looked down at the contract in his hands. "I think everything is in order here," he said brightly, and signed the document.

———

"What were you thinking?" Jack demanded as soon as the elevator doors closed behind us.

"What do you mean, what was I thinking? It worked. They all signed the contract."

"You threatened them."

"And?"

"And now we're a threat," he explained, as if it were obvious. Jack leaned heavily against the wall of the elevator. "The point of that whole conversation was so they *wouldn't* see us as a threat. They'll never leave us alone, now."

"They were always going to see us as a threat," I countered. "The only thing they respect is strength. The contract isn't going to stop them. Fear might."

He closed his eyes and took a deep breath in, visibly reining in his anger. "Maybe you're right," he conceded. "Maybe they'll let us go. Either way, it's done now and we can't change it."

The elevator doors opened, and we stepped out into the lobby for what was hopefully the last time. "Hey," I said, bumping Jack's shoulder with mine. "We won. We got what we wanted. We're retired now," I reminded him. "We can relax. Live a little. Maybe take a vacation, finally."

"A vacation?" he repeated with a hint of a smile. "Maybe a honeymoon?" he asked, throwing an arm around my shoulders.

I slipped mine around his waist. "We'd have to get married first," I pointed out.

"Let's do it," he said, eyes alight.

"What, now?"

"Right now. Go straight to City Hall, get married today. I don't want to wait another minute for our new lives to begin. Start over. Together. Right now."

"As crazy ideas go, this is the best one you've ever had."

CHAPTER TWENTY-ONE: RETIREMENT

Everything was perfect. The sun was bright in a clear blue sky, and a faint breeze carried the scent of flowers over the water. We couldn't have asked for a more beautiful day for a wedding. I still didn't want to be here.

"Do we have to do this?"

"Backing out on me now?" Jack sounded more amused than concerned.

"We're already married. I'm not talking about that. I meant going out there in front of everyone." I felt self-conscious as hell in this frippery of a white dress. The morning dew was already seeping into the hem of the floor-length skirt, and I was sure in a few minutes it would be permanently grass-stained.

"No," Jack allowed, sounding reasonable. "But if we don't, you're the one who's going to have to explain to Amelie that she doesn't get to be our flower girl, since you're the one who agreed to it in the first place."

"This is all Candace's fault," I muttered. When she heard we eloped, she was outraged, and insisted on throwing us a proper wedding. I'd refused immediately, and then she'd dragged Vivienne's kids into it. One pouting lip from the little girl, and I'd caved instantly. "You try saying no to that face."

She was right there, in the front row, with her brother Alain, the two of them the picture of innocence. Behind them, Vivienne chatted with Candi's husband Howard, and Athena's nephew, who was nearly as annoying as Athena herself, was regaling Oliver and his date with tales of his exploits as a boxer. It seemed like cheating to me, since as a Pre-cog, he could see all the punches coming, but given my history with casinos, I had no room to judge.

People were gathering curiously, peeking at the wedding guests standing in front of the arch of trees draped in flowers and white ribbons. As soon as Jack un-hid us, they would be staring at *me*, in the ridiculous dress Candi made me wear, and the flowers I'd let Amelie braid in my hair.

"Come on. Quit stalling," Jack insisted, and dropped the illusion that was keeping us out of sight. We stepped out from behind the trees and started walking.

Sure enough, everyone stopped what they were doing and stared. Some of them even started taking pictures.

"Everybody's looking at us."

"They're supposed to," he reassured me, amused, as we took our place under the trees by the water. We wanted to keep our little spot on the rock overlooking Hernshead Point to ourselves, so instead, we chose the shores of the Turtle Pond, not far from where Jack and I once lay in the grass, looking at clouds and trading stories. Behind us, across the water, Belvedere Castle sat stately and majestic. Between the castle and the water and the trees, the whole thing made a perfect photograph, and plenty of people were taking them.

"I hate this," I whispered to Jack as the officiant started walking toward us.

"I know," he said, brushing a strand of hair back from my face in a romantic gesture that was bound to trigger a million more photographs. "You're doing great," he assured me.

And then I was flying through the air in a tangle of bodies, over the edge of the shore, into the foot-deep water of the pond. Mud and tangled weeds pulled at my arms as I struggled to sit up and figure out what just happened.

Jack sat beside me, looking as confused and mud-covered as I was, and Athena's nephew Hector, who had just tackled us both, sat nearby, looking back at the shore with a grim expression.

"What the hell, Hec-" I stopped and turned at the sound of a loud crash a few feet away from us. A giant tree limb landed in exactly the spot Jack and I were standing a few moments ago.

Hector was a Pre-cog.

On the shore, people were shouting and running across the lawn toward us, but Jack and I just sat in the water and stared at each other, absorbing the knowledge that we would be dead right now if Hector hadn't just saved our lives.

"This is why we can't have nice things," I muttered, as Jack stood and helped me up out of the mud. My dress was weighed down by the water, making it difficult to move.

"At least now we have an excuse to skip the party."

The party. "Candace." She was a heavy Telekinetic, and had very emphatically insisted on this spot under the trees.

"We don't know it was Candi. Oliver's date is also a Telekinetic, and there are a ton of strangers within range."

My eyes scanned the shore, taking in the number of onlookers that had just tripled in size. "We need to leave," I realized. "Now."

Hector slogged over to us, limping. "Twisted ankle," he explained. "You guys OK?" He had to have seen the injury coming, and did it anyway. My opinion of Hector just rose dramatically.

"It could have just fallen naturally," Oliver's date was arguing as we approached. "We don't know that it was deliberate."

Candi looked livid. "That branch did *not* fall on its own," she was insisting.

"It doesn't matter now," Jack cut in before things got out of hand. "We're all safe, thanks to Hector, and that's what's important." Whoever did this was nearby. Anything we said right now would make it back to the Twelve. They wouldn't stop at one failed attempt, and if they knew we suspected the truth, the attacks would come faster.

"I'm afraid you'll have to have the party without us," I said, faking regret as I gestured down at my mud-soaked gown. In an undertone, I asked Hector, "Would you mind giving us a lift to the airport?"

———

I groaned as we watched our flight take off. Through the window, from the gate. The plane that we were not on. "I told you we were going to miss the plane," I sighed in frustration.

"There was nothing we could do about it," Jack reminded me. "We can get another flight."

He was right on both counts. We had gotten into a minor accident on the way to the airport. Hector had managed to avoid a collision by stopping short when a car had barreled through a red light. His rental car fortunately had excellent brakes. Unfortunately, the brakes on the car behind us weren't quite as good.

If not for Hector's reflexes, the speeding car would have hit us hard, and it probably would have been fatal. It could have been a coincidence. People ran red lights all the time. Sometimes people died in car accidents. I didn't think it was.

But if the worst thing that had happened was that we missed our plane, I'd count myself lucky. "Yeah, you're right," I said, turning to look for an airline desk. "I'll go see if I can-"

A loud boom cut me off and jerked my attention back to the tarmac. Outside, shrapnel rained down from a cloud of black smoke above. The remaining half of the plane - our plane, the one we were supposed to be on - plummeted to the ground. It hit with a deafening crash, and was instantly engulfed in flames. If anyone on board had made it through the initial explosion, there was no way they could have survived the fall, let alone the flames fed by a full tank of jet fuel.

People around us began to scream and run, but Jack and I just stared out the window at the devastation in shock. A planeful of innocent people had just died. We were supposed to be among them.

"They wouldn't-" I began.

"They did."

"But there were-"

"I know."

By the time I snapped to my senses, Jack was already scanning the vicinity for other threats. I saw images of our own bodies step forward to go sit in two of the chairs by the gate, and I knew that we ourselves would be invisible. "Maybe we should take the train, instead," he suggested.

"A car might be better," I murmured.

"Why don't I go get us one, and you can call to cancel the hotel reservation."

"No," I said, thinking quickly. "We keep the reservation and buy tickets for the next flight, on our cards. Get the rental in cash." Let them think we were still going to Hawaii. Hopefully they would look for us there instead of blowing up another plane.

He nodded, following my line of thought. "I have enough for the car, but we'll need more cash. See if you can track down a bank in the airport. How much do you think we can take out at once?"

I had no idea. "It'll have to be enough. We should ditch the phones, too. I'll pick up some maps. Which direction do you want to go?"

"Get them all. We can decide on the way."

———

The quiet click of the lock sliding open woke me. I had fallen asleep with a book in my hand, curled up in the afternoon sun. The little cottage we were renting near Vancouver had a lovely sunroom, and a chair that was perfect for reading. I missed my loft with its giant window, but if I couldn't be there, this would do for now.

It was three months since the last time someone tried to kill us, and six months since the plane exploded. I saw on the news that they were calling it a mechanical malfunction, and the airline was now under investigation for their safety practices. We didn't believe that for a second, but even if we had, the subsequent string of assassins would have removed any doubt. So far, we'd managed to avoid killing any of our old friends and colleagues, but every time I worried that we would.

I was starting to think maybe they'd given up. I was tired of running. I liked it here. It wasn't a private island, or even warm, but it was quiet, and safe, and so far, none of Kingfisher's assassins had found us here.

The door was opening silently. I was still groggy from my nap, and my thoughts were sluggish. Jack wouldn't have bothered to be this quiet. Besides, when I fell asleep, he was out on the deck. Blinking away sleep, I checked. Jack *was* on the deck. That meant that whoever had just come in the door was not Jack. I wondered who they sent this time.

Sighing, I told the intruder, "I don't want to kill you, but I will if I have to."

I rose to see who it was this time, but before I could turn, all of the air left my lungs. I tried to gasp, but nothing came. An Aerokinetic, this time. I knew I should reach for his heartbeat, but all of my concentration was fixed on the futile attempt to breathe.

"That's where you and I are different," said a familiar voice. Casey. "For you, this was always just a job. For me, it's a calling." I fell to the ground, still struggling for air. He smiled down on me, gloating. "I always hoped I would get to kill you. You were always so smug. Everyone thought you were the golden child. Sickening." I was dying, and the last thing I heard was going to be this idiot's voice.

There was a certain justice in it, though. I would die as I'd lived. Somewhere along the way, I'd lost count of how many people I'd killed. Maybe I deserved this. Maybe we both did.

"You know what I love about asphyxiation?" Casey asked, as I lay dying at his feet. "There's something so satisfying about watching someone gasp for air. It's painful, it's slow, but it's not messy. You get to watch the panic, and then see the life go out of them, without having anything to clean up afterwards."

Spots danced in front of my eyes. "The delicious irony is

that if you hadn't hesitated, I'd be the one dying at your feet. And yet, here we are-"

Air rushed back into my lungs. I gasped, panting, chest heaving. My vision had barely started to clear when something heavy hit the floor next to me. A body, not quite dead yet. A pool of blood was starting to spread around him, stemming from the knife embedded in his back. Casey's eyes stared into mine as he bled out onto the tile floor.

"You chose the wrong target," Jack informed him, as he leaned over to pull the knife from my would-be killer's back. "She would have let you live."

I sat up slowly, bracing myself against the remnant dizziness. "So much for not making a mess," I said, watching Casey's blood spill across the floor. "This isn't going to stop, is it?"

"No, it's not going to stop," Jack agreed, helping me up. "I guess we should have expected this. As long as we're alive, they'll see us as a threat, and they don't tolerate threats."

"Maybe we should be." I stepped over the body, careful not to get any blood on my clothes.

"A threat?"

"I don't want us to be looking over our shoulders for the rest of our lives. We can't run forever. They'll keep coming after us, and eventually they'll succeed."

Jack looked unhappy about it, but nodded. "It's time to stop running."

———

"You can't be here," Vivienne hissed. "You have to get out of New York. They have half the agency looking for you."

"No one can see us, Vee," Jack assured her. "And out here, no one will hear, either." We were back on our favorite little rock on the edge of the Lake in Central Park, hidden in the winding paths of the Ramble.

"They're never going to stop," I told her. "We can't run

forever. Someone will succeed eventually, and we'll have to kill a lot of our friends in the meanwhile. This has to end. We have a plan, but we're going to need your help, and as many of the others as you think would be willing."

Vivienne looked at her hands. "Some of the others would," she told me. "A lot of them aren't happy about being sent after their own. And people have started to look harder at their own missions. Di, I looked into some of their memories. Fisher, King, Morris, Dane, a few others. The things I saw - I don't even want to tell you some of the things they've had people do. We all knew they weren't saints, but this was beyond what anyone suspected. Most of us want out, but we're all afraid to leave, after what's happened to you. The rest of us wouldn't survive as long as you have."

"Do you think they'd side with us over them, if it came down to it?"

She thought for a moment, counting people in her head. "Most of them will be sympathetic, but they'll side with whoever they think will win. They're terrified."

"And you? We can't do this without you. Are you willing to take the risk?"

"Are you going to win?"

"Yes," Jack said without hesitation.

"Then yes," she replied. "What are you going to do?"

I smiled grimly. "We're going to teach them a lesson.

Chapter Twenty-two: Lessons

The Twelve filed into the boardroom slowly, chattering unsuspectingly among themselves. As far as they knew, this would be a normal monthly meeting. Presumably, they expected to talk about things like killing innocents and stealing priceless gems.

One of the first things Jack and I did after talking to Vivienne was break into their records. It was an easy infiltration and retrieval job for us - you would think they'd have done a better job of hiding their secrets if they ever read our reports. The sight of Jack's face as he read through the details of our past missions would stay with me forever.

They weren't all horrible. In some places, the interests of the Twelve coincided with the interests of others, and we did some good. Among other things, we'd prevented at least three wars, because war was bad for trade. But we'd also stolen scientific research that could have cured millions of people, because it threatened profits. We'd killed peaceful protest organizers and others who had done nothing wrong. We'd destabilized peaceful governments and propped up oppressive regimes.

On some level, we always knew. Life was good for us, so we didn't ask too many questions. We buried our heads in the sand and obediently carried out every mission they gave us, until the truth became inescapable. Neither of us suspected it would be this bad.

We weren't agents. We weren't soldiers doing what needed to be done for the sake of others. We were murderers. Monsters like them.

Starting today, we would begin to make things right. But first, just one more day, we had to be monsters again.

None of them noticed anything amiss as they gathered and sat at the long table. They were all just hazy blurs to my Kinetic sight, but this time it wouldn't matter. This time, we were prepared.

Once they were all seated, I nodded to Jack, and he dropped my disguise. No one noticed me until I pulled out a chair and sat in it. They all stopped, mid argument, to stare at me speechlessly for a moment.

"Good morning, gentlemen," I said, leaning back and propping my feet on the table. You could hear a pin drop. "I'm going to need a volunteer."

"You can't be in here!" one of them blustered. "This is a private meeting. Where's security?" I recognized Weasel-face from last time. You'd think he would've learned to keep his mouth shut.

"Thank you for volunteering." I took the first of the knives Jack was hiding on the table and slammed it into his chest. He died with a look of surprise on his face.

"Lesson number one: your little trinkets are useless. I don't need to sense you to kill you. Do I have your attention, or do you need another demonstration?"

"Where did that knife come from?" someone asked.

"Where's her partner?" someone else muttered.

"Excellent questions, both of them. Very insightful. I encourage you all to consider the answers. There will be a quiz at the end." I took my feet off the table and leaned in.

"Lesson number two: you are not Paranormals. You don't understand us. You see our Talents as parlor tricks that we bring out for your amusement. To you, they are buttons for you to press, weapons for you to point at will." Some of my anger was starting to come through, moving from the cold resolve I'd started the day with into something hot and dangerous.

"To us, this is who we are. It's not something we turn on and off. It's built into how we think, it's part of everything we do. You don't understand that, so you don't understand us, and therefore, you are unfit to lead us."

A man in a black suit snorted in derision. "And you are? You're a glorified hit man."

A second knife caught him in the throat. Blood ran down over his expensive silk tie. "Any other questions?"

Silence.

"Good. Pop quiz: Which one of you ordered the destruction of a plane full of civilians?" All but one of them pointed at a single man, who looked suddenly terrified. He jumped up and ran for the door, colliding with the hidden knife in his way. He dropped to the floor with a surprised gurgle.

"Which one of you ordered the murder of an infant?" They didn't point this time, but their eyes gave them away. They all looked at the blonde man I remembered from our last meeting, confirming my suspicions that it was him. I thought this one might be King, but it didn't really matter now. My knife caught him in the chest and he fell unceremoniously to the ground, gasping. I glanced over - not dead yet, but with that amount of blood, he would be in a few minutes.

"That kid was dangerous!" One of them burst out. "Did you read the prophecy? All of the Psychics panicked when she was born. She would have been the death of us all." He slumped forward onto the table with a knife in his back.

"Yours, at least," Jack agreed, appearing behind him. "But the rest of you have a choice. You all have two options. I believe the first option," he said, gesturing around the room, "is evident. The second option is that you will give us everything you know about this organization and everyone who knows about it. And then you will forget about all of this - literally this time, since you clearly can't be trusted. Vivienne will erase all knowledge of this agency or the existence of Paranormals from your minds. You will live, but you will forget everything you know about us."

They looked at Vivienne who was now standing in the doorway, surrounded by a group of the others. "That's decades of memories," someone protested. "Can you do that without permanent damage?"

Vivienne shrugged. "We'll find out."

"Katie! Do your job! Help us!"

Candi, who was standing beside Vivienne at the front of the crowd, laughed. "And why the hell would I do that? You can't even remember my name." She looked at us. "Can I do one?" she asked, hefting a file cabinet. Candi was the first one they'd sent to find us. She clearly considered it a suicide mission, and refused to do it. Instead, she contacted us quietly, and asked us to help make it look like she'd tried. Clearly, she held a grudge.

"Only if they choose wrong," Jack cautioned.

"Ten thousand dollars to anyone who kills these two!"

"Thousand? That's insulting," someone in the crowd said.

"We're not stupid," muttered someone else, glancing around the room.

"You can have that one," I told Candi, tipping my head toward the man who'd made the offer. She grinned.

"I guess we're all out of jobs, now," Bob commented, wincing at the sound of a file cabinet dropping.

"Not necessarily," Jack said with a smile. "With your help, the organization can continue to exist, with some changes. Under new management."

We'd talked it over, and we both saw an opportunity to wipe the slate clean. If we kept the sort of missions that helped people, and were transparent about what we were doing and why, and treated employees with respect, maybe we could do some good. It wouldn't erase our sins, but maybe we could begin to atone for them.

"George," Jack snapped, turning to look for Montgomery, who was staring in at the room stunned and horrified. Montgomery looked up at Jack when he heard his name called. "Please call a full emergency staff meeting. I want everyone there. As soon as possible."

Montgomery glanced back at the carnage in the boardroom one more time before smiling tightly and saying, "Sure thing, boss."

—

The majority of the agency responded to our summons. The lobby was packed. It was the only space big enough for all seventy-odd agents, which was something to fix later.

All eyes were on Jack and me, standing at the front of the room. I addressed the gathered crowd. "As you have all heard by now," I began, "there will be some changes. The old board has… stepped down." I glanced briefly at the closed-off boardroom. Most of the blood had been scrubbed away by the Aquakinetics, but a few conspicuous stains remained. "Despite itself, this agency has done a lot of good, not the least of which is creating a community and support system for Paranormals. We can do better."

"Starting today," Jack continued, "there will be no more contracts. Employment is at-will, meaning that you can leave whenever you want. All employees will get a base salary that is not dependent on the success of your missions, a standard benefits package, including health and life insurance, and a stipend for training and education. High-performers will be rewarded accordingly, and there will be hazard bonuses for those who choose to take on dangerous jobs."

"And guaranteed vacation time for everyone," I added. "There will be full transparency on the purpose of your missions. You will not be required to take any contracts you don't feel morally comfortable with. You will, however, be expected to adhere to a code of conduct, which includes abiding by all applicable laws, unless the life or wellbeing of agents or civilians are at stake. You will use force only when necessary, and take extreme caution to maintain the secrecy of this organization and the Paranormal community." Now that we had painstakingly wiped the memory of our existence from the minds of the Twelve and their business associates, we wanted to be very careful about who knew about us.

"Anyone who wishes to opt out of further employment, please see Asim after this meeting. He will ensure that your contracts are voided." Jack paused, looking sternly at the crowd. "For the safety of those who stay, the original non-disclosure agreements will continue to be enforced."

"Enforced how?" someone asked.

"Let's not find out," I advised him. "Any other questions?"

"Yeah," said Asim, the lawyer, rubbing his forehead. "In order to dissolve the old contracts, the organization needs to no longer exist. Whatever you're forming now needs to be an entirely new legal entity."

"Is that a problem?"

"Nope. It's all just paperwork, but I need to know what to put on the new documents. I need a name," he clarified when we looked at him blankly. We hadn't thought about this.

"We could name it after the new founders," Lynn's cheery voice rang out, followed by a murmur of agreement.

Jack and I glanced at each other and started to protest.

"Raven Grey? That doesn't make sense," said someone in the crowd.

"Grey Raven," called out someone else.

"Ravens aren't gray," a voice protested.

"And kings don't fish. What's your point?"

Despite our objections, cheers of approval spread through the crowd, and a few people began to clap. We stood speechless for a moment, watching as the applause grew.

Jack and I glanced at each other, wondering what we were getting ourselves into. He grabbed my hand and squeezed it. Whatever it was, we were in it together.

CHAPTER TWENTY-THREE: CRASH

"This is a lot more work than retirement," Jack complained when he saw me leaning in the doorframe.

"Fewer people trying to kill us, though. Most days," I clarified.

He was tired. I could see it in his eyes, in the way his shoulders sagged as he slumped back in his chair. It worried me, but nothing I said or did could convince him to rest.

In the months since we founded the new agency, he had thrown himself completely into the task of rebuilding it into something to be proud of. We'd sat down in the beginning and sorted through the list of things we would and would not do. Personal security, private investigation, and disaster mitigation, yes. Assassination, espionage, and theft, no. It wasn't surprising that Paranormals could do things others couldn't - that was what defined us - but being able to actually leverage those skills into true accomplishments, that was new.

Beyond our direct employees, a community was growing. Families and friends were coming together and forming bonds, now that we weren't set in competition with each other. Something remarkable was happening.

Despite this, or because of it, Jack was working too hard. It was like the weight of his past missions was crushing him, and he needed to do whatever he could to balance them out. He threw everything he had into making this experiment work. I did, too, but I slept sometimes.

I sat on the edge of his desk, placing my body between him and the computer. "You've been staring at that same spreadsheet for five hours. You should take a break. Let's go get some lunch."

His face brightened immediately at the prospect. Standing, he leaned over me and gave me a long, lingering kiss. "Can we bring it back here?" he asked with a grin and a raised eyebrow.

"As long as we remember to lock the door this time. I think poor Oliver was traumatized last time."

"He should have knocked."

I pried myself away from him with some effort. "Lunch first," I insisted firmly.

Five people stopped us on the way through the lobby. Some of them had easy questions, like what color chairs we preferred for the conference rooms, some had hard ones, like how much we should charge for various services, and some just wanted to say hello. We were always at the center of attention, and weirdly, I was OK with it.

Most people had decided to stay. Some, including Vivienne, took it as an opportunity to retire, now that they were free from their contracts, some went off to find other adventures, but the vast majority - almost sixty people - threw their lots in with us.

No one wanted to stay in the old building. Everyone had bad memories there, it seemed. The new office was still under construction, being adapted to our particular needs, but it was going faster with Telekinetic help.

A group portrait of all of us sat prominently in the lobby, reinforcing the idea that this organization was a joint effort. Our names were on the door, and our money was paying the bills, but Jack and I both wanted people to feel that it was just as much theirs as it was ours.

He squeezed my hand as we walked by the picture and the smiling faces. We were building something good here. It made it worth the long hours.

"Any luck with the Mayor's office?" Jack asked as we rode the elevator down.

"Some," I conceded. "We have a meeting scheduled, which

is huge progress. It's hard to get an appointment when you can't tell anyone what the appointment is about, and if I try to explain it over the phone, they hang up."

"I still think it'll be worth the effort. We're going to need their cooperation. They'll come around once they see what we're trying to do."

"Is it?" I asked. "Is it worth the effort? You've barely slept in weeks, Jack. I hate seeing you do this to yourself. You're working too hard."

"I'm working too hard because it *is* worth the effort. We're building something special, here. Something to be proud of. I know you believe in this as much as I do."

"I do, Jack, but-"

Someone bumped into me.

A hand grabbed my arm.

A girl's face looked up at me, and she smiled.

—

Bright lights. White ceiling. Voices.

There was something on my face. I tried to brush it away, but there was something on my arm, too. I struggled to sit up.

"She's awake," I heard someone say. I turned to the source of the voice. A doctor? A Healer? Both? I blinked, trying to clear my head. Nothing made sense.

"Where?" I tried to ask, but my voice was weak and hoarse.

"You're in a hospital," said a familiar voice.

"Vee?" I turned to find my friend. She was standing by the bed, opposite the doctor.

The fog was starting to clear. Everything hurt. My body wasn't moving right. "Slowly," Vivienne told me. "You were injured. You're going to be OK, but you need to take it easy." There was an IV in my arm and a tube under my nose.

Something was wrong. Someone was missing. "Where's-"

The doctor cut me off. "Can you tell me your name?" he

asked, looking at his clipboard.

I ignored him. "Where's Jack?"

No one answered me. I sat all the way up and looked around the room. "Where's Jack?" I asked again.

The doctor looked at Vivienne uncertainly. "Where is Jack?" I demanded a third time, starting to panic.

Vivienne stepped closer and put a hand on my arm. I saw it in her eyes before she said a word.

No.

No no no no no.

"Di," Vivienne began, with a hitch in her voice. "You were injured. Both of you. Very badly. They managed to save you, barely, but they couldn't save him."

No. What? No.

"No," I said out loud. "That's not…." I trailed off as memories started to come. People running, shouting. Pushing past us, and then a loud noise and pain. I clutched my chest, realizing I'd been shot, and reached for Jack.

Oh god. Jack.

He was just here. We were just talking, we were walking to lunch. If I tried hard enough, I could rewind it, go back, this couldn't be real, this wasn't happening. I looked at Vee mutely, waiting for her to tell me that this was a mistake.

She didn't.

"There was nothing we could have done," the doctor was saying. "We barely saved you. The damage was so extensive-"

"Why?" I asked him.

He blinked. "Why what?"

"Why did you save me?"

He looked at Vivienne, confused. "Wh-"

"*Why did you save me if you couldn't save him?*"

The doctor's eyes went very wide. He took a step back, and then two.

Until this, the worst pain I had ever experienced was having the air sucked out of my lungs. I wasn't an Aerokinetic, I couldn't do that, but I wanted this doctor, this man who saved me and not Jack, I wanted him to suffer like that. I could feel the air going in and out as his lungs moved. I couldn't stop the air, but I could stop the lungs. I'd never killed anyone like this. I wondered how long it would take.

Panic crossed his face when he suddenly couldn't breathe. He looked across at Vivienne.

—

Bright lights. White ceiling. Voices.

"She's awake again."

I was lying back on the bed again. I heard footsteps and the click of a door. When I picked up my head, only Vivienne was there.

"What happened?"

"You almost killed your doctor," she told me. "We had to sedate you again. He'll recover, but no one else was willing to be here when you woke up the second time."

Jack was gone, I remembered. "Why don't I feel anything?"

Vivienne's expression was drawn, her lips tight. "Drugs," she told me. "A lot of them. They wouldn't agree to wake you up again without them."

I should feel remorse, but I just felt flat, empty. Nothing mattered anymore. Nothing at all. "Jack is gone," I told her.

"Yes. I'm sorry. There was nothing anyone could have done."

"I know. I remember now." I touched the bandages on my chest. After all of our dangerous missions, it was a few stray bullets from a robbery gone wrong that got us. One punctured my lung, another caught me in the arm, and a third hit Jack in the chest, piercing an artery. For the rest of my life, I would never forget the sight of Jack's blood on the sidewalk, and the life fading from his eyes.

"Are they-"

"In custody. They're still questioning him, but it seems like it was exactly what it looked like. You were just in the wrong place at the wrong time." After a pause, she asked, "Do you want me to take the memory away?"

"No." I refused to part with a single memory of him, good or bad.

She took my hand with pity in her eyes. "I want to tell you it's going to be OK, but I don't want to lie."

Jack was gone. It would never be OK.

—

The morning light was too bright. It poured in through the window, offensively cheerful like the people below. I hated them, every last one of those oblivious, happy people who didn't seem to know that the world had ended. How dare they carry on with their normal lives, when mine was shattered?

I sat in the middle of the bed - our bed - remembering lazy Sunday mornings and long summer nights. Every last inch of this place was filled with memories of him. He came into my home like he'd come into my world, bringing life and color and a sense of belonging that I had never felt before. Without him, everything was pale and empty. Food was tasteless, laughter was gone.

This morning I buried him, and life dared to go on.

I would go on, too. I had to, for him. The last conversation we'd ever had was about how much he believed in what we were doing, how important it was that we succeed. For his sake, I would finish what we started. Other than memories, it was the last part of him I had left.

I would go on, but not here. Vivienne and Candi insisted I stay with one of them for a while, but I knew I wasn't coming back. It was too full of him. Everything connected to him would stay here. There could be no reminders of him in this new life, if I was to function. He left me a task, and in order to do it, I had to lock all of this away and never look back. The handful of things I was taking with me were already at Vivienne's. That just left this - this one, last thing.

A small black box, lined with white. Inside lay a necklace - deep red garnet, shaped like a heart. I was now the only person alive who knew the meaning behind it - a reminder of the two days that shaped everything that came after. The worst and best days of my life. I slammed the box shut, trying to chase away the memory of standing in this exact spot, so many years ago, the exact moment my life had been changed forever.

Time to let go.

I lifted the little box up into the rafters, to a spot on top of a beam that wasn't visible from the ground. Leaving it there, where no one could find it, I got up from the bed and slowly walked the length of the loft for the last time. I paused at the couch, where we'd sat together in rare moments of rest. I ran my hand along the table, that we'd never been able to move from its place in the center of the loft. I paused in the kitchen we'd sat in so many mornings, discussing missions over coffee. I hesitated in the doorway for one last moment.

And then I shut the door on the life I used to have, and stepped out into the harsh light of day.

—

Walking into the office alone for the first time felt like balancing on a tightrope. If I swayed even slightly, let my control slip even a little, I would lose my footing completely and fall. One step after another, past the faces who were trying not to stare, with my head held high, doing my best not to see the pity in their eyes.

I walked into the office that was now mine alone, and sat at the desk. For a moment the weight of it was crushing. I stared down at the massive pile of work in front of me. There was no one to split it with, no one to share the burden, no one to celebrate the victories and laugh at the absurdities. I had to be strong enough to do it alone.

I took a deep breath, and picked up the first stack of papers, to see what tomorrow would bring.

PART 3

2018

Fourteen Years Later

Chapter Twenty-four: Shadow

I dropped the papers onto my desk with a sigh. "Theo," I called through the open door to my assistant. "What is this?"

He dutifully poked his head through the door to see what I was looking at. "It's the bill from the museum for damages from the incident last week."

"Damages? But we didn't cause any of that! We're the only reason the damn place is still standing." The museum incident was shaping up to be a massive headache. It should have been just another case on just another day, but the fallout was spiraling out of control. It would have been better if we'd headed off the whole thing before it started, but even so, our intervention had saved hundreds of lives, and prevented much more extensive damages to the structure itself. "We should be sending *them* a bill," I muttered.

"They don't see it that way."

I drew a deep breath to calm myself so I didn't lash out at Theo. It wasn't his fault, and it wasn't the first time this had happened. Fortunately, after so many years of running this place, this was a problem I knew how to solve.

"Send Grace to talk to them." There was a reason Grace was my Public Relations lead. A Charismatic Empath, she exuded a low level of charm and likeability at all times. If she couldn't talk them down, no one could.

"Grace is on vacation. Shall I send Nico instead?"

Nico wasn't quite as good as Grace, but the nice thing about having a staff of nearly two hundred was having vacation coverage. "Yes, but tell him to loop in the Mayor's office if he needs to."

The hardest thing was keeping them out of trouble. "What's the latest with Alex?" I could see from his expression that it wasn't good. Athena's older daughter, the Clairvoyant, had every inch as much Talent as her mother, but in Alex's case, her visions were actually helpful. She and her partner James were the ones who uncovered the museum plot, just barely in time for us to step in and prevent catastrophe. They had performed well together. I'd have to consider making their partnership permanent.

Once we found James.

It wasn't hard to draw the connection between his disappearance and the museum incident, but that didn't make it any easier to find him. Any one of my agents missing would be a crisis, but this one was particularly hard for me. I felt personally responsible for James. When I'd found him, he was so much like my younger self - relying on his Talent to keep him one step ahead of the con. His particular scam was poker. As an Empath, he had a huge advantage, since knowing how your opponent feels about their cards was half the game. But eventually, he would have slipped up as I had, won one too many times, caught the attention of the wrong people, and landed in trouble he couldn't get himself out of. I'd recruited him myself, and given him a chance at something better, and he'd jumped at it. Since that day, he'd been my best, hardest working, most loyal agent.

I needed to get him back, and without any other leads, a vision from Alex was our only hope of finding him.

"Nothing yet," Theo admitted.

"What's the problem?"

"She's psyching herself out. She blames herself for his disappearance, and it's throwing her off."

At some point, I'd need to have a talk with her about letting personal relationships interfere with her job, but today was not the day for that. "Send her here. I want to talk to her."

He nodded, but continued to hover in the doorway. "What

else?" I asked him.

"Nikki got arrested," he said almost apologetically.

"Again?" Nikki was a very Talented Pyrokinetic, and arguably the main reason the entire museum wasn't destroyed, but she had a knack for getting herself into trouble. "On a job?"

"No. Just a bar fight. Do you want to bail her out?"

I closed my eyes and signed in annoyance. "Fine. But tell her this is the last time we're doing it. Next time, she's on her own."

In reality, I would continue to bail her out of trouble, but maybe we could go a few more weeks if she thought I meant it. It may have been a mistake to send her into the museum, but there was no other way. One Pyrokinetic and one Empath had almost killed hundreds of people. Nikki contained the Pyro, but when the Empath caused a mass panic, Nikki had been in range. The Empath was upstairs in custody, but the Pyro escaped in the chaos, and ever since then, Nikki's fights had gotten more frequent.

That was a problem for another day.

Today, the priority was James. While I was waiting for Alex, I reviewed what we did know in my head. Most likely, James was being held by Sergei Petrov, who appeared to be behind the museum incident. He'd been abducting Paranormals and selling them, and somehow the attack on the museum was supposed to cover his tracks, which didn't entirely add up. We rescued a handful of his captives last week, but Petrov himself was still out there, and I didn't know where. Until we found him, he would keep doing it, and now he had one of *my* people, which was unacceptable. It had to stop.

A quiet knock at my door drew my attention, but I kept my eyes on the screen. Alex's shape stood tentatively in the doorway, but there was someone standing behind her. *Now what?* I didn't need another distraction. I needed a vacation. Or maybe just a lunch break.

"Have a seat," I told Alex, glancing up to see who was with

her.

No one was there.

All of the day to day problems of running the agency fell into the background. I hadn't experienced this kind of disconnect between my Kinetic sight and my vision in a very long time. There was clearly someone standing by the door, male, around six feet, but completely invisible. No one had tried to kill me in years, so maybe I was due, but that wasn't what bothered me. Not at all.

Shadows were supposed to be extinct.

I'd only ever heard of one in existence, and I'd watched him bleed out on a sidewalk over a decade ago. There was no other explanation for what I was seeing, though. If there was another Shadow alive in the world, I needed to know who it was.

Contain, immobilize, interrogate. Get some answers.

My walls were lined with weapons. They were extremely effective at intimidating visitors. Most people thought they were purely ornamental keepsakes from past missions, and most of them were, but a handful of them were there for completely practical purposes. I didn't often need to kill people in my office, but it came up now and then.

The Shadow stepped into the office after Alex, and the second they were both clear of the door, I shut it, locked it, and pulled a throwing knife from the wall behind me. Keeping it at his throat, I told him, "I know you're there. "You may as well show yourself."

The air shimmered.

My heart ached a little at the sight of the light unbending itself, a reminder of days I preferred not to think about. I forced myself to watch as a shape emerged from the shimmering haze. It resolved itself into the form of a man. A very, very familiar man.

Jack.

The sight of his face was like a physical blow. I had taken punches in my time at this agency. In the course of my career, I'd been shot, I'd been stabbed, and once, I'd even fallen off a building, but not a single one of those compared to the pain of seeing his face again. After all these years, I thought I was past this, through this grief and this mourning, through this mind-numbing pain, but I wasn't. I wasn't remotely prepared to see the face of the man I'd lost.

It's not him, I told myself. *It can't be him. Jack is gone, I watched him die.* Over and over in my nightmares, I saw the life drain from his eyes, felt his hand go slack in mine. *Jack is dead, this is just a trick. It's not him.* A Shadow could look like anyone. Someone had looked into my history, found a weak spot, and was trying to exploit it. They were trying to throw me off balance, and it was working.

I stood and walked to the window, turning my back on him. I could still sense him Kinetically, but seeing him with my eyes, even if it was an illusion, was throwing me off. With a breath to clear my head, I forced myself to reframe the scene in my head. This was an inconvenience, a minor threat, an enemy to be neutralized. I would get my answers, I would kill whoever this was, and I would get back to work.

"Whoever you are, if you think I won't kill you because you're wearing that face, you're badly mistaken." *It's not him. It's not him. It's not him.* "Honestly, if it turned out that he's been alive all these years, it would be worse than watching him die the first time."

"Diana."

The world stopped.

The sound of his voice pulled me around to face him. No one, no one could fake that voice. No one could fake the inflection behind it, the way it wrapped around the vowels like a caress. The smooth, silky sound of it, that had whispered so many times in my ear.

I looked closer.

He was older. His easy smile was gone. He looked like he had been worn down by time, battered by the world, and scarred by the same kinds of battles I'd fought over the years. He still stood tall and straight and strong, but there were streaks of silver in his dark hair, and a tired, hollow look in his eyes. He was harder, and thinner, almost gaunt, a ghost of the man he'd been. An impostor would show me the person I used to know, as I remembered him, young and full of life, not this version. This was real.

This was Jack.

Chapter Twenty-five: Ghost

Jack is alive.

Jack was alive and standing here in front of me in my office. The miracle I'd wished for in my darkest moments, the dream I had given up on long ago. Somehow he'd come back to me, after all this time.

Jack is alive.

He was right there, I could see him, I could hear him. A few short steps, and I could touch him, I could cross the distance and throw myself into his arms. But my feet wouldn't move, and I couldn't feel my body. Everything was suspended, frozen in time.

Jack is alive.

Parts of me that had died with him were screaming back to life, clawing their way out of the place I'd buried them, tearing at my iron-clad walls, threatening to pull them down entirely. Pain I hadn't allowed myself to feel was pouring through the cracks in my defenses, washing over me in a flood of unhealed grief.

Jack is alive.

Except.

Fourteen years ago, I buried a body. It looked like him, down to every last detail. I knew every line of his face, every tiny scar, and they were all there, on the dead man that it was now clear wasn't him. There was no one else in the world who could have done that - no one but Jack.

Implications came raining down on me like bricks falling on my head. That meant that Jack had been there, watching, while I stood there mourning him like an idiot. He hadn't been abducted. He was at his own funeral, and he willingly, deliberately fooled me.

I never could have imagined a sense of betrayal this deep. The man I had trusted completely, had known without a doubt would never hurt me, just took the last few shattered pieces of my heart and ground them into dust.

Jack left.

I didn't consciously grab the rest of the knives and hurl them at him, but they flew anyway. The hot, sharp pain I felt a minute ago turned to blind rage. I needed to hurt him, I needed to see him suffer like I did. I needed to watch him bleed.

Someone stepped into the trajectory, and I stopped the knives just in time to avoid hitting the wrong target. Some conscious thought made it through the haze. Alex. My agent. I didn't want to hurt her.

"Get out of the way, Alex." Her voice was like a faint buzzing in my ear as I glared past her.

Eventually some of her words registered. "… find out why he's here… might know where James is."

James. My agent was still missing, and if it was remotely possible that this thread could lead us to him, I had to follow it. No matter what it cost me personally. With a huge effort, I pulled the knives back slightly, letting them stay as a visible reminder.

He spoke again. "Diana, please let me explain. There are things you don't know."

Another spike of rage sent one of the knives flying. It missed his neck by a millimeter, and hit the wall behind him with as much force as I could put behind it. "Explain?" I demanded. "How could you possibly explain this?"

He didn't flinch. "You missed," he said quietly. He knew I didn't miss. He knew I hadn't intended to hit him, and he was calling my bluff.

"If I wanted you dead, you'd be dead," I snapped. "The next one won't miss."

He held my eyes steadily, without fear. "If you were going to kill me, you'd have done it already. And you wouldn't bother with a knife."

Unlike everyone else, he'd seen me kill countless times, and he knew all the ways I could do it. I could have stopped his heart before he said a word, but I hadn't. I couldn't.

I needed to be alone to process this, but first, I needed answers. "Why are you here, Jack?"

"One of the Twelve escaped." The Twelve. Ghosts from the past. I hadn't even thought of them in years.

"That's not possible. We accounted for all of them."

"One of them got away. His name is Xavier King. When we removed the others, we created a power vacuum, and Xavier stepped into it." He was speaking quickly, to get all the words out before I decided I wanted to kill him after all. "On his own, he's far more dangerous than the lot of them together. He started building power the day we formed the agency. He thinks he's descended from the Sun King, and judging by his Talent, it's possible. He honestly believes he has a god-given right to rule, and he's assembling an army of Paranormals to build his empire. Some he recruits, some he abducts, and some he buys from people like Petrov. They are all fanatically loyal, and worship him like a god. *That's* who took your agent."

The Sun King. Louis XIV of France, the legendarily charismatic ruler who expanded the power of the monarchy with the force of his personality alone. It was generally accepted that he was most likely a Paranormal, a Charismatic Empath, specifically. Since Talent was genetic, it was only a matter of time until one of his descendants popped up to cause trouble. Finding out that one of them was the co-founder of Kingfisher was not all that surprising, and it followed that the latest in the line would be a member of the board. It certainly explained the name.

As much as I didn't want to believe him, the pieces fit the current situation. If Petrov was selling Paranormals, there had to be someone buying them.

Xavier King. I struggled to put a face to the name, and failed. He should be dead. Every last one of the Twelve was accounted for, and Fisher and King specifically were confirmed casualties of our takeover. I didn't see how he could have gotten away from me, but stranger things had happened.

Like Jack suddenly reappearing, fourteen years after he died. Another conclusion, falling like a brick. "You've been working for him," I realized. He didn't deny it. "All this time I thought you were dead, you've been there with him, helping him build his little delusional empire." I felt sick with horror. Every second that passed, this got worse and worse.

"He would have destroyed you, Di. You were safe as long as I served him. I traded my freedom for your safety."

I didn't want to hear any of this, but I couldn't stop my train of thought. "You knew I'd never agree, and if you just disappeared, I'd look for you. I had to think you were dead. So you staged it."

I closed my eyes, remembering the aftermath, the long, hard road that followed, the days I didn't think I could go on. The only thing that had held me together was purpose, working to build this place as his legacy - his atonement, as much as mine, or so I'd thought. The betrayal cut deeper than any knife.

"Everything I did, I did to protect you."

The words slipped out before I could stop them. "I didn't need protection, Jack, I needed *you!*" I looked away again. I'd just admitted weakness, and let him see a tiny piece of how much he'd hurt me. It was a mistake I wouldn't make again.

"I don't anymore," I told him, regaining a bit of control. "Was that all you came for? Or did you have something useful to say?" My voice stayed steady, but I could feel my tenuous composure starting to slip. I needed him to leave. I needed everyone to leave me alone for one damn minute so I could fall apart in peace.

"I do, but you're not going to like it." I couldn't imagine how this could possibly get worse than it already was. "You can't go after the Empath. This is a fight you can't win."

He should know better than that. I never backed away from a fight, and I would never, ever leave one of my own behind, no matter the odds. "You disappoint me, Jack."

"I won't apologize for protecting you."

"No," I told him. "For underestimating me."

I didn't need him to protect me. I didn't need anyone. I learned how to fight my battles on my own long ago, because I had to. I would deal with this threat, I would get my agent back, and I would go back to pretending Jack was dead. Just as soon as he was out of my sight. "You should go now."

He didn't move. He just looked at me, like he wanted to say something else. If he said another word, any single solitary word, I would crack. I would break down the middle and split open and I would never be able to pull the pieces back together.

I opened the door. It hit the wall with a bit more force than I intended, but my control was gone. "Get out," I commanded.

He turned to go. *Finally.* I felt my knees begin to give out and put a hand on my desk for support.

"Wait," someone said. *Alex.* Alex was still here. One of my agents had just witnessed this whole thing. That was a problem I could deal with later. Right now, I needed to get them out of here, before it got worse. "Who are you?" she asked. She was putting pieces together, too.

He stopped without turning. "No one," he told her. "Just a ghost." I wondered if he was keeping secrets deliberately, or if lies were just automatic for him now.

She figured it out anyway. "She called you Jack. Jack what? Jack Raven?"

"Jack Raven is dead," I said. "I watched him die." Over and over in my nightmares, year after year. Somehow this was worse. The Jack I knew would never have done this. Maybe I never knew him at all. "I have no idea who this man is," I continued, "but he's leaving. Now."

He didn't react, didn't turn, didn't speak. I couldn't see his face as he silently continued out the door.

"No." I turned to look at Alex in surprise. Her fists were balled at her sides. Her back was stiff, her feet were braced, and her mouth was set in a thin line. The normally fearless woman looked frightened but determined, like she was facing down a dragon.

Me. I was the dragon.

She was terrified of me. They all were.

Very few people knew the story of how this agency was formed. It was the only time I'd actually enjoyed killing, and not even Jack knew that. Fewer still knew exactly what it was that Jack and I did before that. It didn't seem to matter. Somehow, my reputation had grown, and now people obeyed me out of fear as much as anything else. I hated it at first, but it made things easier. People very, very rarely said no to me.

And here was Alex, obviously petrified, but standing up to me defiantly. Willing to take on a dragon for the man she loved. "He knows where James is. If we don't find him before they leave New York, we never will. He knows the enemy. He knows how many people they have and what their defenses are. We need his help. You can deal with him, once James is safe."

For a moment, I saw my younger self staring back at me, and if my face wasn't frozen still, I might have smiled. There was a time when I would have risked anything for Jack. What a fool I was.

No, *Diana* would have done that. She was long gone, buried alongside her lost husband. I was Director Grey now, and my agents needed me to *be* Director Grey. With a deep breath, I put aside all emotion, and turned back to Jack. "You will share your information. You will then leave, and you will never come here again. Is that clear?" There. Calm, controlled. A leader, not a person capable of love.

"I can't do that," Jack answered. Always contrary, never following the rules. I used to love that about him, but now it was in my way.

"Do not cross me, Jack. You, of all people, know what I can do."

"I, of all people, know that you won't." And just like that, with a handful of words, he stripped away my armor and cut to the truth. "They may fear you," he said. "But I know you." More than a decade had passed, and he was still the only one who did.

I could fall apart later. First, I had an agent to save. "Start talking."

He closed his eyes and was silent for a moment. "I do know where they're keeping the Empath," he said, glancing at me. "But you can't go after him."

"Have you lost your mind in the last fourteen years? Or maybe working for the enemy has made you forget the point of everything we worked for? I would never abandon one of my people."

"Then you have to give him back the other one."

He wanted me to trade one life for another. The Empath from the museum incident was a young woman named Isabelle. We were keeping her in containment at the moment, partially because she was dangerous, but partially for her own good. She was obviously traumatized, and had clearly suffered abuse at the hands of someone I now guessed was Xavier. Normally, I'd have no problem with an exchange of hostages, but James had asked me not to send her back. They clearly had some history I didn't know about. I didn't like it, but I'd agreed to his request, and I would honor my word.

"He will see it as an acceptable trade," Jack was saying. "You took his Empath, so he took yours. She's stronger, he's stable. As of right now, you're even. If it's a trade, he'll honor his agreement and leave you alone. But he doesn't like to lose, and if you keep both of them, he will consider it an act of war."

Just when I thought this couldn't get any worse.

I was right in the beginning. This was a negotiation, and Jack was here to throw me off balance. Jack was *still* working for my enemy, against me. This day needed to end, and they all needed to leave. "Tell your boss I won't negotiate. And tell him that if he wants to talk to me again, send someone else next time."

"Wait, Diana, no," he protested, an edge of panic creeping into his voice. "He didn't send me. He doesn't know I'm here. I'm here because I saw the kid come in. I knew you'd come after him, and I know what will happen if you do." He was still lying. Spinning a story, so I could pretend that the time we spent together wasn't based on a lie. "Diana, I gave up *everything* to shield you from him, and you're about to throw all of that away, like it was nothing."

His voice broke a little on the last sentence. It was the first hint of real emotion that made it through his empty mask, and more than anything else, that was what got through to me. He sounded sincere. Despite everything, some part of me wanted to believe him. A bigger part of me wanted to hate him, so I could feel something other than pain. "You lied to me for fourteen years. How can I possibly believe a word you say?"

"Get a Mnemonic, one you trust. Call in Vivienne. She'll tell you that it's all true."

I needed to know the truth. No matter what it was, it would hurt, but I needed to know. Vivienne would give me the truth. She was long since retired, but she would do this for me. And in the meanwhile, everyone would get the hell out of my office.

"Acceptable."

—

As soon as the door clicked shut behind Alex, I flipped the lock, making sure no one could come in. The second I knew I was completely alone, all of my strength drained from me, and I crumpled. My knees went out from under me, and I sank helplessly to the floor.

Jack left me.

I hugged my knees to my chest, curling in on myself like a child. Somewhere in the back of my mind I knew I was shaking, but I couldn't feel it. I couldn't feel anything.

The walls and the ceiling were closing in on me, caging me in, threatening to crush me. I pulled my knees in tighter, trying to shrink into myself, make myself as small as possible.

Everything was a lie.

The one person I knew would never hurt me had just caused me the worst pain I'd ever felt. The ground had been ripped out from under me, the foundation I'd built my strength on was crumbling. When he died, I knew beyond a shadow of a doubt that he loved me. It was all I had to cling to, the only thing that gave me the strength to go on, and now it was gone. He took it from me.

I wrapped my arms over my head, as though that could shield me from pain. Even losing him hadn't hurt this much. Through everything, I knew he was with me in spirit, as I'd built this dream we shared. Every long hour, every exhausting day was worth it, because I knew that if he could, he'd be right here beside me.

It was all a lie.

Jack left me, and now I was truly alone.

Chapter Twenty-six: Truth

A knock sounded on my door. "Director Grey," came my assistant's voice. "Vivienne is here. She's on her way up now." I glanced at the time. It was less than an hour since I sent for her. She must have dropped everything the second she got the call. I shouldn't keep her waiting.

"Thank you, Theo. I'll be right out."

I forced my breathing to slow. In a minute, I would go out there, wearing the rock-hard mask I wore in front of my team. I was a leader, and I could not, would *absolutely not* allow myself to appear weak. My people needed me to be strong for them, and for them, I would be.

It would be better if no one knew who Jack was. Theo would have figured it out instantly. I chose him as my assistant specifically because his Talent gave him the ability to take in every tiny detail, see the patterns, and piece them together into a clear picture. The second he saw Jack, he would immediately recognize him from the photo on the lobby wall.

Vivienne knew, of course, no helping that. Alex knew. James, once we found him, would figure it out, too. In the back of my mind, I recognized the irony that it was the Empath who was missing. While I could maintain the outward appearance of calm, James would see through it immediately.

For the first time, I was glad I had a private bathroom connected to this office. When we first signed the lease, I thought it was an unnecessary indulgence, but now I was grateful for it. I splashed my face with cold water, straightened my clothes, and smoothed down my hair. By the time I heard Vivienne's voice in the hall, I had mostly pulled myself back together. The rage that burned hot an hour ago had settled into an icy shell that wrapped around me like armor. I was back in control, and I wouldn't allow anyone to know that it had ever been otherwise.

Especially not Jack.

—

Theo set them up in a conference room. Jack was seated, and Vivienne stood before him, holding a hand to his forehead like I'd seen her do a hundred times before. There was usually no emotion visible while Vivienne worked, but I could see growing horror on her face. I couldn't hear what she said to him when she opened her eyes, but after a few minutes, she rose and told me, "He's not lying. He's just an idiot."

Not lying. I wasn't sure how I felt about this outcome. On the one hand, if what he was saying was true, we had a massive problem on our hands, but at least we knew where to find James. On the other, the knowledge that Jack truly believed he was protecting me all this time should be reassuring, but somehow it wasn't.

"Do you want to see any of it?" Vivienne asked me, cutting into my thoughts.

I shuddered internally at the thought. Seeing what the only person I'd ever truly trusted was thinking when he betrayed me would be a new kind of torture. "No, I'll take your word for it."

"He may need a little while to recover. I wasn't particularly gentle towards the end."

Keeping my face carefully flat, I gestured for her to follow me to my office. I needed to know everything, but I didn't want to discuss any of it in front of others.

She sat opposite me, watching me warily. "Are you-"

"I'm fine," I said shortly. It was a blatant lie, and she would know it. She'd also understand that I didn't want to talk about it. "Do you know where James is?"

"Petrov is holding him in a basement under City Hall. Someone on the Mayor's staff set him up with an office there."

"Is he safe? Injured?"

"As of the last time Jack saw him, he was fine." She looked at me sternly. "You're stalling."

"Is it as bad as I think it is?"

"Probably worse."

"Fine. Tell me."

"The original founders of Kingfisher, Robert King and John Fisher, were both Talented. Fisher was a Prodigal, hyper-intelligent, and handled business strategy. King was a Charismatic, he handled recruitment and fundraising. All of their descendants inherited their Talent, down to Matthew Fisher and Xavier King, the last of the board members. Fisher was killed with the rest of the board. King escaped."

"How?"

"Jack doesn't know all of it, but there was definitely a Jumper involved."

"Tell me about King."

"Charismatic, *very* strong. He thinks the King line is descended from the French monarchy. Given the number of illegitimate offspring there were, it's completely possible that an unknown branch of that family survived."

The beginnings of a headache were pulsing behind my eyes. "And he thinks this makes him entitled to what? To take over the world?"

"That's exactly what he thinks. In his head, he's a savior that has come to liberate Paranormals from oppression and establish a new world order. He's been building an army for decades. The incident at the museum was meant to be a demonstration of his power, to sway some powerful holdouts to his side. Our intervention has forced him to regroup, which buys us a little time, but not much."

That was a much more logical explanation for the failed attack on the museum. It would have been a very effective demonstration of power - two Paranormals had nearly massacred hundreds of the country's most famous people. Other than me, not many people could kill that efficiently, and my methods were developed to be quiet and not draw attention. Their plan would have been spectacularly visible, and gruesome. The Pyrokinetic was supposed to block the exits with fire and Isabelle, the Empath, would incite a mass panic. She had almost no control, but enough raw power to incite the kind of terror that would make people throw themselves into the fire to get away. The sight of the country's most influential and well-protected people burning alive would send a strong message: no one was safe.

"So he took James in retaliation for us foiling his plans?"

"No. He took James in exchange for Isabelle - one Empath for another. Surprisingly, the abductions seem to be strategic. Her absence created a hole on his team, and she's currently too well-protected. James was not."

My headache was blossoming into truly spectacular proportions. So far, all of this was consistent with what Jack said earlier, which meant he told me the truth. If he was telling the truth about that…

"And Jack? Where does he fit into all this?"

"As you know, he was working for Xavier. When Alex and James started getting close to the truth about Petrov, he recognized them as your agents. He knew that if anything happened to them, you would turn over every stone to find them. If you did, it would result in a direct confrontation, which he believes we would lose. He tried to keep them out of trouble, but then James was taken, so he came to talk you out of going after him."

Exactly what he'd told me.

Before I asked anything else, she said, "Diana, there's something you should see."

"From his memories? No." I could handle hearing about it,

but seeing any of this through Jack's eyes would be too much. "Tell me instead."

She was clearly unhappy about it, but continued. "His memories don't match with what you told me about the day he disappeared. I am certain his were not modified. I checked very carefully. Unless you lied, and I wouldn't blame you, yours were." Watching me cautiously, she offered, "I can look, if you'd like."

She knew how much I hated this process. It didn't matter. I had to know. "Do it. Please."

"Shall I restore the missing ones, if I find them?"

"Yes."

She came around the desk and placed a gentle palm on my forehead. Terrified of what I was about to see, I closed my eyes.

—

I was walking down the street with Jack. We were on our way to get lunch, chattering about work, oblivious to the world around us, when someone bumped into me. A hand grabbed my arm. My instinct was to jerk away, but it was just a girl, maybe ten or eleven, who had lost her balance. Her eyes were striking - one brown and one green, like a cat. She smiled up at me sweetly, and I smiled back.

An instant later, we were in a small, empty room. I barely had time to register what had happened before the girl disappeared and I was alone.

A Jumper, I realized. I'd just been kidnapped by a Jumper. A child. She couldn't have been more than twelve, and she just took me off the street, in broad daylight. But to where?

I reached out around me, but outside the room was nothing, just an expanse of empty space. No doors, no windows, nothing to grab, nothing I could use to get myself free or lash out at my captors. I raged impotently inside the room, screaming for Jack, hurling threats at whoever could hear me, until I picked up the telltale scent of chloroform.

I'd never felt so helpless in my life.

When I woke up, I was in a hospital. Vivienne was there, telling me Jack was dead, and I tried to kill my doctor.

—

My head felt too tight, like my skull was suddenly too small, and it might crack under the pressure. "Thank you, Vee. You can go." I kept my eyes closed against the light.

She made no move to leave. I cracked an eyelid to look at her.

"Do you want to see the rest?"

"The rest of what?"

"Jack's memories of that day."

"No." I still had no interest in seeing inside his head.

"Will you forgive him?" she asked gently.

"I saw him die, Vee," I told her, opening my eyes. "I watched it happen and for years, every time I closed my eyes I saw it over and over again. I woke up screaming in the middle of the night for nearly a decade. The only thing that kept me going was that I knew I was doing what he would want, building the organization we thought we'd make together. It was the last little piece of him I had left, and I threw everything I had into it. I dedicated my entire life to building this legacy for him.

"And then a few hours ago, I found out it was all a lie. The only person I ever loved, the only person I ever truly *trusted*, played me for a fool. So no, I will not forgive him. There are some things you don't come back from."

—

Below City Hall, I listened at a door, annoyed, in the middle of the night. On the other side were two dozen guards, an ambassador, two of my agents, and Jack.

Exactly as both Vivienne and Jack had told me earlier that day, Sergei Petrov had set up an office in a spare room below ground level. He used it as a staging ground for sales to Xavier. In the morning, a Jumper would come and collect James, and once that happened, we had no way to find him. We had to get him out tonight.

Still, it should have been a quick, simple extraction. Jack had talked me into letting him hide me from the cameras. I didn't really want to risk a conflict with the Mayor's office, and if we did this right, no one would even know we were there. But then Alex had insisted on coming, too, and I'd let sentiment win over practicality. Now Alex and James were both captured, and being held on the other side of that door, and I wasn't really sure what Jack was doing.

I should have just come alone.

I could still keep this quiet if I wanted to, but the more I thought about it, the less I liked the idea. If we made it look like James escaped on his own, Jack could go back to his old job and pretend the last few days never happened. While part of me also wanted to forget all of this, there was no way in hell I was letting him off the hook that easily.

That wasn't the main reason I didn't like this plan. Petrov was a human trafficker. He'd been quietly abducting Paranormals and selling them for years. He would answer for that. Tonight.

But Xavier King, wherever he was, was buying them. Petrov was certainly not his only supplier. He probably had people all over the world taking Talents in preparation for his bid for power. That had to stop, too.

No, I would not be doing this quietly. I would be making a statement loud enough for Xavier to hear in his fortress or whatever rock he hid under.

The fact that Jack would be pissed was an added bonus.

The guns were the first things to fix. I reached inside each of them, found the firing pins, and bent them. Without a functioning firing pin, the guns were useless. It was the simplest way for me to disable a firearm, and I'd done it a million times. Next problem.

I might have to kill the guards. I tried not to kill people needlessly, but I wanted information from Petrov, and I didn't want to take the chance of any of them waking up while I interrogated him. And it was obvious what he was doing here. As far as I was concerned, anyone working for Petrov was complicit. Besides, I was sending a message, and I needed to make my point strongly. A room full of bodies was a great way to make a point. I compromised, deciding I would only kill them if they tried to kill me.

Time to make an entrance.

I slammed the doors open. They hit the walls with a satisfying crash. Twenty-four guards snapped to attention, and immediately raised their guns and tried to fire at me. *Oh, well. I gave them a chance.* I enjoyed watching their confusion when their weapons all mysteriously malfunctioned at once. Ever since the night Jimmy died, so many years ago, I really, *really* hated it when people pointed guns at me. No one ever did it twice.

A long, narrow room lay ahead of me. On the far side, a man sat at a desk. Scattered folding chairs filled the rest of the room, save for one clear aisle down the center. The only light came from two rows of bare-bulb fixtures dangling overhead. I reached out and crushed the ones closest to me. They crumbled with a satisfying pop and plunged the area around me into shadow. The monster in the dark was much more frightening than the enemy you can see. The Twelve had taught me that.

The guards were still trying to shoot me. I pressed on the arteries of the nearest two. A few seconds more, and… there. They fell to the floor. I took an unhurried step. Two by two, I dropped the guards and smashed the lights, walking down the aisle between them, staying just outside the edge of the light. I could have taken them all out at once, but I wanted Petrov to have plenty of time to feel the inexorable approach of his own mortality. Other people were missing, and he knew where they were. If I was going to get anything useful from him, I needed him scared.

Broken glass crunched under my feet as I walked slowly up the long aisle. Off to one side, Jack was freeing James and Alex, so I kept my attention on my prey. The man behind the desk struggled to rise, but I yanked his chair into the back of his legs and he fell back into it. His heartbeat was racing. Good. He was almost frightened enough now.

"Hello, Sergei," I greeted him with a smile, as he struggled with the chair. "Please, have a seat. My name is-"

"I know who you are," he bit out. "And I'm not afraid of you." He was, but apparently not afraid enough. Yet.

"Your heart rate says otherwise," I told him. "You and I are going to have a chat." I'd give him a chance to play nice. One.

"I have nothing to say to you, bi-" Clearly, he wasn't interested in playing nice. He was more afraid of Xavier than he was of me, which was unwise, because I literally held his life in my hands. Maybe he didn't realize that. I should make it clearer.

He was wearing a tie. I'd never understand why men voluntarily wore nooses around their necks. I tightened it just enough to be uncomfortable. "That wasn't a question," I told him with a smile. "You and I are going to have a nice long talk about what you've been up to lately." I made sure the fabric pressed on his windpipe enough to be extremely unpleasant, but not enough to interfere with his breathing. I needed him alive.

No matter what Jack said, I would not back down from this fight. Fourteen years ago, Xavier King stole the life I could have had. Last week he tried to commit mass murder, and then he kidnapped one of my agents. I didn't know where he was yet, but I would find him. Until I did, I wanted him to be unable to sleep at night, knowing that I was coming for him. Fear was a weapon, and I knew how to use it.

"And then you're going to deliver a message for me."

Chapter Twenty-seven: Rain

I forced a smile as Alex and James left my office. They would get a happy ending, at least. I was genuinely happy for them, but for me, there would always be a layer of pain underpinning the joy. Their love story had reopened my tragedy.

Outside my window, on a park bench across the street, Jack sat as though taunting me. I could kick him out of my office, but I couldn't stop him from sitting in the park.

On impulse, I grabbed my bag and walked out.

He didn't speak when I stopped in front of him. He just looked up and held my eyes. We stayed like that for a long moment, feeling the push and pull of our years together and our years apart.

"Are you just going to sit here until I talk to you?"

"Seems to be working," he pointed out with a faint smile.

I crossed my arms over my chest. "Why are you still here? Don't you have a tyrant to get back to?"

"No point now," he shrugged. "You just declared war. There's nothing I can do now to stop what's coming."

I rolled my eyes. "And what *is* coming?"

"The beginning of the end. He'll stop bothering to hide. More people will disappear. His army will grow. Eventually he'll go public, and once the world is exposed to his Talent, everyone will fall in line."

"He can't possibly be that strong. I've met him and I don't even remember him."

"He didn't want you to, at the time. He will next time."

"That's absurd. No one can consciously control Charismatic Talent."

"And Kinetic sight can't see bodies," he reminded me. "Even if there are a handful of people who can resist his Talent, we'd be no match for his followers. He's made sure of it. That's why he had to split us up. We could have become a threat."

"Why you and not me?"

"Because you couldn't be controlled," he said with a bitter smile. "But I would do anything to protect you."

"Did you mean any of what you said about this place?" I gestured vaguely back at the office. "Or was that all a lie, too?"

"I did. But when it came down to it, it wasn't the most important thing. You're the only thing that matters, Di. You always were. The rest of the world can burn, as long as you're safe."

"I would never have agreed to any of this."

"I know. That was the problem." He looked at me sadly. "You know, I had this conversation a million times in my head, thinking about all the things I would say to you if I ever had the chance again." He gave a humorless laugh. "This is not how I hoped it would go."

"What did you expect, Jack?" I demanded. "Did you think you'd just show up and everything would be fine? That we'd go back to how things were? You can't just walk back into my life after fourteen years."

"Well, I can't walk away, either. So until one of those things changes, yes, I'm going to sit here and wait."

I turned and walked away, disgusted with us both.

—

Break.

The balls ricocheted around the table, but none sank into a pocket. *I'm out of practice.* The new version of Jimmy's Bar lacked the patina of age, but it was just as empty on a weekday afternoon. I hadn't been back here in ages, but just knowing I had a place where I could escape to, where no one knew to look for me, was reassuring.

One. Side pocket.

I should come here more, if only to check in on Mel. Jimmy's granddaughter clearly had things under control here, but it didn't hurt to drop by now and then to make sure.

Two. Far left corner.

Unlike Jimmy, Melanie knew I was a Kinetic. I wanted to be able to relax here, and I decided to trust her with the truth. She took the news that there was a whole community of Paranormals surprisingly well. 'Explains a lot, actually,' was all she said about it before pouring us both drinks and asking about my day. It was nice to have someone completely outside that world to talk to.

Three.

I was not in a mood to talk today. Now that the danger was past, and my people were safe, I had no way to hide from my rage. It was vast and bottomless, and I didn't trust myself around people until I'd cleared my head and gotten it under control. Nothing else was helping, and pool was my last resort.

Four. Scratch.

It wasn't working. With every shot, my fury grew until my hands were shaking and I could barely hold the stick. *How could he leave?* I didn't bother using my hands to fish the offending cue ball out of the pocket and line up the next shot.

Miss.

I lined up a combo shot and missed again. *How dare he come back?*

With a scream of rage, I Kinetically lifted the offending ball and sent it hurtling into the wall. It hit with a satisfying thud, and embedded itself in the drywall. It stayed, half in and half out of the wall. That felt good. That helped. All fifteen of the remaining balls rose into the air, and hurtled as one into the damaged wall. They stayed too, dotting the blank wall with color like splattered paint.

"Want to talk about it?"

Mel. My anger deflated instantly when I realized what I'd done to her bar. "Mel, I'm sorry, I'll-"

She waved me off from where she stood in the doorway. "As far as I'm concerned, it's your bar, so they're your walls, and you can fling anything at them you want. I kind of like them there, actually. Looks kind of cool. I might keep it like that."

"I told you, the bar is yours." As soon as I had the funds, I had given Jimmy's widow enough to repair the fire damage and rebuild the bar. Neither Helen nor her daughter Jane had the heart to start it up again, but Jane's daughter Melanie did. She stumbled a few times in the beginning, but I'd kept her afloat and she learned quickly from her mistakes. Now it was thriving. Jimmy would have been proud.

"Not how I see it," she insisted. "But that's not the point right now. What's got you all pissed off? I don't think I've ever seen you angry before."

I couldn't begin to explain this situation. "It's complicated."

"Try me," she suggested. "I'm better at relationship advice than the kind of problems you're likely to have, but I'm a pretty good listener." At the look on my face, she added incredulously, "Wait, that's it, isn't it? You didn't tell me you had a new guy!" I'd often suspected Jimmy's family had a weak Empathic gift. Mel could see straight through me as easily as her grandfather could.

"I don't. Not a new one, anyway."

"An old one, then? I thought you were a widow."

"So did I." I sank down on a stool.

She looked confused for a second, and then raised her eyebrows. "He's back?"

I wished I had a better way to explain, but it was too much. "He is."

Keeping a carefully neutral tone, Mel asked, "How do you feel about this?"

She'd make a good therapist. Or poker player. "Honestly? Betrayed. Angry. Stupid."

"Why stupid?"

"When I first saw him, there was this split second where I

was so damn happy." I lifted a couple of blocks of blue chalk off the rail, and idly started swirling them in the air. "Like everything was going to be OK again. And then I realized that if he's been alive all these years, then he's been staying away from me on purpose, and that made it So. Much. Worse." I punctuated the last three words by crushing the chalk, sending tiny clouds of blue dust into the air.

"He must mean a lot to you, if you're this angry."

"He meant everything, once. Now he means nothing."

She laughed. "Well, *that's* not true." I glared at her. "If he meant nothing to you, my walls wouldn't have new decorations."

"I'm sorry about that."

"No, I like them. I'm keeping it. Want to do the other side to match? I have another set."

I shook my head, and then thought about it. "Would you mind?"

Wordlessly, she opened a cabinet and pulled out a square box. "Can you make it so the numbers face out?"

"I will never get used to that," she admitted as I lifted them one by one and sent them flying at the wall. "Tell me about him," she suggested.

"We were inseparable, once. He was my partner, my lover, and my best friend. We lived together, worked together, ate, drank, and slept together. He was the other half of me, and when he was gone, he took half of me with him. It changed me. I'm not the same person I was then. I don't even remember who that person was."

"That's kind of sad, to not remember who you used to be. Maybe you should try?"

"I wouldn't know where to begin," I started, and then realized it wasn't true. I knew exactly where to go. "You know what, Mel? You give pretty good advice."

"It's in the job description," she said with a smile.

—

The rickety metal stairs rattled under my feet. I'd have to talk to the caretaker to make sure he remembered to maintain this side of the building, too. The lower floors held art galleries now, but the attic remained untouched. It was still only accessible by this creaky staircase, and the only key was locked inside it. There were other Kinetics precise enough to open simple locks, but this one wasn't simple, and I was the only one who even knew this was here. I hadn't been back since the day of the funeral. It sat here, gathering dust, undisturbed until today.

The door creaked when I opened it, straining hinges that hadn't moved in years. A layer of dust coated the floor, confirmation that no one had been here. My heels clacked loudly on the hard floors, cutting through the heavy silence. Echoes of happier times surrounded me as I walked through the long space. Breakfasts in the kitchen, dinners at the long oak table, evenings curled up on the couch with a book. Memories overwhelmed me as I approached the window overlooking the park.

I sank down cross-legged onto the floor in front of it, and looked out. Heavy clouds hung over the city, oppressive and bleak. There was no reflection on the surface of the reservoir. It just sat silently, deep and dark and still. I felt like I was sinking in it, pulled down into the depths by the weight of sorrow.

I reached up into the rafters, easily finding my hiding spot and the box I'd left in it. A cloud of dust swirled down as I lowered it to land in my hands. Taking a deep breath, I steeled myself to open it. Out of all the things I'd faced in my life, this shouldn't be the hardest.

I lifted the lid.

The garnet lay exactly where I'd left it, nestled in its bed of white cloth. I lifted it by its chain and held it up in the dim light. The metal was black with tarnish, but the gem itself was deep and red and beautiful, untouched by time. I sat staring silently at it for a long time, lost in memories of good days and bad days, and all the days in between. Days spent with anger and love and joy and pain, all things that felt distant and distorted now, like light through broken glass.

Below, the park was nearly empty. A rumble of thunder sounded ominously in the distance. I heard the rain before I saw it, sweeping in from the west and clattering on the old copper roof. I watched as it spattered on the pavement below, sending pedestrians running for cover. I saw the first drops hit the lake, shattering the smooth surface of the water. Tears started to fall, slowly at first, like the rain, building to a torrent I was helpless to prevent.

For the first time in fourteen years, I cried.

Chapter Twenty-eight: Ducks

He was still there, sitting on that goddamn bench. Three weeks later, and Jack just stayed there, waiting for me to get desperate enough to talk to him again.

Hell would freeze over first.

With difficulty, I pried my eyes away from my office window and forced myself to look at the papers scattered across my desk. Data collected from other agencies and communities across the country and the world, cross-referenced and analyzed by Theo, painstakingly detailing the depth of the hole we were in.

As much as I hated to admit it, it seemed like Jack was right about the consequences of our rescue mission. The last three weeks had been horrific. Paranormals all over the world were going missing, twenty in the last week alone, and I was powerless to do anything about it. Alex still hadn't had any new visions. The information we'd gotten from Petrov led us to one holding facility, where we'd found and freed a handful of people. After that, we had no place else to look.

Meanwhile, there were incidents happening everywhere. On the surface, to the untrained eye, they looked like accidents. To people in the Paranormal community, who knew a Pyrokinetically induced fire when they saw one, they were clearly acts of violence. None of them were quite as overt as the incident at the museum would have been, but everyone knew what they were.

It was a coordinated campaign of terror, and it was working. Between the 'accidents' and the disappearances, people were terrified. They were looking to me for guidance, and all I could think about was the idiot on the bench outside my window.

This is a fight you can't win.

I flung one of my knives blindly into a wall behind me with a yell of frustration. It made me feel a little better, until I looked up. James stood in my doorway, hand raised to knock, staring at the knife that was now embedded in the wall a few inches from his head.

"What do you want?" I snapped at him. James, the Empath, who could pick up my every emotion, was the last person I wanted to see right now. Unfortunately, because he was an Empath, he would immediately know that.

My anger deflated a bit. I should know better than to treat him like this. This was exactly why I took him in. It wasn't his fault, and the curse of his Empathic Talent meant that everyone resented him for knowing what they were feeling, and I would *not* do it myself.

"I'm sorry, James," I corrected myself. "What is it?" Pulling myself away from the window, I returned to my desk.

He gave me a rueful smile, no doubt having followed the progression of my thoughts. "I can hear you from the other side of the building. It's giving me a headache. Anything you want to talk about?"

"No," I snapped at him again, sliding back into anger. *Empaths.*

He came inside and shut the door. "That's not exactly a lie," he said, sitting in a chair across from me, "but it's not exactly the truth, either." Part of his Talent gave him the ability to tell truth from lies. Handy for him, extremely annoying for the rest of us.

"Take the day off, if I'm bothering you that much."

He smiled. Was that pity in his eyes? "You know that's not why I'm here. I want to help. You've helped me in countless ways, and this is the least I can do in return."

I gave him a flat stare. "I don't need help."

"Look, I know you don't want anyone to see that you're upset, but I'm a lost cause. You may as well take advantage of it."

My resolve snapped. "You want to help?" I asked him. "Fix it." I thrust my hand out to him, palm up. With physical contact, he was extremely good at manipulating emotion. "I need a clear head to deal with this situation. Drain away all of this foolishness so I can think."

He stared at my outstretched hand without moving. "I don't think that's a good idea."

Rage was always just under the surface lately, threatening to break through. "I didn't ask for your opinion. Just do it."

His face was set in a determined expression. "No."

James was one of the few people who wasn't afraid of me, but he very, very rarely defied me. "What do you mean, no?" I growled. "I thought you wanted to help?"

He looked at the floor for a minute and then back up. "If I thought this would help you, I'd do it in a second," he said, meeting my eyes. "But, Diana, this is the first time I've seen you feel anything stronger than mild annoyance in the entire time I've known you. A few weeks ago, I watched you kill a roomful of people with less emotion than if someone got your coffee order wrong. That's not good."

"They were trying to shoot me."

"You'd already broken their guns."

Ungrateful wretch. "Would you rather I left you there?"

"That's not the point. The point is that you didn't care. Whether or not they deserved it, you should have felt *something*."

"How dare you judge me?" I demanded. "You would be dead by now if it wasn't for me. Half the people here would be dead. None of this would be here. You'd all still be working for the Twelve, and most of you would be murderers like me."

Murderers like me.

The words hung in the air, echoing in my head. In all these years, I hadn't managed to erase the stain of the things I'd done. Maybe I never would. There was blood on my hands, and no matter how hard I tried, nothing was enough to wash it away.

Maybe it never would be.

"How the hell would you know what's good for me?" I continued. "You have no idea what I've done. What I saved you from." James was looking at the ground, patiently waiting for me to finish my rant. "Are you even listening?"

"Yes," he said. "But I know that none of this is directed at me. I am very aware that I owe you everything. If it wasn't for you pulling me out of my old life, I'd have run out of luck years ago. I'd do almost anything you asked of me without question, and I would like to think I've proven that by now.

"But more than that, I'd like to think that we're friends. And I'm going to talk to you right now as a friend, not as an employee." He paused and got that impish grin that everyone found so disarming. "So please don't fire me for it." I continued to glare at him.

"In all the time I've known you, I've never seen you react like this. I've barely seen you react at all. Now that I've met Jack, I understand why - don't bother to lie. You have a chance, now, to either be happy again, or get closure and move on, but if I take this away, I'd be robbing you of that. I can't do that to you. You're living half a life. You rescued me from myself a long time ago. Consider this returning the favor."

Somewhere in the back of my mind, I knew he was right. I still hated it. "You're fired," I told him childishly.

His mouth twitched upward with suppressed laughter. "You're lying."

The little bastard was lucky he was charming. "Get out of my office."

Obediently, he stood to leave, but paused at the door. "For what it's worth," he told me more seriously, "he's just as bad as you."

—

He was still there the next day. And the day after that. Waiting.

"No, Silvio, I don't have any more information," I snapped,

shifting the phone into my left hand to open the door to my usual morning coffee shop. The leaders of other Paranormal communities were calling me non-stop, expecting me to fix everything. "Yes, we're looking. I'll let you know when we find something."

Pushing my way through the door, I stabbed at my phone to end the call. My shoulder bumped into someone coming out. As I looked up, the young woman touched my arm with one hand in what seemed like a casual, friendly gesture.

Her free hand tipped her sunglasses down, and she winked.

She was out the door before I could even react, and gone by the time I followed her outside, knowing she wouldn't be there. A Jumper. But I already knew that. I'd seen her before.

My heart pounded in my chest and my phone slipped from numb fingers as the image hung in my mind. Two eyes, peering over the edge of dark sunglasses, one brown, and one green.

Hell just froze over.

—

"Tell me about the woman with the mismatched eyes."

Jack looked up at me sharply. "You've seen her? Here?"

It was a sign of how rattled I was that I didn't even try to deflect his question. "Yes. Just now, in the coffee shop. She wanted me to know it was her."

He drew in a deep breath, and let it out slowly. The image of a woman appeared beside me, staring blankly ahead. Her eyes were quite striking, but the effect was deeply unsettling. "They call her the odd-eyed cat, or just Cat to her face. One of the best combat Jumpers I've ever seen. Impossible to fight - she's in and gone before you even know she's there. She's one of the fanatics. She believes he rescued her from a bad situation as a child, and is fiercely loyal. She'd Jump in front of a bullet for him."

"She believes? You don't?"

"Mnemonics," he explained. "I'm not positive in her case,

since it happened so long ago, but I've seen it many times since. A rare Talent is identified, and brought in, and their memories are rearranged to fit the narrative. Somehow, no matter how many times they see it done to other people, it never occurs to them that it might have happened to *them*."

"That's horrible."

"That's the least of it, honestly. I don't know what her exact circumstances were when they found her, but she was *young*. Ten or so." The image of the woman shifted, grew younger, smaller, until a girl stood before me. "She was already good enough to take both of us off the street at eleven." I saw my own form materialize, saw the whole scene play out from Jack's point of view. The girl stepped into my path, bumped into me, and grabbed an armful of my coat. By the time I'd even reacted, both of us were gone.

"And now?"

"Now, she's twenty-five, a master of multiple martial arts, and oversees his personal security team. She rarely leaves his side, so if she's here, it's on direct orders."

"Orders to do what?"

"I don't think he wants to kill you. He might be trying to recruit you."

"If that was it, why wouldn't she have taken me? She could have." I admitted. "Easily. I was caught off guard, and she had physical contact. But she didn't. It makes no sense."

"No," he agreed. "It doesn't. I don't know what game he's playing with you."

———

"Why are we here, Theo?" A woman's voice drifted up from the alley. "Are you sure this is the right place?" Jenna. Not the Jumper I would have chosen, but I trusted Theo's judgment.

"We're here," Theo answered in a tired voice, "because Director Grey told us to come here, without being followed. Jumpers can't be followed."

"But why here?" Jenna continued determinedly. "Why would she want us to come to a random back alley?"

"Ask her yourself," suggested James, nodding at the top of the stairs where I stood looking down at the three of them.

I really hoped I wasn't going to regret this. "No more than two at a time on the stairs," I told them. "Try to be quiet." I stepped back into the loft, leaving the door open behind me.

While they climbed, I took a deep breath to calm myself. These were the people I trusted most. It shouldn't be hard to let them in. I didn't even live here anymore.

Old habits died hard.

If anyone picked up on my discomfort, they didn't show it. James would, of course, but he knew better than to give me away. He just watched me curiously as the other two looked around.

Theo's eyes were huge. I watched him take in every detail, knowing they would be instantly filed away into his infallible memory. He looked at me, and then looked back at the space, clearly trying to connect the two.

"OK, but where are we?" Jenna insisted. "What is this place?"

"My home," I told them, confirming what I was sure Theo and James had already figured out. "Or at least it used to be."

"I always thought this was an investment property," Theo said.

"It is." James raised an eyebrow at me. "Mostly. Have a seat," I told him. We weren't here to discuss my real estate decisions.

James sat beside me at the huge table. "How's Alex?" I asked him, while Theo and Jenna lingered in the open kitchen.

"Still nothing," he admitted. Alex's visions hadn't returned after James was captured. It wasn't that surprising - emotional trauma was known to suppress Talent - but I'd hoped they'd be back by now. We had no way of knowing if they'd ever return.

"How did you even get this up here?" Jenna marveled, looking at the granite countertops.

"Heavy Telekinetics. Can we get started?"

"Are these the original floors?" Theo asked. "How old is this building?"

"Focus, please. That's not why we're here."

"Fine, fine, we're coming." They sat on the far side of the table, opposite James and I, still looking around curiously.

"So," began James, "why *are* we here?"

"We're here because I needed to talk to the two of you without being overheard."

The loft was not my first choice of venue for this meeting. Or my second. Unfortunately, until I had more information, we couldn't discuss things openly in the office, and my studio apartment was way too small for this many people. Since I was never there, it was minimalist - the extent of my furniture was a bed and a small table. This conversation was awkward enough here, so I could only imagine having them all sitting on the edge of my mattress.

Jenna snorted. "And I'm the taxi," she said. "Figures."

I looked at her sharply. "You're here because Theo trusts you. Don't prove him wrong." Stopping myself, I recalibrated. Intimidation wasn't going to work with Jenna. She Jumped in and out of dangerous situations every day. She was our best rescue Jumper, partly because she had no fear. "And because I trust you, too. You would still be in the alley if I didn't."

"Talk about what?" James cut in.

"Someone is watching us. At least, watching me. And I think they have inside help."

"You think we have a spy?" Theo asked, finally focused on the problem instead of my apartment.

"I think we have someone reporting my movements back to Xavier's team." I outlined what I knew about Cat.

"It could be anyone," Theo said. "Not just staff. It could be the security guard or the guy at the newsstand. Anyone."

"Find out what you can. Quietly. If they realize we're looking, they'll just run. I want to know who they are, and what they know."

"And then what?" Jenna cut in. "We find the spy, maybe we buy ourselves some time. It's not going to stop him. He's going to keep picking us off, one by one. We're sitting ducks." I looked at her appraisingly. "What? Someone has to say it." As usual, Theo was right. She was a good addition to the conversation.

"You're right," I said, surprising her. "On both counts. We need to be brutally honest with ourselves and each other to figure this out."

"What I don't understand," James mused, "is how he managed to do all of this without anyone noticing. Without *us* noticing."

"We weren't looking for it," Theo explained. "And his people did a really good job of covering his tracks. Paranormals tend to have short lifespans, so it's not remarkable when one of us disappears. Or dies. Especially if their family members have clear memories of seeing them die."

Like I did. "Mnemonics?"

"Some of them. Not everyone we've spoken to had modified memories."

I would do anything to protect you. "Jack."

"It's possible." It seemed a lot more than possible. He was perfectly capable of faking more deaths than just his own. I wondered what else they'd made him do, over the years. What it cost him.

"Who's Jack?" Jenna asked Theo in an undertone. I really didn't need anyone else knowing about him.

Picking up my dismay, James said, "Look, the good news is that a lot of people who were thought to be missing or dead are alive."

"True. But the bad news is that they're all working for the enemy," Jenna pointed out, distracted from questions I didn't want to answer.

"So what do we do?"

"What *can* we do?" Theo asked. "He's like a phantom. We have no idea where he is, or when he'll strike. Even if we did, what could we possibly do to stop it? What little information we do have suggests he has thousands of people on his side. We're massively outnumbered. If we fight, we'll lose. And the more time we wait, the more people will disappear, and the stronger he'll get." The stark assessment was even more disheartening coming from Theo. "I'm sorry, but you said to be brutally honest."

This is a fight you can't win.

It was true. We were all sitting ducks, myself included. Xavier's Jumper could have easily taken me today. She'd done it before. There was nothing I could do about it then *or* now.

Except… she hadn't. The question was, *why?*

Chapter Twenty-nine: Talk

"What does he want?" I said without preamble as I sat at the cafe table across from the woman in sunglasses. She was sipping an iced latte, wearing yoga pants and a tank top. To anyone passing by, she looked like she was on her way to the gym. I recognized her attire for what it was - the battle gear of a combat Jumper, light and non-restricting.

She looked at me in silence for a moment, then smiled and slid her sunglasses on top of her head. To all appearances, we were a couple of old friends, meeting for an afternoon coffee. "To talk," she said.

She extended a hand, palm up, inviting me to take it.

I just stared at it. "Does he really think I'm that stupid?" If I took her hand, she could Jump me anywhere she wanted. On the other side of that Jump, there would be either a Mnemonic, waiting to erase my memories, or a loaded gun.

With an unconcerned shrug, she said, "Suit yourself," and vanished.

—

I sat staring at the empty chair for so long that the barista came over and handed me a coffee. "Your usual. On us," she told me. "You look like you need it."

I was Diana Grey, Telekinetic ex-assassin who toppled the old Paranormal power structure and set up a new order. The lives of everyone around me were in the palm of my hand. I had nearly two hundred Paranormals at my command. Communities all over the world looked to me for guidance.

And my barista had just taken pity on me.

"Thanks, Gloria," I said with a grateful smile. "I do."

I took a sip, utterly at a loss. For the first time in many years, I was starting to feel like I was in completely over my head. There was no way I could go with Cat to talk to Xavier. It was an obvious trap. I couldn't let him keep taking people, either, but I was helpless to stop him. I was losing this fight, and I had absolutely no idea what to do.

I needed to think, and in order to do that, I needed a clear head. The coffee was helping, but there was something else that would help more.

—

Mel stood in the doorway of her bar with her arms crossed over her chest and a forbidding expression on her face. "You need to leave."

"What?" After everything else, Mel's sudden hostility hit me hard.

"You see that man over there?" she asked, nodding to someone across the street. "He's been there for days. When I open, he's there. When I close, he's there. I don't know what kind of trouble is following you, but I can't have it here. I have kids to take care of. Please just go."

I looked to see who she was talking about. There was a man across the street, leaning against a wall and smoking. When he saw me watching, he tossed the stub of his current cigarette to the ground. Before it landed, it burst into cinders, and fell to the pavement in a cloud of ash. He pulled out a second one, and with no visible means of lighting it, the end started to glow.

Pyrokinetic.

My blood ran cold. Someone with his Talent could burn down this entire building - this entire block - in minutes. It had been happening all over the city lately. There was absolutely no reason why a Pyrokinetic should be here. To the best of my knowledge, Mel

197

had no connection to the Paranormal community. This was an ordinary bar, in an ordinary neighborhood, of no particular significance to anyone.

Except me.

This was personal now. He was targeting me, and until I gave him what he wanted, everyone who knew me would suffer. This had to stop.

"You need to get out of town for a while," I told her. "Go on vacation. Take the kids, take your whole family. Buy the tickets in cash. Don't tell anyone where you're going. Do you understand?"

She didn't look happy about it, but she nodded. "How long?"

I pulled a card from my pocket. "Call this number. Ask for Theo. Tell him you're a friend of mine. He'll tell you whether or not it's safe to come back."

"Will my bar be here when I do?"

She deserved the truth. "I don't know."

—

Theo answered my call on the first ring. "Where are you? Your 10 AM meeting has been waiting for an hour."

Oops. My encounter with Cat had driven everything else from my head. It wasn't important now. "Cancel it. I'm on my way back to the office, I'll be there in twenty minutes. I need to see you and Jenna in my office when I get back. Set up a video call. Leave the security open. Print out the connection details, please."

"Print? Like on paper?"

I laughed. "Yes, on physical, dead-tree paper. Bring it with you to my office."

—

They were waiting for me when I arrived. I glanced at the page

Theo handed me, and nodded approvingly. Digging in my desk drawer for a pen, I spoke seriously to Jenna. "Take this to the cafe downstairs. There's a woman there wearing sunglasses and yoga pants. I want you to hand her this paper, and then *immediately* Jump back up here."

"Sunglasses?"

"Yes. Big, black sunglasses."

"And yoga pants."

"Yes."

"Is this that Cat woman? The Jumper?"

"Yes."

"What if she's not there?"

"She is. I saw her on the way in." She looked like she wasn't taking this seriously, so I added, "Consider this a high risk job. She is dangerous and unpredictable. I'm sending you specifically because I trust you to get yourself out of bad situations. Trust your instincts. If anything seems off, get out, with or without the paper. Do you understand?"

Focused now, she nodded. "Got it."

"Good." I picked up a pen, and scrawled three words on the mostly blank paper.

Fine. Let's talk.

CHAPTER THIRTY: LIGHT

The wanna-be monarch's face filled the screen. I expected Xavier King to be ugly. Somehow, I thought that his nature would seep through into his looks, and I'd be able to read it in his face. Logically, I knew it didn't work that way, but I suppose too many movies had colored my internal assumptions.

I'd also thought he'd be older. He had touches of gray in his hair, much like Jack did now, and Jack was the last thing I should be thinking of at a moment like this. I shook my head, refocusing on my enemy's face. The few threads of gray in his hair mixed with the blonde, looking like strands of silver and gold. His bright, confident smile reached his piercing silver-blue eyes. The faintest hint of stubble dusted a strong, masculine jaw.

No, the face that was projected onto the conference room monitor was anything but ugly. He looked like the proverbial prince, ready to ride off on his white horse and lead his troops into battle.

He also looked familiar. "I killed you."

I remembered him now. He was the one who'd ordered the death of an infant. The one whose predecessor died suddenly. I'd last seen him bleeding out on the floor of a conference room.

"It's alright, my dear. I forgive you." His benevolent beam warmed my heart. "It wasn't your fault. You were the hand of Fate, moving me where I needed to be."

For a second, I felt proud to be a part of that, and then I remembered to resist his Talent with a conscious effort. "And how did I do that?"

"You showed me the error of my youth. Until that glorious day, I was content to hide in the shadows, like we all do. But you didn't hide. You stepped forward and took power, and showed me the strength we could have, if we were brave enough to wield it. You taught everyone in that room that Paranormals can only be led by one of our own. And I alone lived to remember that lesson."

"Pretty sure that's not what I said," I muttered. "How did you survive?" I asked aloud.

"Providence. Destiny. I'm told that if your knife was a fraction of an inch to the left, I would have died instantly. I nearly did anyway, but I managed to signal for aid in time. My people are quite efficient." I struggled to remember the scene. Xavier had fallen to the floor, hidden from sight by the table, still shielded by the Kinetic damper he wore. In theory, while Jack and I were still occupied with the others, a very precise Jumper could have gotten in and out without notice, if they were small enough to hide under the table. Like, say, a ten year old girl with mismatched eyes.

That explained how he got out, but, "There was a body." It occurred to me that neither Jack nor I were involved in the cleanup, and very few of the others knew what the board members looked like. Still. "We counted."

"Yes, regrettable, that." He looked like the memory pained him. He shook it off quickly. "My double. Chad, I believe. He was proud to make the sacrifice for the benefit of our people. He understood as I do that we were meant for greater things," he continued. "*I* was meant for greater things. As I lay dying, listening to your speech, I realized that I had to rise above the mediocrity that generations of my ancestors had settled for. They hid from what they were. After that day, I knew I couldn't deny my heritage anymore. I had to wear it like a crown."

He held his head high, as though someone might step up behind him and bestow an actual crown upon it. I could picture it, him sitting on his white horse, majestically draped in a flowing cloak. It was a beautiful sight. I wanted to see it.

I physically shuddered, as if it would help me shake off his influence. Holding on to hard facts for balance, I reminded myself, "You sent me to kill a baby." Everyone in the room looked at me. "I didn't do it," I assured them. James looked relieved, while Theo and Jenna looked disappointed in me. I wasn't the only one feeling the effects of his Talent.

"You and I are the same, Diana. You know as well as I the hard choices a leader must make. Sometimes we must commit an act of evil, to achieve a greater good. This organization you have built does good things, but do not forget that it was born in blood. We must tear down the old to make way for the new. It is the way of the world."

I glanced down at my hands, imagining the blood they were stained with. Who was I to judge him?

Wait. No.

"You bought people," I remembered with an effort. "You erased their memories and forced them to serve you. You tried to destroy a museum, and murder hundreds of people." It was an effort to remember. "You took my husband from me."

His laugh was musical, paternal and yet magnetic. "You still don't understand, do you? I freed you from him. He was holding you back, hiding your brilliance in the darkness. Once you were out of his shadow, I watched you blossom into the leader you were always meant to be."

He smiled brightly, and his eyes glowed with the promise of his vision. "I want a world where none of us have to hide. Where Normals know and respect us, and we don't have to disguise what we are. I want to see us all step into the light, and take our places in the sun."

Maybe I had all of this wrong.

Half of my life was spent in fear. For two decades, I believed that if anyone ever found out what I was, my world would crumble, that I would be killed, imprisoned, forced into servitude, some of which was not far from the truth. I couldn't help but wonder what my life would have been like if I hadn't been taught to be afraid. There were so many things I might have accomplished, if the world were different. Somewhere, right now, there were hundreds or thousands of kids just like me who were terrified, hiding their Talents and wasting their potential.

Xavier could change all of that.

"We have much in common," he continued. "We both built up teams of extraordinary people. You are an exceptional leader, a general, and you've done remarkable things with the limited resources you have. Imagine what you could do - what we could do - with more. We Paranormals have among us the best minds, the strongest warriors, the most skilled craftsmen. With Normals running things, we have war, and sickness, and suffering. Once we are in charge, we will transform this world into a paradise. Think how far we could advance humanity, what we could achieve."

It was a beautiful picture. I thought of all the times I had been frustrated by my limitations, and all of the people I hadn't been able to save. "We will change the course of history. You can be a part of building the future, if you choose. Come, Diana, it's time to stop hiding. Step out of the shadow, and into the light. Come stand by my side, where you belong."

"You want me to join you? Be your general?"

"No, my dear. You are so much more than that. I want you to be my queen."

The screen went black. I felt the sharp pain of loss as his face disappeared from my view. Crying out in dismay, I looked around angrily to find James holding the disconnected power cord in his hand with a grim expression. "I think we've heard enough of that."

I became aware that there were others in the room, as reality settled back into place. It hurt.

"Holy shit," said Theo, at my side. The look of reverence on his face was being replaced by horror. Jenna looked dazed.

James nodded. "I've never seen anything like that before.

It's unbelievable. I'm mostly immune to Charismatics, but even I felt that." He shuddered.

"That's some Talent," Theo marveled. "Now I understand why the French monarchy lasted for 800 years." Their conversation buzzed distantly like flies in the back of my mind.

"Diana? Are you alright?" James's voice cut through my reverie.

Without a word, I got up and left the room.

———

Jack was sitting in his usual spot on the bench. He looked over at me expressionlessly as I sat beside him.

"I spoke to Xavier," I told him, staring at the ground.

Jack was silent for a long moment. "Did he ask you to join him?"

I looked up at him, watching for his reaction. "He asked me to marry him, actually."

There it was - a crack in the mask. He looked like he wanted to throw something, break something, or throw up. After a moment, he forced his expression back to neutral.

"And?" he asked finally. "Will you?"

"Technically, I'm already married."

"Technically, you're a widow." He watched me warily. "What are you going to do?" he asked.

The vision Xavier painted was beautiful. All my life, I'd dreamed of a world where Paranormals could live openly and unafraid. We were safer now than we used to be, as long as we kept quiet around Normals, but it killed me that it was still necessary. Xavier was offering the future of my dreams, and I wanted it. I wanted it so very badly. I wanted it so much that I was willing to throw away everything I cared about to have it. I wanted to leave everyone that ever mattered to me and run to his side.

"I'm going to kill the bastard," I told Jack with a snarl.

I had almost fallen for it, and for that, he had to die.

Even knowing what he was, having every warning of what

I was facing and taking every precaution, I still nearly succumbed to his Talent. The rest of the world didn't stand a chance.

The slow smile that spread across Jack's made my heart skip a beat. It was the first real smile I'd seen on his face since he came back, and it held the memory of everything we once shared. "There's the woman I married," he said with gentle affection. "I knew you were still in there." It was a surprisingly intimate moment, and it caught me off guard. For an instant, I forgot my anger, and I felt that inexorable pull toward the man that was once the other half of my soul. One smile, and I was weak again.

I shook it off. I wasn't falling for *his* charms, either.

"The first problem is how we're going to get in," I said brusquely, diving into logistics. "It's probably nothing we haven't dealt with before, but I don't want to be surprised."

"We?" he interrupted.

Xavier had a truly extraordinary Talent. I'd never seen anything like it, and it explained why people flocked to his cause. That introduced a weakness - the force of his personality was probably what was holding everything together. Without him, it would fall apart. All I had to do was cut the head off the snake.

Unfortunately, he also had an army.

There was no way I could beat him in a direct confrontation. Even if I called in every resource available to me, I would lose, and many lives would be lost in the process. He was rich, powerful, and well-protected. Killing someone like that would be nearly impossible - for anyone but the two of us. Killing the rich, powerful and well-protected was what we did.

"We," I confirmed. "You know as well as I do that it's the only way. There is no one else in the world who is half as good at this kind of mission as we were. There's no other way. It has to be us. We go in, we take him out, we leave."

Jack shook his head sadly. "I wish it were that simple."

"There must be some way in. We've done this a million times before."

"Getting past his physical security is not a problem. There's an entrance no one knows about, it's unguarded, and it will lead us straight to him. That part is easy." He grimaced. "Getting close enough to kill him… that's impossible."

"Nothing is impossible."

"Don't you think I've tried? Hundreds of times, maybe thousands, I lost count. He's never without his bodyguards, and they'll see us coming a mile away."

"We've gotten around bodyguards before."

"Not like these. He has Pre-cogs and Empaths around him at all times, and Cat almost never leaves his side." He ran a hand through his hair in frustration. "It's impossible to get to him. The Pre-cogs see you coming, she gets rid of you. If she doesn't feel like killing you, she'll just remove you from the situation. Every time I got remotely close, I wound up in the middle of nowhere, miles away. Sometimes ten feet in the air."

"You can't remove a threat you can't see."

"That's what the Empaths are for. They can identify hostility a mile away. Kinetics may not be able to see us, but it's impossible to hide from an Empath."

Except that it isn't, anymore.

I almost laughed out loud at such an ironic coincidence, before I realized there was nothing accidental about it. There was a direct line of cause and effect. Fourteen years ago, Xavier had ordered the murder of a child based on a prophecy. Today, that child was a teenager, and that prophecy was about to unfold. And in the process, I'd get to torture Jack, just a little bit.

"Why are you smiling?" he asked with a wary look. "What are you thinking?"

I grinned. "I'm thinking we should go visit an old friend."

CHAPTER THIRTY-ONE: DRAGON

Jack stared dubiously at the cottage, nestled back in the woods of New York State. "Will you tell me where we are now?" We'd done some planning on the two hour drive north from the city, but I wanted this part to be a surprise. Maybe it was petty, but I figured I was entitled to a little pettiness, all things considered.

"Remember that last mission they tried to send us on?"

"The child? Like I'd forget." He trailed off, looking at the cottage, taking in the twinkling wind chimes, the haphazard garden, the brightly colored trim and shutters. Jack had never been here, but Athena's eccentric personality shined through every inch of her home. I enjoyed the look of horrified realization as he figured out where we were. And why. "You can't be serious."

"The baby grew up. She's fourteen now, and an astonishingly good Bender. Like nothing I've ever seen before."

"Does she know?" he asked.

"That we were sent to kill her? Or why? Or what happened when we didn't?"

"Any of it."

"No. And she can't find out," I warned. "She's just a kid, Jack. None of it was her fault."

"She's a dangerous kid. What was it the Psychic said? *The Dragon comes*, *bringing death and destruction*."

"Dangerous to who? That Psychic was working for Xavier. Maybe it was his death she predicted." The door to the cottage opened, and a kaleidoscope of color came hurtling towards us. "Too late to back out now," I added with a vengeful smirk.

"Jack!" Athena proclaimed as we got out of the car, "It's been ages!" Jack glared at me over her shoulder as she enveloped him in a giant hug. I gave him a little smile and a wink. "Come in, come in! I was just pouring tea. Angelina made cookies just this morning." I wondered what she made them from.

Benders could transform matter, morph it into a different shape or substance - which in Angelina's case, included cookies. Most Benders were minor Talents, and tended to be artisans of one kind or another. The most successful were the rare few who could transmute dense metals. They typically became jewelers, transforming base metals into gold or silver, and were typically quite wealthy.

Angelina was on a whole other level. A few months ago, she'd managed to transform a normal coin into a mildly radioactive metal like the one we used in our containment cells for Mental Talents like Empaths - except Angelina's version was far more effective. Instead of requiring masses of heavy bricks inside the walls, a single small coin completely negated Mental Talent in a three-foot radius. Once she realized it didn't work on her mother's Talent, which was Temporal and not Mental, she got bored, gave it away, and moved on to other things.

The coin went to Vermont with Isabelle, the woman we'd freed from Xavier, setting off this whole chain of events. Thanks to Vivienne, Isabelle now had no idea she was a powerful Empath, and no memory that Talents existed at all. She had chosen that life for herself, and from what Vivienne said she'd been through, it was a kindness. More importantly to me, it took an unpredictable, powerful Talent off the board. *That* coin needed to stay exactly where it was.

Unfortunately, it was the only one of its kind in existence. In order to carry off this mission, I had to convince her to make two more. I left Jack to distract Athena while I slipped off to find the girl. I was pretty sure Athena wouldn't approve of what I was about to do, but these were dire circumstances. I found the girl hunched over a desk in her bedroom, working on something that involved gears. Other than the workspace, it looked like the bedroom of any teenage girl, full of pastel colors, string lights, and band posters.

"Hey, Lina," I greeted her with her preferred nickname. "What are you working on?" If she was surprised to see me, she didn't show it. She kept working on her little clockwork... thing.

"What do you need?" she asked, bluntly cutting off my attempt at small talk.

"Why do you think I need something?" I hedged.

"You wouldn't be there if you didn't."

Hard to argue with that. I decided to go with it. "Do you remember you made something for your sister, once? Something that disrupts mental Talents?"

"I didn't make it for her. I made it for me, and it didn't work, so I gave it to her." She sighed, rolling her eyes in annoyance. "You need another one, don't you?"

"Two, actually." We could make do with one, if we stayed close together, but it would be better if we each had our own. "Name your price."

The object she was working on jumped three feet into the air, landed on the table with a loud thunk, and started to scurry away. She caught it easily and held it down, continuing to tinker with it. "I don't think you can afford it."

I laughed, deciding I liked this kid. "Try me," I suggested.

She looked at me thoughtfully, then came to a conclusion. "I'll decide later."

"I need them now."

"I'll make them for you now. I'll decide later what I want in return."

That was a very dangerous proposition. I'd never agree to trading an unspecified favor under normal circumstances. These weren't exactly normal circumstances, but still. "Why would I ever agree to that?"

"You don't have a choice." She looked at me pointedly.

"You're in charge of a huge organization of very Talented people, you have more money than you know what to do with, and yet you're bargaining with a teenager while your boyfriend distracts my mom. If you had any other option, you'd be doing that first."

Direct, observant, and clever. She had read the situation and come to exactly the right conclusion. Her Talent clearly wasn't her only asset - she was also smart, pragmatic, and completely willing to leverage someone else's desperation for her gain. Putting myself in debt to this girl seemed like a terrible idea, and yet, she was right. I had no choice. "You drive a hard bargain. How soon-"

She tossed something sparkly at me. I caught it out of reflex and looked at it. It was a painted necklace in the shape of a bright pink cat. Looking at the back, I saw that under the chipped paint, the metal had taken on a dull gray cast. "There's one," she said, rummaging around a drawer.

"You had one already?"

"I made it while we were talking. My mom got me that necklace and I hate pink, so you can have it. Here," she said, pulling something else out of a drawer. "You can have this, too." She turned it over in her hands a couple of times, and tossed that one at me, too. It was another charm, but this one was shaped like a cartoon dragon.

My breath caught in my throat as understanding hit me.

The dragon comes.

Lina wasn't the dragon in the prophecy. Lina *made* the dragon in the prophecy. In the back of my mind, I heard Athena telling me that prophecies never mean what they say.

"How do I know these work?"

"You don't. But I do. So if they don't work for you, you don't owe me anything. But don't even think about cheating me. My brother-in-law is an Empath, and he'll know if you're lying," she told me sternly. "And he's more afraid of me than he is of you, so I trust him. Remember, you owe me a favor now." She sounded like a teenaged crime boss.

I held out my hand seriously. "It's a pleasure doing business with you, ma'am."

She shook it, and gave me a genuine smile. Despite her earlier brusqueness, I had the sense that I just made a friend. Treating her like an equal was the right call. Her age probably made people underestimate her, which was something I'd experienced more than a few times myself. In both of our cases, it was a grave mistake. "I hope to see you at the agency in a few years," I told her.

"We'll see," she said with a one-shouldered shrug. She went back to her project and continued working as though I wasn't there. I caught a hint of a smile as she turned away. *Yes, I think I like this kid.*

Up until today, I'd mostly avoided her. Despite what I said to Jack about none of it being her fault, I'd always resented her. She was the catalyst that blew up my life, and ripped Jack away from me. When we argued that day, Jack told me, *'if it's a choice between you and a nameless stranger, I will choose you every time.'* I couldn't make the same choice, and because of that decision, I lost him. In my worst moments, in the dark hours of the night, I wished I could take it back. Today was the first day I truly felt like I'd made the right choice.

—

I slipped the two charms into my pocket as I walked back into the kitchen, where Athena was regaling Jack with some convoluted story about rabbits. After a long effort, I managed to pry him away from her and out the door.

"Are you going to tell me what that was all about now?" Jack asked once we were outside.

I tossed him the dragon pendant. He caught it and turned it over in his hands, looking for some significance to the trinket in his hands. "It blocks Mental Talents," I told him.

He looked at the cottage, and back at the charm. "The dragon comes," he breathed, putting together the same pieces I had. Watching his face change was amazing. His eyes widened in astonishment as he realized what it was and what it meant. With these charms, we would not only be immune to Xavier's Talent, we would be hidden from his Empath bodyguards. With these charms, we had a shot.

"Looks like Athena was right," I said with a smile. "Prophecies never mean what they say. Which one of us do you think is Death, and which one is Destruction?"

He threw his head back and laughed. It had been so long since I heard that sound. It was like music, soothing and heartbreaking at the same time. I wondered how long it had been since the last time he had laughed like that. With a weird twist in my chest, I tried to remember how long it had been since I'd laughed like that, and couldn't.

When he looked back at me, his eyes were filled with unexpected hope. "This might work," he said in amazement.

"This *will* work," I corrected, unable to stop smiling back.

The light in his eyes transformed him. He'd given up, I realized. Coming back to me when he did was just an attempt to buy time. He went along with my plan, but he never thought it would work. Now he did.

He took a step toward me, to throw his arms around me and hug me out of sheer joy. He did it without thinking, moved by the muscle memory of doing it a thousand times before. My reaction was also reflexive. I pulled back, flinching away from him.

He saw me flinch.

I saw my reaction register on his face, saw him remember that everything had changed, and that even if we won this fight, the past could never be undone. I watched the light in his eyes drain away. For a moment I'd seen the man I fell in love with so many years ago, and now he was gone again. With a tight, sad smile, he turned away, tucking the charm into his pocket and got into the car without another word.

I stared up at the sky for a long moment, feeling the cool evening breeze on my face, and a heavy weight in my chest. It hurt. I wondered if it would ever stop hurting.

CHAPTER THIRTY-TWO: REFLECTIONS

Having my team in the loft with me had been hard enough. Having Jack here was another thing entirely. We'd come straight here from Athena's cottage, wanting to get started on the planning immediately. Theo, Jenna, Alex, and James would be here soon, but for the moment, it was just the two of us in the home we'd shared for nearly ten years. Every square inch of it held a memory, and I could see every last one of them reflected in his eyes.

I tried to ignore him as he wandered the space, pausing here and there. When he got to the end of the long, heavy table, he stopped and traced the surface idly with one finger.

"What are you thinking?" I asked despite myself.

"I don't think you want to know."

"Tell me anyway."

"I was wondering if you still had that dress," he said with that sideways smile I could never resist.

I did still have it. There was absolutely no reason I should, but it was hanging right over there in the closet along the far wall, with all of the other things I couldn't let go of.

I should lie. I should tell him I got rid of it long ago, but I couldn't quite form the words.

The clatter of people on the stairs outside saved me from having to answer. Theo came in first, took one look at the two of us, and immediately turned to leave again. He ran headlong into Jenna, immediately behind him, who said loudly, "What the hell, Theo?" and pushed past him. It effectively broke the moment, and I was grateful for the distraction as the rest of them piled in.

When James came in, Jack's expression grew hard. "What's he doing here?"

"Oh, for crying out loud," James said, throwing his hands up in disbelief. "Still?" I glanced back and forth between the two men, bewildered, and looked to Alex, coming in behind him, for help. She had a hand over her mouth, and was visibly trying not to laugh. I thought I heard Theo mutter something unflattering about straight men as he unpacked his laptop onto the table.

I decided I didn't want to know.

"Who's this guy?" Jenna asked, eyeing Jack. Something about the way she was looking at him made me suddenly very aware of the beat of her heart and the surge of her pulse in her veins.

I caught the look of alarm James threw at Alex, and the way Alex shook her head warningly as she wrapped an arm over her friend's shoulder and said, "Long story. I'll fill you in later."

They were all gathered around the table, leaning over Theo's laptop before I even said a word. "What are we looking for?" Theo prompted, saving me from having to respond to any of it.

"We're looking for the Palace at Versailles," Jack answered.

"That should be easy to find," Alex answered, looking confused.

"Did it move?" asked Jenna, still looking back and forth between me and Jack.

"Not the original," Jack explained. "A replica. In a remote location."

"No, really," said Theo. He looked up from the keyboard and his face fell. "You're serious?"

"He built himself a palace in the middle of nowhere? An actual palace?"

"It fits the personality," James pointed out.

"He calls it New Versailles," Jack continued. "It's an exact replica of the original, as built for Louis XIV."

Theo looked at James. "Please tell me he's lying."

"'Fraid not," James replied. "Absolute truth."

"He really thinks he's descended from Louis XIV, doesn't he?" Alex commented. "Is it true?"

Jack made a face. "Does it matter? He thinks he's the rightful king, he's decided not to limit himself to France, and he's got the power to back it up. His family history doesn't really matter."

"It matters to him, though," James mused. "Bring up the original?"

A few keystrokes later, Theo had a satellite map of the real palace displayed on his screen. "Did he include the gardens?" Theo asked. "Between that and the building itself, it's a very distinctive footprint. If we can narrow it down a little more, we might be able to find it from satellite images."

"The palace gardens yes, but not this part here," Jack said, pointing at a spot on the screen. Theo slapped his hand away. "The big courtyard is there, and some of the auxiliary buildings, like the library."

"And you have no idea where it is? Not even what continent it's on?"

"I can tell you it's surrounded by mountains, but not more than that. Only the Jumpers are allowed to know the location, and that's the only way people can get in or out."

"How many Jumpers does he have?" Jenna asked incredulously. Jumpers were one of the rarer kinds of Talent. Out of the hundred ninety-two people in the agency, only a handful of them were Jumpers.

Theo ignored her. "What about the climate? Is it hot, cold? Are there seasons? Does it snow?"

Leaving the rest of them to figure it out, I wandered away from the group, gravitating toward the window as I always did. I stared out for a long time, trying to reassure myself that I was doing the right thing.

Being in this place reminded me of the long years I spent

alone and hiding, terrified to go outside or let anyone see what I was for fear of being caught. I thought of the parents I'd never known, all the friends I'd lost because people - Normals especially - hated those who were different.

We'd made great strides since then. The community that surrounded the agency gave us all a support system, both emotional and practical. But there was so much more that could be done.

With the resources Xavier could give me, I could change the world, and take the little safe haven I had created here and expand it everywhere. We could all live, and grow, and prosper out in the open, without fear. The concept of royalty was an outdated anachronism, but power was every bit as real and relevant as it had ever been. Now that I had Lina's charm to protect me from his Talent, it cast the whole situation in a new light. With the kind of influence he was offering me, I could fix so many things.

This was an opportunity I'd never get again.

My reflection in the glass stared back at me. Over these last few weeks, I had seen a side of myself that I didn't like. Part of that pretty picture was about control. I felt completely powerless when I lost Jack, and it changed me. I never, ever wanted to feel that helpless again. My need for control led me to keep the agency in an iron grip.

After a while, I stopped caring about the cost. *Necessary evils*, Xavier had called them. It started with taking down the rich and powerful, killing a few to save many. Dismantling the old agency had required blood to be spilled, but they were evil men, and it was for the greater good. A few weeks ago, I casually killed a roomful of guards and hardly gave it any thought. How long before I was willing to murder innocents? How long before I was the one giving orders to blow up planes, or kill a child? Would I know where the line was? Would I cross it anyway?

There it was, the ugly truth that Xavier showed me. I didn't know. If I was honest with myself, the reason he disturbed me so much was that he was too much like me - a funhouse reflection of my darkest parts. He was a vision of my future if I continued down the path I was on. When this was over, that was another problem I'd have to address.

"Everything OK?"

I jumped, startled to find Alex standing behind me. "What? Yes," I waved her off.

"It must be strange to be back here again."

"It's fine."

Taking her cue from my tone, she turned to go.

"Alex."

She stopped and faced me again. "Yes?"

"Is everyone afraid of me?"

The look on her face was as clear an answer as I could ever hope to get. Alex was a terrible liar. "No," she stumbled, "people aren't *afraid* of you. Everyone respects you, of course, but not-"

"Found it!" Theo's triumphant shout saved us both for the rest of her sentence.

"Go ahead," I told her. "I'll be there in a minute."

She fled.

I stared at my reflection in the window one last time, thinking about the past and the present, and trying to see the future.

———

In the center of a satellite photo, there a handful of distinctive shapes in an otherwise remote valley. The first was a stately cluster of orderly gardens, roughly laid out in a grid. The two center squares on one side held an odd-shaped building, like a U wrapped around a large courtyard, with two long wings leading out from each side. Next to the neatly landscaped grounds was a second large area that was its complete opposite. Where one was carefully laid and ordered, the other had no rhyme nor reason, with meandering paths winding around scattered ponds without any visible pattern. If it wasn't completely incongruous with the surrounding forest of densely packed pine trees, I might have thought it grew there naturally over time.

The third area was the largest. Centered around a rectangular pool of water was a large flat area. It was surrounded on three sides by rows of buildings that resembled barracks. In the center, several large groups were assembled. "How many people would you say are there?" I asked Theo.

"Thousands at least, when you add them all up. Maybe tens of thousands. Those buildings could house twice that if necessary."

I put a hand on the back of his chair to steady myself. It was one thing to know, abstractly, that there was an army. It was something else entirely to see it. In the back of my mind, I always thought the word 'army' was hyperbolic, and I was looking at proof that it wasn't. "Tens of thousands of people, all Paranormals, fanatically loyal to one man," I breathed. "That's horrifying. No one should have that much power." *Not even me.*

"Do you understand, now?" Jack asked softly from behind me.

"I understand that we can't Jump directly in," I said, glossing over his point. "There's no knowing what we could land in the middle of. He could have sentries everywhere. We should Jump to a point at least a mile away, and hike in, to make sure we're not seen. You said you know a hidden way in?" I asked Jack.

"Yes. Right here," he said, pointing to a spot on the screen. Theo slapped his hand away again. "Right there," he continued, "is the entrance to a tunnel that goes into the main palace. It leads directly to the king's bedchamber and bypasses all the gates and guards. The original was a secret way for the king to visit his wife and mistresses."

"How do you know all this?" Jenna interjected.

"I listen," Jack said with a quick glance at me. "The door is hidden behind a tapestry between rooms, maybe twenty feet from his bed. It's about a twenty minute walk. If we start at five

AM, we should get there around five thirty. No one is permitted to wake him until at least seven. Plenty of time to get back out before they find him. Usual method?" he asked me.

"It's the quietest," I agreed. "No chance of him waking up and calling for help. Quick, quiet, no indication it wasn't natural." I explained to Theo, "People don't seek revenge for a natural death. Jenna can drop us here," I continued, pointing to a clearing a mile or so away. Theo slapped my hand away.

"Perfect," Jack continued. "We won't want to hike in the dark, so we can start tomorrow afternoon. We walk in from there, stay here and rest until early morning," he said, indicating what looked like a building in the middle of an overgrown tangle. "It's about ten minutes from the tunnel entrance. We can leave all our gear there-"

"Hold up. What?" interjected Theo. "Leave your gear?"

"We have to leave everything behind," I explained. "No weapons, no phones, nothing. Lightweight clothes. As far as we know, I'm still the only Kinetic who can sense bodies," I glanced at Jack for confirmation and he nodded. "But they can pick up what we're carrying. We have to go in with nothing." Theo started to protest, so I added, "we've done this before. We know what we're doing."

He still looked horrified, but Jack went on before he could object again. "If it goes well, we'll get out the same way and collect everything. We'll call for extraction from the same point."

"And if it doesn't go well?" Jenna asked.

I looked at Jack and shrugged. "If it doesn't, we won't need extraction."

Chapter Thirty-three: Forgotten

The transition from dense woods to overgrown garden was subtle. After an hour or so of hiking, I started to make out older trees that were set in an unnaturally straight line, as though they were planted. They were overgrown with vines, but I could still make out the remnants of what was once a path alongside them.

Jack seemed relieved when we found it. He guided us along the half-there path more confidently now. As the path became clearer and more open I could make out what looked like ruins off to either side. Occasionally there were empty spaces, as though they had been carved out deliberately.

We came to a crossroads, at the edge of a small lake. One road led along the edge of the water, and the other across a low stone bridge that looked mostly intact. To the right, a tall structure that looked like it might have once been a tower stood guard over the silent lake. To our left, an empty area of packed dirt sat forlornly.

"What is this place?" I asked, curious and disturbed at the same time. It must have once been beautiful, but now it was eerie and unsettling.

"A mistake," Jack told me. "A fatal one, for the person who built it. About a century after the main palace was completed, Marie Antoinette had a separate estate built for herself. On one side, there's her main little palace, with ornamental gardens, and then there's the hamlet. She wanted to pretend to live as a commoner with her friends, so she had a make-believe peasant village built on the far side of the grounds."

As he spoke, the place transformed. In front of me was an idyllic pastoral scene, straight out of a fairytale. The tall structure to the right transformed into a delicate domed tower, with arched windows and a staircase winding around it. The empty space to the right sprouted a stone structure with a thatched roof and a trellis. Behind us, neatly trimmed hedges lined the path, and on the other side of the pond, I could make out a water wheel attached to a similar building. Across the bridge was a cluster of more little houses, all looking artfully quaint. It looked like a theme park.

He dropped the illusion, and it was once again the decaying, overgrown space we'd walked into. "Xavier hates Marie Antoinette. In his version of history, she and her husband were usurpers who destroyed the monarchy. He maintains that Louis XIV had a child before he married his first wife, and that Xavier's ancestors were directly descended from her. None of his legitimate children displayed any Talent, which is a point of much speculation. A handful of his many illegitimate ones did, but the crown passed through the legitimate line. Without a Charismatic holding it together, the monarchy dissolved in two generations."

Xavier was wrong. It wasn't the lack of Talent that caused the fall. This was the inevitable result of setting one group of people above another. Unequal classes of people create divisions that lead to resentment, discontent, and eventually, bloodshed. It might be years, or decades or even centuries, but eventually, it would all come crashing down.

"So what happened here?" I asked, looking around at the rotting structures.

"Xavier wanted the palace to be recreated as it was when his ancestor lived here, not as it exists now, but nobody told the architect this. The hamlet was half built when Xavier found out. He immediately executed the architect, and put someone else in charge. Fortunately for us, the tunnel we're going to use tomorrow was one of the first things built, and I'm pretty sure no one but me even knows it's there. No one comes here, or even talks about it, because they're too afraid of making Xavier angry. Everyone tries to pretend it doesn't exist."

I caught sight of movement across the water. "Then who is that?" I asked, pointing. A small figure stood and waved at us. As he came around the lake, I could see it was a child, no more than ten or twelve. "And why can he see us?"

Jack smiled. "That's just Marcel," he said. "They try to pretend he doesn't exist, either." The boy was covered in mud up to his knees, which were scraped and scratched. His clothes were torn and smeared with dirt, and there were a couple of leaves in his hair. A cat, as dirty and bedraggled as he was, followed in his wake.

"Hello, Marcel," Jack said in an amused tone. "Did you fall in the lake again?"

"Hi Jack! I caught a frog. Would you like to see?" he asked, holding it out to show us. He glanced at me curiously, but didn't seem concerned by my presence.

"Next time," Jack promised. "We're in a bit of a hurry." Jack waved me forward. "This is my friend. She's visiting for a bit, and I wanted to show her around."

Marcel tilted his head at me curiously. The cat got up and walked over to me, circled me once, and then rubbed against my legs, smearing mud on my clothing. Tentatively, I reached down and stroked its head. It purred, and returned to Marcel's side. The dirt-covered child smiled up at me. It was impossible not to smile back. "Just stay away from the mill, there's a fox hiding in there. I think she's about to have kits."

Jack nodded solemnly, and promised we'd leave her in peace. Marcel ran off happily, with the cat trailing close behind.

"Who is he?" I asked when he was out of earshot.

"Xavier's biological offspring. At one point, he decided that he needed an heir, found a woman with a compatible Talent, and Marcel is the result. Fortunately for Marcel, Xavier had no interest in an actual child, so he's mostly ignored here. He's been raised by a series of nannies out here, away from the court. Only a handful of people even know he exists."

"What happened to his mother?"

223

"She thinks he was stillborn," Jack said. "The result of a regrettable one-night stand."

"That's horrible," I said with disgust. "Did she even consent to any of this?"

Jack grimaced. "She thought she did. Consent is complicated with Charismatics. But she didn't know she'd have to leave him here. Elena. I have no idea what happened to her."

"That's disgusting."

"At least she got out. I could tell you worse stories," he said, looking away. I wondered again what he'd seen and done in his time here. "But I won't. Come on, we're almost there."

A little farther along the lake was a larger building, a little more complete than the others. A long, curved row of supports held up nothing, but led to a two-story structure. The walls of the first floor had mostly rotted away, but the second floor was more intact, and even had the remnants of a roof. We climbed up to the most sheltered area and settled in to wait and rest until it was time to leave.

It all felt so familiar. Working with Jack again, I found myself falling into old patterns of behavior and thought, and it was bringing back things I didn't want to remember. I had a partner, once. I had someone to rely on, someone to share the burden, someone I could trust to be there when I needed him.

At least, I thought I did.

All over again, I relived the devastating loss, the years spent alone, and the betrayal of seeing him appear in my office. With every minute that passed, my fury grew, until it was all I could see.

"Go ahead," Jack said from the other side of the room. I'd set up my bed - really, just a thin blanket on the floor - as far from his as possible. He laid his out on the east side, facing the rising moon and the lights of the palace in the distance, while I looked out into the darkness over the lake. I stood with my arms crossed over my chest, back to him.

"Go ahead what?" I had no patience for guessing what he meant.

"Yell at me. I can feel the anger pouring off you. Anger clouds judgment, and causes mistakes. Half the reason we worked so well together is that we were a team. If we go in divided, we'll fail. There are a million ways this could go wrong, so we need to trust each other. So let's have this out now. Say what you have to say."

"There's nothing to say." I continued to stare outside at nothing.

He laughed. "That's a lie."

"A lie?" I demanded spinning around. "How can you talk about lies? I trusted you, Jack. I trusted you and you lied to me." I didn't want to have this conversation. I didn't want to have any conversation with him at all, but it seemed like my mouth had other ideas. The words came out of their own accord, whether I liked it or not. "You *left* me. You abandoned me and left me to pick up the pieces and try to move on. How do you expect me to trust you after that?"

"You think I wanted to?" he shot back. "I had no choice," he said, emphasizing each word individually. "How many times do I have to say it before you believe me?"

"There's always a choice."

He shook his head. "Should I have let them kill you, instead?" His voice was raised now, too, and some of his own pain and anger was seeping into his tone. "They had a gun to your head. I could watch them blow your brains out, or I could do what I was told. You call that a choice?"

He wasn't making sense. "What gun? What are you talking about?"

"Vivienne didn't show you?"

"She restored my memories. I wouldn't let her show me yours."

He shook his head. "You were unconscious. You wouldn't

remember."

I knew I had been taken, and trapped, but he was right, I didn't remember anything after that. Vivienne thought I should see his memories. Maybe I should have listened to her. "Tell me now."

"Cat took us off the street," he began, head tilted toward the ground. "She took you first, so I had time to panic. By the time she came back for me, I was desperate to find you. And then she brought me to a room where I could see you." The image of my own body, sprawled on the floor, appeared between us, viewed from above, at a distance. "You were already unconscious. I got to watch helplessly while they beat you half to death and shot you." I watched as people appeared around my unconscious form, saw the scene unfold as he said it. When the bullet passed through my chest, I involuntarily touched the scar I still had in that exact spot. "And then they put the gun to your head." I had been so close to death, and I never knew it.

The scene vanished. "By the time they even told me what they wanted, I would have done anything to get you out of there. I would have traded my life." He smiled bitterly. "They didn't want my life. They wanted my soul. So I did what they said. I couldn't watch you die."

My anger began to slip, but I held on to it. "And afterwards?" I threw back at him. "Once I was safe, when there wasn't a gun to my head?"

"There was always a gun to your head!" he shouted, looking directly at me now. "She took you once, she could do it again. They fed me pieces of information, just enough that I knew they were watching you. To make sure I never forgot that the minute I stepped out of line, they would pull the trigger."

"And in fourteen years, you never had any chance to let me know you were alive? To send me a goddamn *note*?" I hated the way my voice cracked on the last word.

"And what would you have done?" he asked. "If you found

out I was alive and being held against my will?"

"I would have looked for you!" I shouted.

"Exactly," he snapped back, stopping me. "You would have moved heaven and earth, and you would never stop until you found me. Tell me I'm wrong, Di. Tell me you wouldn't have put everything you had into looking for me, because that's what I would have done for you." I couldn't. He was right, we both knew it, and there was no point denying it. "And you would have died trying."

"You don't know that!"

"I do, Diana. I knew what he had in his arsenal, and I knew what you had in yours. It wouldn't have even been a fight."

He sighed and turned away, looking out the window, toward the lights in the distance. I could see defeat in the way his shoulders sagged, and realized how much his bargain had cost him. How it had broken him. "How did you know? Were you watching me this whole time?"

"Always," he said, staring out the window. "I watched you grieve. I watched you hurt. And then I watched you forget and move on."

"You weren't watching very closely, then. Because I never did. I just got better at hiding it."

Silence stretched, awkward, agonizing, and impenetrable. Some part of me wanted to forgive him, but if I did, I would lose my anger, and all I would have was pain.

"Why?" he asked after a moment, turning back to face me.

"Why what?"

"Why didn't you move on? Find someone else? You thought I was dead." I understood what he was really asking. He wanted to hear me say that I never got over him, that he was the only one I'd ever loved. He wanted to know if, after all these years, I still loved him. If there was hope.

It was more complicated than that. "You think you know the answer. But you're not going to like the truth."

"Tell me anyway."

"Do you remember the time Casey found us in Vancouver? How he pulled the air from my lungs?"

"I do. I also remember killing him for it."

"When I lost you, it felt like that. You were my air, and once you were gone, there was nothing left to breathe. So I learned how to live without breathing.

"Nothing is worth that. Love is great in the beginning, but after everything, when you weigh the good and the bad, it doesn't balance out. When I look back, the pain outweighs the joy. If I could take it all back, I would, and now that I know better, I'm not about to do that to myself again." Even as I said it, I knew it was a lie. But I felt like a wounded animal, needing to lash out, make him hurt as much as I did.

"So you regret it?" he asked, turning away from me. "All of it? You wish we'd never met?" I could see pain in the stiffness of his shoulders, and I knew I'd hit my mark. The two of us could hurt each other more than anyone else ever could. We could shred each other to pieces, ripping open old wounds, tearing until there was nothing left. I didn't know how to stop.

A gulf of time and pain lay between us, so vast and deep that I couldn't see the other side.

"It doesn't matter now."

CHAPTER THIRTY-FOUR: MIRRORS

The entrance to the passageway was in the center of a flat, round tiled floor on a small island. Getting here was easy - a short walk along an overgrown path - but the island itself was positioned to be visible from the main estate, where Marcel lived with his caretakers. There was nothing between the two but a patch of grass and a small stretch of pond. I wondered how many times he'd fallen into this one.

There was supposed to be a small neoclassical temple here, dedicated, appropriately, to the goddess of love. The farthest they'd gotten on the temple was the platform on which it was intended to stand, before the poor architect met his fate. A round flat plinth sat in the center, where a statue would have been. Jack moved the stone aside as quietly as possible, while I kept watch in the pre-dawn gloom. No one could see us, of course, but sound carried over water, and anyone in the vicinity could hear the scraping sound of stone on stone. Fortunately, no one did, and after a few nervous moments, we went in.

An ornate spiral staircase led down into the darkness. Our flashlights revealed an opulent space, protected by the elements, unlike the ruins above. Aside from a few places where tree roots had broken through, it was mostly intact. The stone had kept the animals out, and the tiled passageway was clean and free of bugs and debris. I could dimly make out erotic mosaics lining the walls.

We moved as quietly as possible until we found another staircase leading up. Leaving the flashlights behind, we climbed until we came to a dark, curtained area. Beyond the thick tapestries, I could feel open spaces. The room to the right was empty, but the one on the left contained a few backless chairs and a heavily canopied bed.

It was unoccupied.

"He's not there," I whispered to Jack.

He shifted uneasily behind me in the dark. "We should bail and come back tomorrow," he said. "Stick to the plan."

Beyond the empty room on the right, the dim sound of voices echoed from a room beyond. "There are people out there. Let's just look around before we go. I want to see it."

"Just look," he repeated. "Nothing else." When I hesitated, he added, "You have a tendency to go off script. Promise me we're just going to look."

"Yes. We're just looking around for a minute, and then we'll go. No one will know we're here."

We stepped silently through the curtains, Jack hiding us from sight, and Lina's charms hiding us from everything else. When I saw what lay on the other side, I stopped dead in awe and disgust. It was the most absurdly opulent room I'd ever seen. Two enormous crystal chandeliers, easily four feet across and twice as high, hung from an arched ceiling. Around the top edges, the walls were lined with a long row of raised figures, painted shining gold. The ornamentation continued down, draping around large glass doors that interrupted an expanse of Renaissance paintings and mirrored panels. A carved marble bust glared balefully from its perch beside a door.

"Is this for real?" I whispered to Jack.

"It gets worse," whispered back. I couldn't see how.

On the other side of the open doors to the right, people milled about a long chamber. I stepped cautiously into the room, cutting carefully through the crowd. Jack trailed behind me.

He was right, it was worse. This room was exponentially more over the top than the last. The painted murals extended up to completely cover the high, arched ceilings with scenes of war and victory. Dozens of the same immense chandeliers we'd seen in the other room hung like giant crystal spiders in three neat rows, spanning the long space. One side of the room was lined with mirrors reflecting the orange glow of dawn that poured in through the huge glass doors on the other side. Smaller chandeliers dripped from pillars atop gold-painted figures of naked women. The legendary Hall of Mirrors, or rather, a cheap modern reproduction.

On the far end of the room, a raised platform dominated the space. Silver statues lined the steps leading up to an immense silver chair, a physical manifestation of the ego of two powerful men, three centuries apart. On the ridiculous chair sat Xavier, holding court.

There must have been hundreds of people here, dressed to the nines at six in the morning. Every face in the room was turned toward him, gazing in rapt adoration, almost zombie-like in their devotion. If I could just get close enough, this whole ordeal could be over, but he was still out of my range.

The crowd was too dense to get any closer without risking bumping into someone. Frustrated, I ducked into an alcove by one of the big glass doors, straining to see over the heads of scores of people mindlessly worshiping at the altar of his vanity.

A semicircle of attendants stood at attention behind him - no doubt his bodyguards. I recognized Cat just behind his right shoulder, hovering protectively with a hand on the back of his chair. On her right stood a thin, wiry man who was watching the crowd - probably one of the Empaths Jack had mentioned. Another two people sat at his feet, probably Pre-cogs, ready to step between him and danger.

My enemy, the man who stole my life from me, was right there. The rage I felt the night before began to build again, this time, aimed where it belonged. My hands clenched in impotent fury. Jack tugged on my wrist, telling me it was time to leave. Every ounce of my being fought it. He was right there. I could see him, I could almost, almost reach him.

"Diana," Jack warned quietly. "We have to go."

The more he urged me to leave, the harder I resisted. He was *right there*. Adrenaline was flooding my system now, bringing every inch of the room around me into focus. Every golden bust, every hanging crystal on every massive chandelier, every pane of-

Glass.

Jack grabbed my arm now, and started pulling me toward the exit. "Whatever you're thinking, stop. We need to go now." I yanked free from his grasp. There was no way I was leaving now. Not when I finally had a clear shot. It wasn't the quiet assassination we had planned, but I could kill him right now. I would get to watch his blood flow down the arms of the silver monstrosity he sat on, and seep into the pristine carpet under his feet. He was too far for me to reach directly, but that wouldn't matter.

Jack was whispering urgently in my ear, but I barely heard him. "Diana, no, there's-"

Glass shattered.

Every pane on every door, every mirror lining the walls, all of it cracked and pulled away. Each hanging crystal splintered into shards. For a second, a cloud of glittering, sharp projectiles hovered above the crowd, and then hurtled toward the would-be king. People screamed and ran, adding to the chaos. The man I hated more than anything else in this world stood and watched his approaching death.

When I hit the edge of my range, I hurled them with all of the strength I could muster, and watched as momentum did the rest. A thousand shards flew toward my enemy - and crashed loudly against an invisible barrier at the edge of the steps.

"- bulletproof glass," finished Jack with a groan.

The Pre-cogs hadn't even moved. At a word from Xavier, Cat stepped forward, put a hand on his arm, and they both disappeared. The crowd was fleeing past us, jostling us and making it impossible for us to escape. Rage turned to horror as I began to understand how big of a mistake I'd just made.

"What happened to 'just looking around'?" Jack demanded.

A hand grabbed my arm roughly, and then I was in a small, enclosed room with Jack, two Jumpers, and the man I'd failed to kill.

"Welcome," Xavier said graciously. "I've been expecting you."

CHAPTER THIRTY-FIVE: MISTAKES

Xavier sat behind a carved wooden desk, with one hand resting lightly on a gun. Behind him, well-lit displays showcased trophies, which I now recognized as the French Crown Jewels - assorted crowns, a sword resting on a high shelf, and the hand-on-a-stick that Oliver asked me to free from its box on my very first day of work at Kingfisher. In the middle, perfectly lit to bring out each facet, mounted on the end of a heavy spike called a cravat pin, was a smoky blue diamond.

The diamond *I* stole for him.

I couldn't imagine hating anyone more than I hated the man in front of me. Reaching out, I looked for veins and tendons and flesh to tear apart, but there was nothing. He wasn't there. None of them were, not Xavier, not Cat, who was now standing behind me, not Jack or the Jumper now struggling to hold him. Not even the walls were there.

I was blind.

The entire room must have been lined with Kinetic dampeners. I could see everything with my eyes, but my Kinetic sight showed me nothing but void. My mind went blank. For the first time in my life, I couldn't feel *anything* around me, and it was terrifying, like part of me was missing.

Pain shot through my shoulders as Cat twisted my arms behind my back and shoved me roughly into a chair. Something looped around my neck and yanked me against the high back of the chair. Another tie wrapped around my torso, pinning my arms to my sides, holding me tight against the chair.

Jack landed roughly in the chair beside me, struggling while Cat tied my wrists.

He looked at his servants. "You may go."

The man standing over Jack vanished immediately. Cat did not. "Sir, I don't think-"

"I said leave us," Xavier repeated with a note of command. "I wish to have a private conversation. You have done well, and I'll be perfectly safe. I will call when I need you."

Cat gave me a look that promised pain, but vanished obediently from sight.

Xavier looked at Jack and frowned with annoyance, as though Jack were a pebble in his shoe. Before I could even react, he picked up the gun on his desk and fired. There was the jarring crack of a gunshot, the acrid stench of gunpowder, and then the bright tang of blood pouring from Jack's chest. His head fell forward and the weight of his body sagged limply against the ties still holding him in place.

Jack.

I couldn't breathe. Nothing worked. My limbs were frozen, my lungs stopped moving, even my heart stood still. Shocked and powerless, I watched the man I loved above everything else in this world die.

Again.

I should scream. I should shout and rage and tear at the bonds that kept me from his side. I should feel something. Instead, I was empty. Hollow. Clear. All of my tangled, complicated feelings unraveled, leaving me alone with my naked truth.

It didn't matter that Jack left. It didn't matter that I'd spent the last decade half-alive and closed off from the world. The pain, the betrayal, the raw, brutal fury, none of it was important. What mattered was that Jack was the only thing in the world I ever really cared about, and that no matter what happened, no matter how angry I was or how loudly I raged at him, I would love him until I died.

And now that didn't matter anymore, either.

It was my fault. Despite his warnings, I let anger cloud my judgment. Instead of sticking to the plan, I acted impulsively, thinking I could rely on my Talent to get me through any situation, as it always had before. My overconfidence, my arrogance, cost me everything. Jack was dead, and it was my fault. He died believing I didn't love him, and that was my fault, too.

"Now, then. Shall we talk?"

I blinked, remembering that Xavier was here. Air returned to my lungs, my heart began to beat again, feeling came back to my limbs. There was one thing that mattered after all. Xavier had just made the biggest mistake of his life. Jack was dead, and I had nothing left to lose.

I turned my head slowly to look at him, and smiled. "Yes. Let's talk."

"That was quite an entrance," he said, sounding impressed. "People will be talking about that for years. And no one will ever fail to take you seriously." He beamed at me. "You're off to a wonderful start, my dear. Well done."

Either he was utterly oblivious, or he fully expected his Talent to work on me, with the corpse of my murdered husband sitting three feet to my left. Maybe it would have. It probably had worked many times before, and somewhere in this building there might be people who had looked past the bodies of their loved ones and fallen at his feet in adoration. I might have lasted longer than the others, knowing exactly what it was I faced, but I would have succumbed eventually. No matter how hard I tried to resist, I'd wind up worshiping blindly at his altar along with everyone else.

Except I had a little pink cat tied to my ankle.

Clearly, Lina's gift was working, because despite the massive amount of Talent he was throwing at me, I still wanted nothing more than to watch his expression as I tore out his throat with my bare hands.

But he didn't know that, and that was the one advantage I had. If I could keep him talking, I could figure out a plan. "Thank you," I said, forcing a smile.

He appeared to be convinced, but he still had his hand on the gun, which was resting on the desk, now pointed at me. "You will come to understand the vision in time. Surely you must see that we are different from the Normals." He said the word like just the sound of it disgusted him. Like they were something stuck to his shoe. "We are better."

"Of course." There were so many ways I could kill him, if I could only use my Talent. Without it, my options were limited. Still, there had to be a way.

"It is a travesty that we must hide in fear. Lesser beings rule the world, because together they are stronger than one of us alone. United, we are strong. All we need is a leader, someone to pull us together, and we can conquer. We can lead humanity into a new age of enlightenment." I wondered if the 'humanity' he was talking about included everyone, or just people with Talent.

"And that's you?" I asked, still thinking. I broke through a Kinetic dampener field once before. All I did was snap a few threads, but I did it, and I was a lot more motivated now.

"Exactly! I was sent to be the ruler that will lift us up," he went on. I tuned him out. He seemed perfectly content to talk about himself without any interaction from me, and I needed to concentrate.

I let my eyes unfocus. The room mostly felt empty, but there was something - yes, there - a faint shadow of something round-ish behind him. No, oval. The diamond, the hardest thing in the room. From there, I made out the shelf and then the wall and followed it down to the floor. Whispers of substance touched my mind. The desk. Big and bulky and solid. The gun on top of it, hard metal. I couldn't make out the hand resting on it, but the fabric of his suit was like the faintest veil. I followed it up his sleeve, shoulder, shirt collar.

Tie.

I only needed two points. Two tiny, tiny points, one in the knot at his neck, one on the hanging tail. Silk was strong, and the fabric would hold. I strained to catch just a few threads, but it was like grasping at spiderwebs.

"Don't you agree, my dear?" The sudden distraction broke my concentration, and it all slipped away.

"Of course," I murmured, swearing inside.

As soon as he started talking again, I looked for the diamond. Now that I'd done it once, it was easier the second time - wall, floor, desk, gun. The sleeve was harder, but I found it, and traced the line up again until I found the tie. Two points.

Now or never. I gripped the threads as tightly as I could and pulled with all my might. His left hand went to his neck and tugged absently at his tie, pulling it from my grip. I had to distract him until I could get a better hold.

Minutes ago, my anger and hubris had clouded my judgment, and I'd made a fatal mistake. Perhaps I could goad him into the same thing.

He was saying something now about Normals being born to serve us, and how only he could restore things to their proper order. It would be easy to manipulate him. His buttons were right there on the surface, waiting to be pressed. And it would be fun.

"Are you really that stupid?" I asked, letting my contempt show on my face. He looked like I'd slapped him. "Do you honestly expect me to follow a useless idiot like you?"

"So you've made your choice, then?" he asked, his hand shifting slightly over his gun. I had to be careful. I didn't plan to get out of this alive, but I needed to take him down with me, and being shot was not going to help with that. Still, I needed him angry, and I'd been shot before and survived.

"There was never a choice to make," I told him with a derisive laugh. "If you actually thought I would lower myself to join you, you're even dumber than I thought." *Diamond, wall, floor.*

I could see his anger rising in him. His face turned red and he spluttered for a moment. "I offered you a crown!" he burst out.

Desk, gun, sleeve.

"I have no use for a crown," I said dismissively. *Collar.* "I know who I am. I have nothing to prove." *Tie.* I traced the knot, looking for the right points to pull. I grabbed a few threads… he moved and I lost them again. "Crowns are meaningless. They're an outdated anachronism from a barbaric age. The world has moved past the concept of royalty. In the end, you're nothing but a meaningless, insignificant, spoiled brat, raised to think you were inherently superior, when in reality, you're not special at all."

His face was turning purple, and I was starting to enjoy this. "All of your money, all of your status and privilege, and this is the best you can do?" *Desk. Gun. Sleeve.* "I came from nothing, and yet here you are, begging for my help." *Collar.*

Tie.

"You should beg for my mercy, instead." I had the knot.

I pulled.

The silk held, and this time, my grip stayed firm. The fabric tightened around his neck like a noose. Both of his hands flew to his neck and pulled at the tie. For a moment we struggled as he gasped for air, and then he ripped it from my hold again.

But it didn't matter, it didn't matter at all, because behind him, I saw the most miraculous, beautiful sight I'd ever seen.

The air shimmered.

I laughed out loud from pure joy. Xavier seethed. Giddy with glee, I told him, "In the end, you made the same mistake as everyone else. Would you like to know what it was, before you die?"

"I don't make mistakes!" he blustered, arrogant until the end.

"You assumed *I* was the threat."

His brow furrowed in confusion, but his eyes flicked over to Jack's lifeless body. It picked up its head, winked, and dissolved into the body of the Jumper that Jack struggled with earlier. My eyes moved back to the space behind Xavier's chair, where my beloved, who I would kill in a very painful way when this was over, stood behind him. Xavier, finally catching up, spun his chair to face Jack.

With a dark smile, full of fourteen years of quiet hate, Jack drove a weapon through his heart. Jack held his eyes for a moment, watching with satisfaction as his life drained away. Then he yanked the weapon from his chest, causing blood to fountain from the wound, drenching them both. As he stepped back, I finally saw what he held.

It was the long, heavy cravat pin, attached to the smoky blue diamond he held in his hand. Our eyes met over the body, and I laughed with joy - not that Xavier was dead, but that Jack, beyond all hope, was alive.

"Nice distraction," he said, wiping the pin on Xavier's sleeve.

God, I missed him.

CHAPTER THIRTY-SIX: FALL

Jack watched me warily as he walked around the desk. Silently, he untied the ropes holding me to the back of the chair. "Sorry that took so long," he started. "He had a gun pointed at you," he explained. "I had to wait until he took his hand off it." He knelt in front of me and started unbinding my wrists. "I couldn't risk him figuring it out. Your reaction had to be genuine. If he suspected anything, he would have called for help, and we'd lose this chance. I have to say, though, that little speech was the mos-"

The second my wrists were free, I grabbed his head with both hands and kissed him. Pulling back slightly, I told him, "If you *ever* die on me again, you'd better actually be dead, or I will kill you myself."

"Last time," he assured me, nodding a little dazedly.

"I lied," I told him, kissing him again. "I never regretted a minute of it. Not for a second. And the reason there was never anyone else is that no one could possibly compare to you." I rested my forehead against his. "I haven't forgiven you yet-"

"Yet?" he interrupted, smiling.

"Yet," I admitted. I would, eventually, and we both knew it.

"I'll just have to spend the rest of my life making it up to you."

"It better be a good, long life," I informed him, letting him draw me into a deep, lingering kiss.

A shout of alarm yanked my attention away. Cat stood over Xavier's body with a look of horror on her face. She glanced around the room, taking in the dead Jumper slumped in his chair, Jack and I wrapped around each other and covered in Xavier's blood, and a look of insatiable hatred crossed her face. It promised vengeance, slow, painful, and gory.

She leaned over Xavier's body and they both vanished. A second later, deafening alarms began to blare. An incongruously calm voice repeated, "Danger. We are under attack. Evacuate immediately and report to mustering points."

Jack turned to me regretfully, and said, "We should get out of here. Continue this conversation later?"

"Definitely," I promised. Reluctantly, I released him. "But you're right. We should go." I looked around for an exit, and didn't find any. "Where's the door?" I asked.

He grimaced. "There isn't one."

"Who builds an office with no door?" I demanded.

"Someone with an excess of Jumpers at his beck and call. We're several floors underground. It's the only way in or out."

"There has to be something," I said, starting to search more seriously. "A hidden door, or a button or a switch somewhere."

Someone paranoid enough to build an underground office would not depend on a Jumper as the only way to get out. There had to be another exit. A secret door only he would know about. I checked the frames of the paintings for hidden hinges, but I still didn't have access to my Talent to see if there was anything beyond. Jack began searching the desk, running his hands under the edge.

"How much time do you think we have?" I asked him.

"She probably took him to the infirmary," he reasoned aloud. "It'll take them a while to convince her they can't save him, but as soon as they do, she'll be back for us. We need to get out of here." He rifled through the drawers, and stuffed a few things in his pockets. I moved to help him search the top, pushing papers aside. A familiar pattern caught my eye, painted on the surface. Heart pounding, I swept everything off the desk so I could see the entire design. It was round, divided in quadrants, with a long winding path that looped back and forth between them, ending at the center.

A labyrinth.

"Oliver's box," I said out loud.

"What?"

I scanned the wall of trophies behind the desk. A sword, a crown, the empty space where the diamond had been. And off to the side, a painted wooden hand on a scepter, holding up two fingers.

I pointed at it. "The hand was in a box."

"What?"

"I need a magnet!"

Jack was watching me with concern, as though I'd suddenly lost my mind. Pushing him out of the way, I rifled frantically through the top drawer, sifting through pens and paper clips. "On my first day at Kingfisher, Oliver asked me to open a box for him. It had a locking mechanism shaped like a labyrinth, just like this. There was a ball inside. You were supposed to trace it with a magnet to open it. I opened it for him, and that thing," I said, pointing at the hand on the shelf without looking up, "was inside it."

One of the pens didn't have a point. *Aha! Found you.* Holding my breath, I traced the pattern on the desk with the fake pen. When I got to the center, I heard a faint click inside. An answering click sounded inside the wall opposite the desk. One of the panels swung forward silently. Jack pulled it open, revealing a staircase on the other side. He looked back at me in astonishment. "Have I ever told you you're amazing?" he asked with an adoring grin.

"A few times," I said with an answering smile. "But I never get tired of hearing it."

—

The stairwell stretched in both directions, wrapping around a central hole. A dim light came from what might be a skylight above, but below, it descended into darkness. The whole thing smelled like…

"Propane?"

Jack's eyes lit up with a dangerous gleam. "I always wondered where this was."

Outside the room, my senses were beginning to return, and I pulled the door shut. We started upwards. A few stairs up, we heard a frustrated scream from inside the room. Cat had returned to find an empty office. If she knew about this stairwell, or figured it out, we'd have nowhere to run. I climbed faster.

After five or six flights, we emerged into daylight. There was no glass at the top of the stairwell, just a raised cover to keep the rain out. The whole thing was an air shaft, venting the propane fumes from the leaking tank.

We were on the roof of the palace, probably directly above the Hall of Mirrors. It was a broad flat space, slanted only slightly down toward the rail. Below, the formal gardens were rapidly filling with people obediently reporting to their muster points. An army was massing all around us, forming a perimeter. We were three stories above ground. Even if we somehow managed to find a way down, we'd have to sneak through that army. We were stuck here, and without the phones we'd left back in the cottage, we had no way to call for help.

"Did you know Xavier smoked?" Jack asked, casually pulling a lighter out of his pocket.

"I didn't," I said, keeping one eye on the crowd and one on Jack.

"Terrible habit," he commented with glee. "Very dangerous." He pulled a handful of cigars out of his pocket where he'd shoved them and lit them one by one. The stench of burning tobacco competed with the overwhelming smell of propane, and I started to see where this was going. I stared at him in disbelief as he held the lit cigars upside down to catch as much of the bundle on fire as possible. When he held five flaming brands, he turned to me and asked, "Ready to go?"

Eyes wide with equal parts astonishment, admiration, and

horror, I asked, "Have I ever told you you're insane?"

"A few times, but I never get tired of hearing it," he answered with a wink.

The rest of the building should be empty by now, except for one person. "Cat's probably still down there looking for us."

"I sure hope so."

He dropped the lit cigars into the pit. Fascinated, I watched them fall, a handful of dim sparks against the darkness. They might all go out before they reached the bottom. There might not be enough of a leak to matter, or enough of a spark left in the cigars to catch. Even if the leaking propane lit, it might not be enough to ignite the whole tank. But if there was...

A flash erupted below, answering the first and second questions. A loud boom answered the third. The building began to shake as its foundation collapsed underneath it. Jack's grin was enormous as he grabbed my hand and we started to run along the roof.

"How big is that tank?" I asked as we ran.

"It runs under the entire foundation."

I married a madman.

Behind us, a gout of flame erupted from the air vent. Below us, to the right, the black and white tiles of the courtyard began to buckle. On the left, shouting began to rise from the crowd.

I ran faster.

Chapter Thirty-seven: Library

We quickly ran out of roof. A right at the corner, and then a left past the tall spires of the huge chapel, and then there was no place left to run. I glanced over the edge. The ground was fifty feet below us, and the side of the building was too steep to climb down. Behind us, the destruction was widening. Most of the building had fallen in. The courtyard was gone.

People were shouting in alarm and dismay, and judging by the sounds, someone must have spread the word that Xavier was dead. All around, Telekinetics were fighting a losing battle to hold up the walls. Despite their efforts, the epicenter was widening, swallowing more of the building as it expanded. As I watched, the chapel roof caved in, its spires sinking gracefully in on themselves.

"*The Dragon comes, bringing Death and Destruction,*" Jack quoted from where he stood beside me. "*Empire crumbles and voices wail in mourning.*" He gazed down at the wreckage, holding a gold-cased phone in his hand that was probably Xavier's. "Hey Theo," he said after a moment. There was a pause. "No, you can't talk to Diana right now." Another pause.

The entire central building had now collapsed, and the long span of the wing we were standing on was rapidly following it. "That's great, you can tell her all about that when we get back." The roof lurched underneath our feet. "Speaking of which, we could really use a lift right now." Pause. "I turned on location tracking on this phone. Can you get our position from that? Including elevation? That part is important." Fifty feet away, the roof was sliding down into the hole.

"Theo!" I shouted into the phone. "Jumper. Now!"

Jack calmly hung up the phone and gazed out over the wreckage with me. He slipped an arm around my shoulders. Either they would get here in time, or they wouldn't. Nothing left to do but wait. I wrapped my arm around his waist and leaned my head on his shoulder as we watched the palace fall.

I felt someone appear behind me. "Director -" a voice began, and then cut off. I turned to see Jenna staring past us in awe. She looked at us, and then back at the wreckage. I saw her take in our blood-soaked clothing, his arm around me, and the screams coming from the ground below as we stood together on the rapidly collapsing roof. Another section fell in as she stared. "What the hell did you *do?*" she said in an awed tone.

There was no way this story wasn't going to be all over the agency by morning. If I thought people were afraid of me before, this was going to cement it.

"Jenna?" I prompted gently as the surface beneath us began to shudder. "We should go now."

She blinked, and her eyes returned to me. "Back to the office?" she asked in a distracted tone.

"No," Jack interjected grimly. "We're not quite done yet." He pointed to a long facade on the opposite side of the wreckage. A specific building lit up with a bright glow as Jack twisted the light around it. "Take us there."

———

The library of New Versailles was virtually indistinguishable from the surrounding brick facades. It was far enough from the palace itself that only a faint rumble could be felt here. This seemed to me a smarter place to put an office than the flashier areas that made such obvious targets.

There was no one stationed outside, presumably because they'd all run to the palace. No one challenged us when we entered through the main door. Jenna was slightly disappointed when we left her outside, but she didn't argue. I wasn't sure what this next encounter would bring, but I didn't want another body to protect. Or a witness.

"Don't kill this one," Jack cautioned me as we climbed the stairs. "We need her help."

"Who is she?"

"They call her the Professor. She is - was - Xavier's chief strategist."

I was skeptical. "Why would she help us?"

"Because she's smart."

"Why do we need her help?"

"Two reasons. First, I don't want to have to hide forever. That," he said with a nod back the way we came, "was not quiet. Cat saw us, would have told others, who will be looking for revenge. Once we make her see reason, the Professor can help diffuse that."

"Can I at least threaten her a little?"

He grinned. "By all means," he agreed, dropping a kiss on my lips.

"What's the other reason?"

"We just created another power vacuum."

The halls were empty, and we saw no one as we approached the door to an office on the third floor. No Kinetic dampeners, which was an oversight. I made out five people inside, four of whom carried guns. I hated guns. While Jack knocked, I took a minute to disable them all.

"Come in," came an accented voice from inside.

I followed Jack in. The four guards stood silently at attention, one in each corner. Aside from them, the office looked like it belonged to an actual college professor. Shelves lined the walls, covered with books varying from ancient tomes to shiny new paperbacks. The large desk was so covered with papers and scattered pens and other assorted things that the surface was completely hidden. Globes and maps and busts of historical figures filled every remaining space.

At the center of it all, Xavier's chief strategist sat behind the desk. Even sitting, it was clear that she was tall and graceful. Close-cropped dark hair framed a delicate face with smooth dark skin. She wore an elegant white blouse, and small round glasses perched on the end of her nose. She peered over them briefly, and then went back to her papers.

"Hello, Jack," she said in an accented voice. "I thought you might come, when I heard the noise. I didn't think you'd bring the butcher, though," she said with a dismissive glance at me. "Disappointing." She gestured, and a guard raised his gun and pointed at me. The trigger clicked uselessly. I laughed. She frowned and gestured again, and the three others tried to fire at me and failed.

I couldn't resist. "I thought you said she was smart."

"Just stop," Jack told her. "You know who she is. You know who I am. You know you can't overpower us. We just want to talk. For now."

She looked us over dismissively. "And why would I bother talking to you?"

"Because you know it's over. You can't hold it all together without him."

Her eyes narrowed. "Marcel-"

"Is twelve," Jack interrupted sharply. "And hates you."

"No," she said with a smile. "He's afraid of me. There's a difference. Marcel will do what I tell him."

"You can't run an army with a terrified child at its head."

She raised one eyebrow in challenge. "Can't I?"

Something about her looked familiar. "You're Ayo Abara," I realized aloud. "Youngest graduate of Oxford in the history of the school. Dual PhDs in Biology and History by the age of sixteen. Single-handedly advanced the fields of physics and genetics more in three years than the previous twenty. You literally wrote the book on Paranormal Talent." She looked bored as I listed her accolades. "So much intelligence, so much possibility.

You could be using it to make the world a better place, and instead, you used it to prop up a madman."

"What do you think I was *trying* to do?" she snapped. "The world is run by idiots. I could solve so many problems, if only people would do as I say." She paused. "You think that imbecile built this? All he cared about was having people fawn over him. I got him to pull himself out of obscurity, and he thought it was his own idea. I built an empire. You kill people for fun. Do not dare to judge *me*."

No wonder Jack said we weren't done. Just like Xavier, she thought she was doing the world a favor. "You're destroying lives. Ripping apart families and loved ones."

A flash of anger broke through her calm demeanor. "And what of my life?" she snarled. "What of my family?" With a visible effort, she regained her composure. "I didn't set the rules to this game. I just played it best."

"And lost," Jack said flatly.

Her lips pursed. "Only because of your disobedience. If you'd done what you were told, things would be different right now."

"You know, I think that's the nicest thing you've ever said to me."

Before she could reply, I broke in. "Doesn't it bother you that no one knows? You did all the work, he got all the credit. Don't you want-"

The increased heartbeat was the only warning I had. The man behind us moved so fast, I had no time for finesse. I ripped at his arteries, spraying the room with blood. Abara glanced at the few drops on her pristine paperwork in disgust, not even looking at the man now lying dead on her floor.

Her unrepentant glare told me she hadn't accepted defeat yet. She would keep trying, and the longer this went on, the more people would die. I needed to make an impression on her, or this would never end. Glancing at the few drops of blood on her desk, I understood how to get through to her. In this immaculate, isolated office, she didn't see the cost of war. Violence was theoretical to her. Academic. Death didn't enter into her domain.

Death *was* my domain. And since he wasn't using it anymore…

Looking into the dead guard's chest, I felt for his heart. It was harder when it wasn't beating, and I'd only done this once before, and then by accident, but I found it. One good pull, and it flew from his chest, splashing blood on the expensive-looking carpets. I let it hover grotesquely for a moment, above the desk, dripping onto her pristine paperwork.

"You're smart," I acknowledged. "But you're wrong about one thing. I don't enjoy killing, and I don't do it casually. I'm very, *very* good at it, but I use it as a last resort." I held her eyes so that she was sure to understand the threat. "I only do it when I am forced."

I let the heart fall. It landed on the desk with a splatter, sending a fountain of blood across her white shirt. She startled, and then looked back up at me in frozen horror. The heart twitched once, sending a spray of red across her glasses.

"Do I have your attention, *Professor*?" I asked, holding her eyes. She nodded. "You have a choice. You can be our ally, and together, we can accomplish many things. Or you can be our enemy." I let my eyes flicker back to the gory mass between us. "Do you really want to be our enemy, Professor? Think it over carefully."

Eyes wide, she asked, "What do you want of me?"

"Contain the fallout," Jack instructed. "Pin it on someone else, say it was all a tragic accident, I don't care what you tell people. The two of us were never here. There is no revenge to be taken."

"Cat knows. And the Healers. They can be reasoned with, but Cat will come after you. There is nothing I can do to stop her."

"I don't think she will," Jack said with a cold smile. Abara's eyes widened at the implication. I wondered what their relationship was.

"Speaking of Cat," I continued. "Restore all modified memories. Return anyone who wants to leave to their homes. No more disappearances, and no more acts of violence."

"We all know most people will get bored without Xavier and leave. Let them. Let it die from attrition, and don't try to rebuild. If anyone remains voluntarily, use them to actually help people. Our teams can work together.

"If you keep your word, you will never see us again. If you don't…" I paused with a glance at Jack and smiled. "I suppose you won't see us either way."

Chapter Thirty-eight: Legends

"Thank god you're back," Theo gushed at me the second we appeared in the office lobby. "Anderson hasn't reported in, and Flores needs backup, and-"

"Theo."

He stopped short, still wild-eyed and frantic.

"It can wait."

He took in our expressions, our blood-soaked clothing, which was now starting to get cold, and our joined hands. With what looked like a huge effort, he forced a smile and nodded.

A crowd was gathering, whispering furtively behind us. On another day, I would care what they were saying, but right then, none of it seemed important. Without so much as a glance backwards, I led Jack down the hall to my office, once again grateful for the extravagance of the full bathroom attached to it.

I didn't bother undressing before stepping into the large, walk-in shower. The freezing spray was a welcome shock when it hit my upturned face and began to soak into the fabric of my shirt. Cold water washed the blood from my clothing, from my skin, from my soul. *Maybe it's enough now.* Streams of red swirled at my feet, circling once and then flowing away. I let water pour over my face, my hair, my body, and I slowly began to feel clean. *Maybe the scales are finally even.*

The water was already getting warm when Jack stepped into the enclosure behind me, and wrapped his arms around my waist. I leaned back into him, feeling his warmth, his strength, surrounding me and tethering me to the world.

"I missed you," I told him, turning to face him. A decade and more of longing and pain and sorrow, distilled down to three words.

He tucked me against him and rested his head on top of mine. A familiar gesture, long forgotten. "I missed you, too," he said against my hair.

Pulling back slightly, I looked up at him. My fingers traced the scar that now ran along the side of his jaw, and I wondered how it got there. So much time, lost forever. Years wasted, that we could never recover.

Suddenly, I was just so *tired* of being sad. I was tired of being angry. Maybe I could just... be.

"I watched you die today," I reminded him.

"I know. I'm sorry. There was no other way."

I looped my hands behind his neck. "As I recall," I said, idly sliding my fingers into his hair, remembering feeling the it between my fingers, and the warmth of his body against mine. "You said you'd make it up to me."

A spark flickered behind his eyes. "And I will," he promised with that wicked smile I could never resist. "Every day."

"I intend to hold you to that," grinning back. "In fact, I think you should start making it up to me right now."

He leaned close, until there was barely space between us. "And how, *exactly*," he murmured, "would you like me to do that?" The spark in his eyes told me he knew the answer already.

"I'm sure you'll think of something."

"Nope. Say it out loud," he whispered against my lips. "Be specific."

Jack was alive, and I was remembering how to breathe.

—

"What are you thinking?" he asked as we sat together on the wet tile, tangled in each other.

"I'm wondering if I'm going to wake up and find that you're still gone, and this was all a dream."

He chuckled, and the motion of it reverberated through my body, into skin and muscle and bone. "If so, you have some pretty weird dreams," he told me as he laughed.

I glanced over at the diamond, still in its gory setting, discarded with our sodden clothes on the bathroom floor. Jack had shoved it carelessly in a pocket when he untied me, and we'd forgotten about it entirely until we got back. "Should we give it back?"

"It would be difficult to explain why we have it."

"True." I looked around at him. He had a wistful look on his face. "What about you? What are you thinking?"

He kissed the top of my head. "I'm thinking I should have run away with you when I had the chance. Taken that rock, gotten on a plane, and disappeared. Lived happily ever after with you." It was such a lovely thought. A long-forgotten dream of peace.

I turned to face him, struck by an idea. "Let's do it."

"What?"

"Let's go. Disappear, live happily ever after." I could picture it - a cottage on the beach, a path down to the water, and no one but us. "We can find an island somewhere, just the two of us. Let's actually do it this time. The world can fend for itself."

He looked carefully at me. "You're serious," he realized. "Don't you have an agency to run?"

"No." I hadn't told anyone yet, but I'd made up my mind. As I thought about it, I became more and more certain it was the right decision. "I can't be the one to run it anymore. I'm going to hand it over to Theo."

"Why? I mean, I'm not complaining, because I want you all to myself, but you put your soul into this place."

"Xavier was right about one thing. I'm too much like him. I let the ends justify the means. I accomplish the goal, and I don't care that much about how it gets done. We set this up to help the Paranormal community. How long before I'm building my own army and blowing up museums for 'the greater good'?"

"You're nothing like him." There was a vehemence in his voice that I'd never heard. Hate. Pure, dark, and brutal. Someday, maybe he'd tell me more about what he'd been through. But not today.

"I'm a little like him. But just a little. I'd like to keep it that way." The closer I came back to the person I used to be, the more I realized how far away I'd gone. "Besides, Theo can handle it," trying to convince myself as much as him. "I can consult. Advise as needed. Occasionally."

"So you're retiring?" he asked. "Running away and leaving all of this behind?"

"If you'll come with me?"

"Diana, if you wanted to go live at the South Pole with the penguins, I'd go with you."

"I like the island plan better," I said, leaning in to kiss him again.

—

When we finally returned to the lobby, clean, sated, and dressed in spare agency clothes, a large crowd already filled the lobby, celebrating the return of friends and colleagues who had disappeared. It seemed that Abara kept her word, and people were rapidly being returned to their homes. Someone found champagne, music was playing, and the missing people were welcomed home with hugs and tears of joy.

Jack's fingers were intertwined with mine as I steered us to a small couch in the corner. I couldn't seem to stop touching him, finding little excuses to make contact, always keeping him somewhere in my field of view. We still had things to work out, and I didn't expect everything to be perfect immediately. For now, though, I could just relax for a minute. Breathe.

I tried to keep out of the spotlight, but almost immediately, a curious crowd gathered around us. Everyone seemed to know who Jack was. Rumor had it that he'd been undercover this whole time, laying the groundwork for our victory, which was sort of true. The more sentimental were calling it a tragic love story, which made me laugh.

Somehow, the story of the fall of New Versailles had spread almost instantly. Jenna had apparently snapped a few pictures of the wreckage while we were talking to Abara, and at this point, absolutely everyone had seen them. Several people saw us come in, covered in blood and dust and holding hands. My reputation had already spun out of control before this, and his was now growing rapidly. I fully expected both of us to be urban legends within the week.

"Did you really kill Xavier King?" someone asked me.

"Technically, Jack did," I clarified, smiling up at him.

He shook his head. "It wouldn't have worked without your distraction," he insisted, gazing down at me affectionately. "Which was brilliant, by the way."

I became aware of the silence surrounding us. Everyone was staring in horror at the two of us. Apparently, gazing into each other's eyes and reminiscing about murder while cuddled up on a couch at a party was not something normal people did. Jack noticed the sudden quiet as well. "What?" he asked the surrounding crowd. "Was it something we said?"

I laughed, feeling genuinely happy. I was pretty sure that half the reason everyone was so freaked out was the sight of me smiling and laughing. They'd have to get used to it. "You see?" I said to Jack. "This is why we need to retire."

"Retire?" Theo squeaked. "You're retiring?" His voice carried over every other sound in the room. All conversation stopped, and every head turned toward us. *Oops.*

"You've been practically running things here anyway," I reassured him. "You don't need me."

"Yes! Yes I do!" His voice went up a couple octaves.

"Don't you own the agency?" someone asked. "If you leave, how do we get paid?" Nikki, blunt as always. And Theo's problem, now.

"The operating funds will stay to run the agency." I assured them all. "Theo will run the day to day, and we can be silent partners."

"We?" Jack asked with a raised eyebrow.

I shrugged. "Half the startup money was yours," I pointed out. "And your name is on the door, too. Legally, it's half yours."

"Legally, I'm dead," he reminded me.

People were shifting uncomfortably again. I stifled a laugh.

"What will you do, then?" asked James from where he stood with Alex.

"I could sell the loft," I mused.

Theo spun to face me with wide eyes. "Don't you dare."

"That would take time," Jack pointed out.

"True. I really want to be on a beach by this time next week. We could be jewel thieves," I continued, enjoying the reaction of the crowd. "We were pretty good at that." Maybe this legend thing would be fun.

"That won't be necessary," Jack told me. "You know that Xavier paid me, right?"

"Oh? What's the going rate for a soul these days?" I teased.

"Enough that you won't have to resort to a life of crime," he assured me, dropping a kiss on my forehead. "Not again, anyway."

EPILOGUE

"How much time do you think we have until they get here?" Jack speculated as we stood atop the widow's walk on our new home. The breeze off the ocean tempered the hot Caribbean sun, and it felt wonderful. From here we could see the beach stretching for miles in either direction, our sprawling little complex of patios dotted here and there with a handful of guest houses, and the bridge leading back to the mainland. It wasn't the tiny cottage on a desolate island like we'd planned, but it suited us. It was a perfect compromise - privacy without complete isolation - and we loved it.

The bridge and the extra space meant that guests could visit when we wanted them, like today. "Theo's coming with Jenna, so they could arrive anytime. Vivienne, James and his in-laws should have landed half an hour ago, so we probably have another twenty minutes or so." I leaned back into his arms, liking the direction of his thoughts. "Think it would be enough time?"

He pulled me close, and held me like he'd never let go. "It will never be enough time."

The crunch of tires on gravel made me groan. I broke away and looked down the long driveway to see a white car pulling up to the house. Athena popped her head out the window, waving wildly. I forced a smile and waved back.

"Continue this conversation later?"

"Definitely."

―

"Is that what I think it is?" Alex asked, eyes wide. I followed the direction of her gaze. She'd noticed our new paperweight.

"That depends on what you think it is," Jack replied vaguely. Removed from its setting, the large diamond was less conspicuous, but not by much.

"Isn't that thing cursed?" asked Lina, coming up beside her.

"Only if you wear it," I clarified.

"Didn't work out so well for its previous owner," Jack observed, leading the three of us out to the deck. I took a seat at the table beside James, rescuing him from his new mother-in-law. Athena was grilling him about something. I suspected it might be grandkids.

"Any word from your brother?" I asked, cutting into the conversation. James's brother was keeping an eye on Isabelle for us. Her new situation was a good solution, but it needed monitoring, and Brian had volunteered.

"I spoke to him yesterday, actually. She seems to be settling in well on the farm. No signs of problems with her memory." This was the first time Vivienne had ever given someone an entirely new memory, and we weren't entirely sure how it would go.

"And the coin is suppressing her Talent? Completely?"

"Seems to be. She's so much better off without it. It's nice to see her happy, for a change." He tilted his head at me with a smile. "It's nice to see you happy for a change, too. A little weird, but nice."

I looked over at Jack, who was chatting with Lina near the door. He was still a little wary of her, so I was relieved to see him making an effort. "I saw a cake inside with your name on it," he told her. "Is your birthday coming up?"

"It's today, actually," she informed him.

Jack let out a surprised laugh. "You were born on Bastille Day? Seriously?"

Lina's brow furrowed. "What's Bastille Day?"

"It's a French holiday," he explained. "To celebrate the fall of the monarchy." We'd chosen to have our housewarming party on July 14th deliberately. It was a delicious sort of irony. If anyone had caught our little inside joke, they hadn't commented.

Lina wasn't interested. "Ugh. History. Boring."

Amused, he asked, "Really? What sort of things do you like?"

She warmed to the topic. "Dragons! They're so much cooler."

Jack's eyes flickered toward me at the mention of dragons, but only briefly. A beautiful, green dragon appeared on the table. It was intricately detailed, with iridescent scales and translucent wings, and I was once again amazed at Jack's skill. It jumped into the air and circled her head. She reached for it, and disappointed when her arms passed straight through.

"That one was pretty," she admitted, "but I can make a better one."

My eyes got wide. I was pretty sure I knew where this was going. Jack didn't. "Yeah? Let's see." *Oh, well. He has to find out eventually.*

"Angelina!" Athena said warningly, like it was something they'd talked about before. Lina rolled her eyes at her mother in the way that only a teenager could.

She picked up a glass from the table. It shaped itself into a dragon with stained-glass wings. Jack smiled and started to compliment her, until it blinked, launched itself into the air and landed clumsily on his shoulder. It made a sound like a cat with a hairball, and a little shower of sparks fell out of its mouth. Then it launched itself into the air and flew off, and Angelina jumped up to chase it.

Jack met my eyes with a freaked out look on his face. I smiled and shrugged apologetically.

"What's not to be happy about?" I replied to James.

Alex came up behind him. "We have something for you," she told me with a mysterious smile. "A housewarming gift."

"I made it!" Lina chimed in, forgetting all about her escaping animatron.

"It was a group effort," James corrected. "The idea was Theo's, Alex did the design, and yes, Lina made it."

I let Jack open the long, thin package. On seeing it, he smirked and suppressed a laugh. He turned it around so I could see.

It was a wooden sign, the sort of thing you'd hang out in front of your house. It was beautifully done, with graceful, curving letters, and an intricate design involving apple trees. When I read what it said, though, I wanted to strangle them all.

The beautiful letters spelled out 'New Avalon'. The symbolism wasn't lost on me. Avalon was the resting place of Arthur, the legendary leader who would return to lead his people in an hour of need.

"I'm not coming back," I insisted.

"Of course not," said Alex, struggling to keep a straight face. Jack was practically falling over with laughter.

"I hate you all," I told them.

"She doesn't," James said in a completely unnecessary aside.

I glared. "I'm not coming back," I repeated.

Any further argument was cut off by the sound of a doorbell. Jack got up quickly to answer it. It had to be Theo and Jenna. They could have just Jumped directly to the deck, but Jenna always insisted on ringing the bell. She'd had some awkward experiences she didn't want to repeat.

Sure enough, they bustled through the back door a moment later, Theo holding a bottle of wine and Jenna a potted plant. Theo looked absolutely exhausted. I took the wine from him and handed him a cocktail, which he took gratefully as he sank into a chair.

"Any word from Abara?"

"Nothing new. She's keeping her promises, but otherwise staying out of sight."

"And Cat?" I'd asked him to keep an eye out for signs of her, just in case she reappeared in search of vengeance.

He shook his head. "She may have been caught in the explosion, or may not. Either way, there are plenty of others still out there, so you should stay in hiding for a while. It's been less than a month."

"Fine by me," I said, gazing out at the ocean. Staying right where I was seemed like the perfect plan.

"I did find someone else, though," Theo said with a nervous glance behind me.

I turned to see Jack standing in the doorway with a familiar-looking child. The last time I'd seen him, he'd been covered in mud but happy and healthy. Now, he was noticeably skinnier, and obviously terrified.

"Theo, what is this?" I asked, my voice dangerously low. He had to know how I'd react to having this child, of all people, in my home. He shrank back and looked to Jack for help.

"This is Marcel," Jack told the now silent crowd. They were all staring at the boy, who was trying to hide behind him. "He's not used to this many people," Jack explained, "so he's a little shy."

I looked from Jack to Theo, who now looked like he wanted to hide just as much as Marcel did. "Don't blame Theo," Jack insisted. "I asked him to check."

Before I could respond, I heard the sound of something shattering. I looked over at the source, to see Alex standing with her face full of shock, and one of my new glasses in shards at her feet. James was watching her closely. They exchanged a glance, his eyes got wide, and he immediately walked over and crouched down next to Marcel.

"Hi!" he said to the frightened boy with a friendly smile. "I'm James." He held out his hand to shake Marcel's. I could tell he was trying to establish contact, so he could make the boy feel more comfortable, but Marcel stared at the hand like it might bite him.

"I was just about to walk down to the beach. Would you like to come with me?" The boy said nothing. "It's just over that way. Have you ever seen the ocean?" Marcel shook his head. "It's very quiet down there. Not as many people," James said with a conspiratorial nod towards the rest of us.

Lina hopped up. "I'll go, too." She was a perceptive kid. She obviously saw the storm clouds gathering above my head, and didn't want to be anywhere near them when they broke.

James stood and held out a hand. "What do you say?" Marcel looked from James to Lina, and then hesitantly up at Jack. When Jack nodded encouragingly, the boy looked bravely back at James, and took his offered hand. The second they made contact, tension visibly drained from the child, and I knew that was James, making him feel safe and welcome.

I wasn't sure I wanted him to feel safe and welcome here. Marcel was dangerous. He had Xavier's genes, so he most likely had Xavier's Talent, and that terrified me. I didn't want him in my home, in my life, or anywhere near my loved ones.

James ushered both kids down to the beach. "What kind of name is Marcel?" I heard Lina ask as they walked down the path. "Can we just call him Mars?"

"Like the planet? That's kind of a cool name. What do you think? Do you like it? Can we call you Mars?" Their voices trailed off as they disappeared down the path.

As soon as they were safely out of earshot, I rounded on Theo and Jack. "What the hell are you thinking, bringing him here?"

"I'm thinking that he's a scared child who has no place else to go. He's just a kid, Di," he said, using my own words about Angelina against me. "He hasn't done anything wrong."

"He's a dangerous kid."

"All the more reason to raise him in a loving home with a supportive family, so he makes the right choices. If he's here, we can watch him, and keep him away from people like Abara." That same logic was exactly why Lina was here, and it was hard to argue with. That didn't mean I had to like it.

"He doesn't understand what's happening," Jack continued. "All he knows is that his entire world was just turned upside down, everyone he knew abandoned him, and he's terrified."

"They just left him there," Theo added. "As far as I could

tell, he's been there this whole time, living off what was left behind. Alone." I felt a sliver of kinship with the child. I knew what it was like to feel abandoned and alone, and he was even younger than I'd been.

"Who is he?" Alex cut in. She was staring after her husband and the two kids.

"He's Xavier's biological child," Jack explained.

"Does he have the same Talent?" Jenna asked, cutting to the heart of the matter. Xavier's abilities were dangerous. If Marcel had them, too, we could be in exactly the same situation in a few years, facing another would-be tyrant with another army of fanatic followers.

"If he does, he hasn't shown them," Jack told us. "They wouldn't have left him there if he did." He was raised by nannies, I remembered. Did they all just leave?

"If he did, we wouldn't be sitting around discussing his fate, either. We'd be falling all over ourselves to help him," Theo pointed out.

"Trauma has been shown to suppress Talent," Vivienne mused, with a glance at Alex. "It could show up later. But it also skips generations, sometimes. He could be completely harmless."

"Well, he can't stay with us," I objected. "At some point, he's going to find out that we killed his father and blew up his home. And we're retired," I added pointedly. My vision of our future together did not include a twelve-year-old child. It was selfish, but I thought we'd earned a bit of selfishness at this point.

"We'll take him in," Alex interjected.

I thought about the feral child I'd seen by the lake, and tried to imagine him assimilating into a normal school. "Are you sure about this, Alex? This will be a big shock to his system. That kid is going to be pretty traumatized after what he's been through."

"All the more reason to give him a safe space. James is quite good at helping people process trauma. I should know."

"Don't you have to talk this over with him?"

"We've already discussed it."

"When were you going to tell us your visions came back?" Athena asked her, amused.

Alex snorted. "Like you didn't already know."

"You had a vision?" I asked Alex, surprised.

She smiled. "We weren't sure when or how he'd show up, but yes, we've been expecting him."

It made sense. James had some immunity to Charismatics, since they were closely related to Empaths. Now that her visions had returned, Alex would see any problems coming far ahead of time. There was no one I'd trust more to raise this kid.

They were all watching me, waiting for my reaction. "What are you looking at me for?" Part of stepping back from authority was relinquishing control. It didn't come easy, but I was working on it. "It's not my decision. It's up to Alex and James."

"Well, now that that's settled, let's eat! I'm starving." Theo rubbed his hands together, looking at the food. I gathered the pieces of the shattered glass and moved them safely out of the way. Maybe I could get Lina to put them back together for me later. She owed me for the one she turned into a dragon.

As the party resumed, I noticed Athena standing quietly by the rail, staring down toward the water. She hadn't expressed an opinion on Marcel one way or another, which was unlike her. Normally, she had something to say about everything. Right now, she looked uneasy and unsure.

I stood beside her at the railing. Below, James was watching as the two kids splashed in the waves. I was struck for a moment by how much raw, unknown potential was down there on that beach. *Empire crumbles, and voices wail in mourning.*

"What is it?" I asked Athena quietly.

She shook her head uncertainly. "There's something," she said. "Something about those two together," she told me.

I felt a chill despite the hot summer sun. "Something good

or something bad?"
"Something."

BOOKS BY LISA J. MORGAN

—

Closer to the Sun

Book One: Shattered

Book Two: Shadows

Book Three: Secrets (Coming Soon)

—

www.lisajmorgan.com

FROM THE AUTHOR

This one is close to my heart. It developed alongside *Shattered*, parts of it woven in and out of the same storyline. It spun out of a single line of dialogue, spoken by one side character to another, and then the heartbreaking story of these two people took on a life of its own and demanded to be told. I've loved writing it, and helping them come alive on the page.

I thought it would be bittersweet to close the chapter on this particular book, but their story feels whole and complete now, and I finally feel that I've captured on the page the picture I had in my head. I can walk away knowing that I'm leaving them exactly where they need to be.

Besides, no story is ever truly over, and this is not goodbye. We'll see Diana and Jack again, along with new friends and familiar faces as the series continues.

Sign up to keep up with news, and get snippets, side stories, and other short fiction at http://www.lisajmorgan.com.

As always, thanks for reading,
LJM

Coming Soon

Secrets

Lisa J. Morgan

Closer to the Sun
Book Three

Sparrow Beaumont's life is not exciting. She likes it that way. Her little farm in rural Vermont is thriving, and if she could only get her shy, sexy neighbor to notice her, everything would be perfect. Life is good - until the day strangers show up in her little town looking for someone named *Isabelle*.

Soon, her quiet world goes up in flames, and she finds out that her entire life is a lie, and all of her memories were carefully constructed to protect her - from herself.

Now Sparrow is on the run with a man she barely knows, trying to uncover her own secrets before the past she can't remember catches up to her.

Printed in Great Britain
by Amazon

CLOSER TO THE SUN
BOOK TWO

LISA J.
MORGAN

Ivy Tower Books, LLC
www.ivytowerbooks.com

ISBN: 979-8-9889761-5-8